SPECIAL MESSAGE TO READERS

This book is published under the auspices of

THE ULVERSCROFT FOUNDATION

(registered charity No. 264873 UK)

Established in 1972 to provide funds for research, diagnosis and treatment of eye diseases. Examples of contributions made are: —

A Children's Assessment Unit at Moorfield's Hospital, London.

•

Twin operating theatres at the Western Ophthalmic Hospital, London.

•

A Chair of Ophthalmology at the Royal Australian College of Ophthalmologists.

•

The Ulverscroft Children's Eye Unit at the Great Ormond Street Hospital For Sick Children, London.

You can help further the work of the Foundation by making a donation or leaving a legacy. Every contribution, no matter how small, is received with gratitude. Please write for details to:

THE ULVERSCROFT FOUNDATION,
The Green, Bradgate Road, Anstey,
Leicester LE7 7FU, England.
Telephone: (0116) 236 4325

In Australia write to:
THE ULVERSCROFT FOUNDATION,
c/o The Royal Australian College of Ophthalmologists,
27, Commonwealth Street, Sydney, N.S.W. 2010.

Caroline Gray is a pen-name for bestselling author Christopher Nicole. Born in the West Indies, the author's historical fiction includes the bestselling five-volume Caribee series. Nicole has won international acclaim for his work under several other pseudonyms, including Max Marlow, Alan Savage and Andrew York. He lives with his wife, Diana, also a novelist in the Channel Islands.

The Phoenix is the second volume in the brand-new Colonial series, following *The Promised Land*.

THE PHOENIX

In 1973, Joanna Orton is one of the most prominent businesswomen in the City. Beautiful and self-assured, she is universally respected — and for that reason, hated and even feared by many. But she is betrayed by her third husband, Dick, whose sales of the shares she gave him cost her the control she values above all else. And when a casual love affair turns sour, Joanna inadvertently causes the death of her lover. As she faces a lengthy prison term, she must call on all her courage and determination to somehow climb out of this desperate situation . . .

Book Two of the Colonial Series.

Books by Caroline Gray
Published by The House of Ulverscroft:

FIRST CLASS
HOTEL DE LUXE
WHITE RANI
VICTORIA'S WALK

Colonial Series:
THE PROMISED LAND: Book One

CAROLINE GRAY

THE PHOENIX

Complete and Unabridged

ULVERSCROFT
Leicester

First published in Great Britain in 1998 by
Severn House Publishers Limited
Surrey

First Large Print Edition
published 2000
by arrangement with
Severn House Publishers Limited
Surrey

British Library CIP Data

Gray, Caroline, *1930* –
The Phoenix.—Large print ed.—
Ulverscroft large print series: general fiction
1. Large type books
I. Title
823.9′14 [F]

ISBN 0–7089–4182–6

Published by
F. A. Thorpe (Publishing) Ltd.
Anstey, Leicestershire

Set by Words & Graphics Ltd.
Anstey, Leicestershire
Printed and bound in Great Britain by
T. J. International Ltd., Padstow, Cornwall

This book is printed on acid-free paper

‘Build me straight, O worthy Master!
Staunch and strong, a goodly vessel,
That shall laugh at all disaster,
And with wave and whirlwind wrestle!’

Henry Wadsworth Longfellow

Part One

Crisis

'Have ye sinned one sin for the pride o' the eye or the sinful lust of the flesh?'

Rudyard Kipling

1

The Storm

The knock on the cabin door had Joanna Orton alert in an instant. She had not actually been sleeping, she had been listening to the whine of the wind and the slapping of the waves against the hull, the reassuring growl of the engines beneath the deck. She sat up switched on the light. 'Come.'

The steward opened the door only a few inches; however attractive a woman Joanna Orton might be, she was the boss, and her privacy was not to be intruded upon. 'Compliments of the captain, Mrs Orton. He says it will be necessary to alter course.'

'Tell him I will come up.' The steward closed the door, and Joanna thrust her feet out of bed. The motion of the ship was more severe than she had supposed when lying down, and she had to clutch the grab rail to stop herself from falling over, while she reached for her clothes, deciding against the dress she had worn for dinner in favour of shirt and pants and deck shoes. She ran a brush through her tangled golden hair, slid across the floor to the door. The cabins on board the *Caribee Queen* opened directly into the lounge and, as she had suspected might be the case, three of the passengers, two women and a man, were up, sitting in the armchairs anchored to the floor, drinking coffee and attempting to look unconcerned.

They turned sharply at the sight of the owner. 'Oh, Mrs Orton,' exclaimed one of the women, 'is there any danger?'

'None at all,' Joanna assured her.

'Someone was talking about a hurricane,' ventured the man.

'There is a hurricane, Mr Lamason,' Joanna said. 'But it is a good way off. We are about to alter course to make sure it remains a good way off.' She smiled at them, brightly, and recalled that her first husband, Howard Edge, the man from whom she had inherited this shipping line, had reassured her in just that manner on the night of their first real meeting . . . was it really thirteen years ago?

She went outside, the door held for her by the steward. Instantly the wind plucked at her, scattered her hair, whipped her shirt to and fro. Even in the darkness she could make out the whitecaps racing by. She put the breeze at perhaps thirty knots, not yet half the strength of a hurricane wind, but sufficient to create lumps and holes in the sea, into which from time to time the freighter plunged or rolled, almost losing way with jarring force. She climbed the ladder to the bridge, where again the door was held for her by an anxious second mate. Once inside, the quiet was almost startling, but the sound of the gale still surrounded this little haven of peace. 'Is there a problem, James?' she asked.

She and Captain Heggie had known each other for all of those thirteen years, as he had watched her grow from a frightened young girl into this confident, mature and most successful woman. Yet whenever she elected to sail with him, as she did whenever possible, he always knew a sense of responsibility that was almost disturbing. 'I hope you approve, Joanna,' he said, and spread the weatherfax print-out in front of her. She gazed at the chart of the North Atlantic, and the swirling angry mass that occupied the centre of it, several hundred miles north-east of Barbados, their last port of call. 'Damn thing has dipped south in the last hour,' Heggie explained. 'So I've been forced to do the same.'

Joanna nodded. She had been involved in Caribbean — and thus Atlantic — shipping long enough to know that they needed to keep the storm to their left to avoid the greatest wind strength. There had in fact been a suggestion from their Barbados agent that they should delay their departure from Bridgetown, but the *Caribee Queen* had a full cargo of rice and sugar from Guyana, not to mention eleven fare-paying passengers, and the route was a competitive one. Besides, all they had to do was keep their distance, which, with modern navigational aids and facsimile prints-out, was not difficult. 'How far?'

'Two hundred miles.'

Close enough for the outlying gales to batter them, but sufficiently far from any real trouble. 'I approve. Tell me what you expect.'

'Presuming the storm holds its present course and speed, we should pass it in about two hours' time, at a distance of about one hundred and eighty miles. Then we will be drawing apart at about thirty miles an hour, and we will be in the safest quadrant, so that by dawn we should be able to to resume our course. The whole diversion should take about eight hours, but that will, I'm afraid, make it probable that we shall be a day late arriving at Plymouth. Unless you wish me to increase speed considerably.'

Joanna considered, as she glanced at the ship's chronometer; it was a quarter to three. But *Caribee Queen*, although her favourite of the six ships that composed her small company, was also now the oldest. She would not wish the old girl to tear her heart out. She had honeymooned, the first time, on board this ship. Besides, as this autumn of 1973 drew to a close, there was all this talk about fuel prices going up as a result of the Seven Days War between Israel and the Arab states in the Middle East and, perhaps as important as any of those, she was in no hurry to get home to the crisis she knew was awaiting her. 'We'll be late, James,' she said. 'I'll explain it to the passengers. If I can be a few hours late, so can they.'

'I'm sure they'll co-operate,' Heggie said. His feelings for the owner were similar to hers for the ship: like most men who sailed for Caribee Shipping, he worshipped her.

'Call me again if there's any change in the situation,' Joanna said, and went to the leeward door.

'Take care,' Heggie advised.

Joanna blew him a kiss and went down the ladder.

By now all the other passengers had assembled in the saloon. There were eleven of them; four men, five women, and two children, all looking anxious despite the reassuring presence of Steward Demont, handing out cups of coffee and glasses of milk.

'Oh, Mrs Orton!' they seemed to chorus.

'Are we all right?'

'Will the weather get worse?'

'Should we put on our lifejackets?'

'Are there any ships close by?'

Joanna smiled at them. 'I do assure you that there is nothing to be the least concerned about.'

'But the captain called you to the bridge!'

'Captain Heggie wanted my approval of the course he is adopting, which is to give the storm the widest possible berth. I approved. I'm afraid this means that we may be a few hours late docking in Plymouth, but we will certainly have a more comfortable voyage. Now, I am going back to bed, and I strongly recommend that you all do the same. By the time you wake up tomorrow morning the storm will be behind us.'

'Is it really a hurricane, Mrs Orton?' asked one of the children.

'Yes, it is. But we are not going to get involved in it. Good night.'

Demont followed her to her cabin door. 'Can I get you anything, Mrs Orton?' he whispered.

'Yes. Once they go back to bed, bring me a large brandy.'

'Yes, madam.' He closed the door, and Joanna kicked off her shoes, but did not undress, instead lay beneath the covers, staring at the deck head above her.

Even in normal circumstances, she valued these voyages on board her ships. They were as much to revisit her Guyanese roots as to get away from Dick and her family, to rest from her job as Chairman and Managing Director of Caribee Shipping, and to escape the responsibilities of being one of the City's most exciting tycoons. This was at least partly because she was still so young — she would be thirty on her next birthday — and remained, she knew, an extremely attractive woman. With her golden hair, which she still wore long, at least in bed, and her clipped features, her full figure, which remained under control although she was twice a mother, she graced any gathering, or any newspaper or society magazine.

But it was also, she knew, partly because of the slightly sinister aura that surrounded her like a cloud. Because of her husbands, and their manner of departing this earth. Howard Edge, old enough to be her father when she had been a teenager and they had first met, had been widely known as a rake and man about town, as well as a successful shipowner. When he had divorced his wife to marry a girl less than half his age, and one who, in addition, came from no reputable English family but from a distant corner of the crumbling empire, it had caused a sensation.

Which had grown when, only a few weeks later, he had died, accidentally but violently, and had, even more sensationally, willed his entire estate to his bride of a fortnight.

Poor Howard had, of course, not expected to die so suddenly and at such an early age. He had been looking to the future. And the future had suddenly been dumped in Joanna's lap, at the age of twenty. When, at such an early age, she had refused to concede an inch in her possession and therefore control of the company, even when it was revealed that Caribee Shipping was in a desperate financial state, sensation had piled upon sensation. The tabloids had rubbed their hands and waited for the coming catastrophe. And had been forced to bite their tongues. She might have been only twenty, but she had understood her assets as well as her liabilities. Arab money had put Caribee Shipping back on its feet. Perhaps the City was getting used to Middle Eastern investment. But they had not expected her actually to marry her Arab benefactor.

That had been to soar to the top of the tree. Many had wondered, sometimes audibly, just what a beautiful young English girl had to do to be the wife of an Arab prince. They would have been surprised, and no doubt disappointed. Hasim ben Raisul abd

Abdullah had been the most perfect gentleman, in and out of bed. The most perfect husband too, in that, although enjoying a multi-millionaire income as Qadiri ambassador to Britain, he had allowed his wife to continue with her 'hobby', as he called it, of managing the shipping line; had, in fact, interfered with her life very little. Which was not to say he had not brought an utterly new dimension to her views on sex. But their marriage had been fatally flawed, as perhaps they had both always been aware. To marry a foreign, Christian woman, Prince Hasim had had to give up his rights to the throne of the Emirate of Qadir, owned by his family. He had seemed willing to do this, but when his father had died, to be succeeded by Hasim's younger brother, the intrigues had begun. There were many Qadiris who wanted Hasim rather than Mutil as their ruler. Efforts had been made to persuade him to re-enter the political arena.

Joanna had never been sure just what that would have entailed. The repudiation of his Christian wife? Hasim had loved her so desperately she did not think he would have done that, not even for a throne. In the event, the question had never arisen. The Emir Mutil had adopted the age-old Arabian method of dealing with his enemies and potential rivals — even if they were half-brothers. Joanna did not suppose she would ever forget the door of their London flat being thrown open while she was celebrating her twenty-sixth birthday, and the three men standing there, each armed with a tommy-gun. She would never cease hearing the shrieks of terror and pain from all around her as the room had been sprayed with bullets. She, and all the women present, had been unhurt; the assassins only wanted any man who could possibly be involved in an attempt on the Qadiri throne. But the slaughter had been sufficient. And she had once again been left a widow.

That had set the seal on her notoriety. And with the withdrawal of Qadiri money from her company — it had turned out that Hasim's millions were all Qadiri millions; he had had little to leave his widow — another crash had been expected. But she had again been saved, by another long-time admirer. With strings attached, to be sure, but nothing involving bed or marriage, at least for the time being. Thus she had married again, hastily. Dick Orton was her oldest English boyfriend, a relic from the days before even Howard had moved into her life. She had been certain that, at last, she was marrying for love. Third time unlucky. Because she now knew, as perhaps did everyone else, that this third marriage had been a mistake, and was now becoming a disaster. There was the real reason for her being on board this ship at this time; she had needed to think about her marriage. They had loved each other, at least in bed, for a while. But they lived, and moved, and above all, thought, on different wavelengths. She was managing director of a thriving little shipping line and, though he worked with her at Caribee Shipping as a co-director, he remained a clerk at heart, more interested in making sure the shillings and pence added up on a balance sheet than in considering how the pounds might be spent to best advantage. Dick existed in a miasma of apprehension at the risks of the shipping world, both physical and financial, and of the bubbling energy and vitality of his wife, which he did not possess and could not share.

Perhaps that was why she had not been a mother for him. She knew this had been a disappointment, although he was a good father to both Helen, her daughter by Howard Edge, and Raisul, her son by Hasim. But Dick viewed both the children with vague suspicion, as if fatherhood, even once removed, of such a disparate pair was bound to involve him, eventually, in catastrophe.

Perhaps he was right.

But those uncertainties, weaknesses, became nothing compared with the report she had received two months ago. It had been like a slap in the face, although, as it had been she who employed the private detective in the first place, she had been pretty sure something was going on. But being pretty sure is not quite the same as being made certain. No wife can accept that a husband to whom she has given everything — too much, Joanna thought grimly, when she considered the share settlement she had made on him — is cheating. How she wished he had accompanied her on this voyage. She had invited him to. She had felt that a month alone together, or at least surrounded only by strangers, might enable them to level the mountain that lay between them. But he had declined to come, and beg she would not do. Nor would she change her mind about going herself. She found it important, even necessary every so often, not merely to voyage in one of her own ships, but to revisit the land of her birth, Guyana, the land where her father had been shot to death, where Howard had drowned. To suppose she received inspiration from such a sad background could never be right. Rather, these pilgrimages, made once a year, reminded her of who and what she was and, perhaps, gave her a sense of direction.

Dick did not like ships or the sea. Or far-off places. Or, presumably, hurricanes, even at a distance. And he did like being in London. He was wealthy, good-looking . . . available? Well, she thought, one of these days he might get a shock. Because a decision was hardening in her mind.

Demont brought her the brandy, and she sipped it, sitting up and trying to read a book, but too conscious of the weather outside to concentrate. Storms at sea gave her a feeling of exhilaration, of directly challenging nature. As if anyone could do that. One did what the *Caribee Queen* was doing; sneaked around the edges and hoped to go unnoticed, well aware that the force generated at the centre of a hurricane was more powerful than several hydrogen bombs all dropped at the same time. When she had finished her drink and switched off the light, she kept seeing that swirling white mass on the centre of the print-out, and she could imagine the wind strength, well over a hundred miles an hour, whipping even these deep and slow-moving seas into a frenzy of white-topped ferocity.

She awoke with a start, surprised at having been asleep, and was immediately aware of silence. The morning, for it was getting light beyond her ports, was exceedingly noisy, from the wailing of the wind to the battering of the waves on the hull, but that in itself was not disturbing. The really disturbing factor was the silence from below her, the absence of the reassuring sound of the engine, throbbing upward through the ship. She sat up, and was half thrown from her bunk with the violence of the movement. *Caribee Queen* seemed to be rolling scuppers under. Half the things on her dressing table had accumulated against the baffles; one or two had fallen over on to the cabin floor.

She switched on her light, dragged on her clothes. As she did so there came a buzz on her interphone. She fell across the bunk reaching for it.

'Joanna?' It was Heggie.

'What in the name of God has happened?' she shouted.

'The engine has been closed down,' Heggie said, not altogether keeping a note of panic out of his voice. 'There has been a burst fuel line. It may take an hour or two to repair.'

'I'm coming up.' Joanna slammed the phone down, staggered to the door, only then realising she was barefoot. But she didn't have the time to stop and look for her shoes; she could hear anxious voices from the saloon. The passengers had again accumulated, staring at her, only half awake and terrified, a huddle of pyjama-and nightgown-clad sheep. 'Please,' she said. 'We have had to stop the engine for a few minutes. We'll be underway again soon enough. But until then, I strongly recommend that you return to your bunks; the movement may be violent.'

To give credence to her words there was a roar as a larger than usual wave burst on the side of the now inert ship, forcing her over, while green water splashed on the saloon windows. The women started to scream, the children to wail, as they desperately clung to the chairs and tables to avoid being hurled across the room. 'Bed!' Joanna shouted at the men. 'Get them back to bed.'

She left them to Demont, opened the lee door, and climbed the ladder to the bridge. In daylight the morning was terrifying. The waves were very big, looming monsters topped with several feet of foaming white, as she had imagined in her sleep. Normally those threatening waterwalls would fall behind as the ship surged ahead. Now they were hurling themselves at the vessel like a succession of infantry battalions, intent on destruction. As she reached the bridge, a wave broke over the bow, forcing it down, sending water curling over the forward hold to break against the lower superstructure. For a moment Joanna's heart seemed to stand still, as the ship hesitated before coming up again, but then she seemed to toss her head, sending the water flying to either side, and prepared to meet her next adversary. Joanna was clinging to a stanchion just inside the door. Now Heggie came towards her, and half dragged her across the heaving deck to the chart table. 'Where is the storm?' she asked.

He prodded the chart of the North Atlantic, where he had made two marks. One was the hurricane, which in the four hours since she had last looked had advanced some fifty miles, more south than west. 'My God,' she muttered, peering at the little cross on the chart. 'And this is us?'

Before the breakdown, *Caribee Queen*, her speed reduced because of the weather, had moved hardly more than the same distance, just north of east. She was now some hundred and fifty miles south-west of the storm. All things being equal, she should be east of the swirling mass by mid-morning, in the safe quadrant, but because of the breakdown she was fast entering the second most dangerous quadrant of the storm. 'Will it keep on coming south-west?' she asked.

'Could be, at least as far as Barbados. Once

they pass through the Windward Islands, hurricanes usually sweep up to the north, either for Cuba and the Bahamas and the East Coast, or for the Gulf of Mexico and then Texas or Mexico.'

'None of which is going to matter much to us,' Joanna said. 'How long will the engine take?'

'Four, six hours, Chief Bartlett says.'

'Shit,' Joanna muttered, and looked at the clinometer on the bulkhead indicating the amount of roll. At the moment, *Caribee Queen* was rolling through a ninety degree arc, some forty-five degrees either way. Joanna knew that if a ship ever rolled sixty degrees she was unlikely to recover. That didn't bear thinking about. 'But at least we'll be underway when that mess gets here. Supposing we don't move, how close will it come?'

'On this course, the eye would pass us about seventy miles to the north.'

'Which means . . . ?'

'We'll have winds of over a hundred miles an hour, seas of maybe thirty to forty feet, rainfall measured in feet rather than inches.'

Joanna took a deep breath. 'Can we survive that?'

Heggie licked his lips. 'Not without power.' Then he grinned. 'We'll have power.'

'But it'll still be tight?'

'Oh, yes, Joanna, It's going to be tight. I've spoken with Barbados. Well, they're nearest. But they're two hundred miles away and expecting a direct hit. There's nothing they can do to help us.'

'And London?'

'I've spoken with Peter Young. He's in a highly agitated state.'

Peter Young was Caribee Shipping's company secretary. He had been Howard Edge's right-hand man when Joanna had first drifted into his orbit; since Howard's death he had remained at her shoulder, rather like a surrogate father. She sometimes felt that was how he saw himself. 'But there's nothing he can do to help either,' she suggested.

'We're rather in no man's land, out here in the middle of the Atlantic. Peter did say he'd have an ocean-going tug standing by at Gibraltar, just in case.'

'Just in case of what?'

'Well . . . ' Heggie pulled his nose.

Joanna went down to the engine room, escorted by Malan, the third mate; Heggie felt he should remain on the bridge. In the bowels of the ship the motion was not quite so severe, but it was difficult enough negotiating the ladders, and she was aghast when she reached the last catwalk. The normally pristinely clean chamber below her was covered in oil, and the men working on the broken piping looked like fugitives from hell, also smeared with oil and with their half naked bodies gleaming with sweat — the heat was intense. 'You'd better stay here, Mrs Orton,' Malan recommended, and himself went down to alert Chief Bartlett that the owner wanted a word.

Bartlett climbed the ladder to join her. He looked tired, and there was oil on both his uniform and his unshaven face. 'What happened?' Joanna asked.

'Old age, I reckon. That engine has done a few miles.'

'When was it last overhauled?'

'Last year, Mrs Orton. But it's not always possible to tell what's going on inside a pipe, if you follow me.'

'But it can be repaired?'

'Oh, aye, it is being repaired. Trouble is, it's a longish job, and a messy one. To remove the fractured joint and replace it, we have to block off the pipe further down. We're doing that now. Hence the spillage.'

'Captain Heggie said something like four hours,' Joanna said, hopefully.

Bartlett pulled a face. 'Nearer six.'

She looked at her watch. 'Just in time for lunch.'

'If anyone feels like eating.'

'Be a dear and have it done by then, Chief,' Joanna said. 'I suppose you know we have a whopper breathing down our neck. Nine hours to contact. That's three o'clock this afternoon. But we'll be feeling it long before then.'

He grinned. 'You mean we're not feeling it now?'

Joanna returned to the now empty saloon; the passengers had taken her advice. Demont was in his galley, doing various things; he seemed able to keep his balance no matter how violent the rolling. 'All service is free, as of this moment and until further notice,' Joanna told him. 'Anything they want.'

'Yes, ma'am,' Demont agreed.

She sat at one of the tables, moving to and fro with the ship. She had long ago got over any tendency to sea-sickness, but she couldn't stop her stomach rolling every time a wave smashed into the ship and sent it, and her, reeling. If they came through this without some structural damage it would be a miracle. She breakfasted, precariously, then took her own advice and went back to her bunk. It was very tempting to be up on the bridge, but she knew everyone was doing all they could, and the presence of the owner would only be a distraction. Besides, she had no wish to look at those waves again.

She actually dozed off, wedging herself between the bulkhead and the leeboards with pillows, so that she was not thrown about, and awoke with a start at the sound of a crash. And that had not been a wave, she knew instinctively: it had come from inside the hull. She kicked the pillows away, sat up and promptly fell over again. The ship was well over. That was the normal extent of a roll, but she wasn't fully recovering. Oh, Jesus, she thought. She had to climb uphill to reach the door. Even in the galley things had shattered, and Demont was cleaning up.

'What's happened?' Joanna gasped.

'Something's gone below, ma'am.' Demont was his usual imperturbable self.

'Mrs Orton . . . ' one of the male passengers appeared in a doorway.

'Is everyone all right?'

'I think so. But . . . what happened?'

'I'm going to find out and let you know.' The ship staggered under another blow, and Joanna slid across the saloon to the leeward door. When she opened it, she gasped in horror. The sea seemed very close, seething green and white only a few feet below the rail. She clawed her way up the ladder to the bridge, found First Officer Lewis in command. 'Where's the captain?' Joanna shouted.

'He's gone below, aft,' Lewis said. 'Something's gone wrong down there. We think it's in the after hold.'

Which was filled with bags of rice. Joanna grabbed the telephone, punched the number, looking at the clinometer while doing so. The ship was centred at ten degrees to starboard, and was still rolling through a ninety degree arc. That meant at the bottom of the starboard roll she was fifty-five degrees over. And the hurricane hadn't got here yet. She looked at the chronometer: ten-fifteen. The seas hadn't really increased a great deal, kept down by the pouring rain that was limiting visibility to the length of the ship. But they would over the next couple of hours. 'Heggie,' said the voice.

'Joanna. Report, please.'

'Some of the cargo has shifted. We're working on it.'

'Be careful,' she told him, unnecessarily. If one of the crew, or the captain himself, were to be pinned by the mountainous rice bags shifting back the other way . . .

'It's under control,' Heggie assured her.

Joanna hung up, clung to the nearest grab rail, as the ship rolled again. Now it was indeed scuppers under, despite the blanketing effect of the rain. 'Ever been in a hurricane, Mr Lewis?' she asked.

'No, ma'am, that I have not. You?'

She shook her head and wet hair scattered across her face. She realised she must look a sight. 'Well,' she said, 'maybe we'll miss this one.' The time was eleven.

Fifteen minutes later the rain stopped and visibility improved. Joanna wished it hadn't. Now they could suddenly see for miles, and there was nothing reassuring to look at. The sea was an unending vista of big, breaking waves, and the sky was crowded with lowering black clouds, racing by. 'Fifty knots of wind recorded.' Third Officer Malan was back on the bridge. 'And rising.'

Caribee Queen lay half on her side, like a half-tide rock, being buffeted by every wave, several of which were breaking right over her. She was in mortal danger, and the temptation to shout that to the world, to send a mayday, was enormous. But the radar revealed no ships within fifty miles of them, and they could not ask any vessel to enter a hurricane quadrant. She went back down to the saloon, where the passengers had reassembled. Uninvited by the crew, they had donned their lifejackets, and were sitting in a miserable huddle, being served drinks by Demont.

'Mrs Orton!' they shouted at the sight of Joanna.

'Is this boat going to sink?'

'I hope not,' she said.

'Have you called for assistance?'

'There is no assistance,' Joanna told them. 'This is our problem, and we'll sort it out.'

'I am going to sue,' one of the men declared.

'That is your privilege, Mr Martin,' she said.

'Engines breaking down,' Martin said. 'In a storm. That is criminal, Mrs Orton. Criminal. There are women and children on board.'

'Yes, Mr Martin,' Joanna said, wearily. A large than usual wave broke, and there was a chorus of screams. But *Caribee Queen*, after going right over again, almost righted herself. 'Oh, thank God,' Joanna said.

'What does that mean?' Martin demanded.

'That the cargo that shifted has been put right,' Joanna said 'Demont, I think I will have a glass of champagne.' She smiled at her passengers, brightly. 'Won't you join me?' They all accepted, even Martin.

'It's amazing how quickly they'll recover, once we're in the clear, Mrs Orton,' Demont whispered.

But they weren't in the clear, yet. Joanna joined an exhausted Heggie on the bridge. 'When I get hold of the bugger who loaded that rice,' he growled.

'I don't suppose he allowed for this amount

of rolling.' She peered through the windows at the turbulence with which they were surrounded, at the massive waves smashing themselves against the hull . . . even inside the bridge it was necessary to shout above the whine of the wind. 'How we've survived so far without structural damage . . . '

'We haven't,' Heggie told her. 'We've lost several lengths of railing, and both motor launches have carried away. That leaves two oar-propelled boats. Just enough for everyone on board. But they couldn't live in these seas anyway.'

Joanna felt sick, for the first time that she could remember. Of course, even the motor launches would hardly survive, but just to know they were *there* . . . The phone buzzed, and Heggie picked it up. 'This had better be good,' he said. And then grinned as he looked at Joanna. 'It is good. The Chief says he is ready to restart the engine.'

Joanna's knees gave way, and she sat in the captain's chair, hanging on to the sides as the ship rolled deeply yet again. But a moment later there was a rumble from below. 'Now,' Heggie said. 'I propose to run like hell, to the south-east. It'll mean a roller-coaster ride, but it's our only way out.'

Joanna nodded. But she knew the dangers. *Caribee Queen* was three hundred feet long.

In normal circumstances that was considerably more than the average wave length, and thus once she had power there was little chance of her being overwhelmed. But some of these waves were more than three hundred feet, and if, running before the wind, she were to bury her bows too deeply while her stern was being lifted by the following wave . . . of course there was no risk of the ship being pitch-poled, that is, capsizing stern over bow — she was simply too big — but if the propellers were lifted high enough so that they could not grip for longer than the average very brief cavitation period, she might well go out of control. The alternative was to risk being overwhelmed by the hurricane. 'You do whatever you think is best, Captain Heggie,' she said.

The captain called up two more coxswains to share the coming wrestle with the helm, then he spoke with Chief Bartlett, explaining exactly what he was going to do. 'I will need instant responses, Chief.'

'You shall have them, skipper,' Bartlett promised.

'Shall I speak with the passengers?' Heggie asked.

Joanna shook her head. 'I'll do it.'

The ship was now gathering way, and the movement was vastly more easy, although still violent enough, but they were still steering across the face of the storm.

The passengers were again gathered in the saloon, where Demont was endeavouring to serve lunch, consisting of sandwiches and soup. 'There's no way I could keep any cutlery on the table,' he explained.

Holding on to a chair, Joanna faced them. 'I know you'll all be pleased we're under way again. But I must tell you that the delay has meant we are too close to the storm. So we intend to run away from it.'

'Won't running before this wind be very dangerous?' Martin again.

'It won't be as dangerous as trying to steam into it, Mr Martin.'

'Because you're afraid that engine will break down again. I am — '

'Going to sue,' Joanna said. 'You've already promised that. I'll eat in my cabin, Demont.'

He followed her a moment later with her meal. 'Maybe he'll get washed overboard,' he suggested.

'Then his family will probably sue,' Joanna pointed out. 'We can handle him, Demont.'

'I reckon you can, Mrs Orton.' Like all of Joanna's employees, he had over the years discovered a tremendous faith in her ability to handle every problem. 'Mr Connor would like a word.'

'Not another complaint?'

'Probably, ma'am. Shall I send him off?'

Joanna shook her head. 'Must co-operate with the passengers, Demont.'

Demont held the door, hanging on to the bulkhead as he did so, and Connor staggered in. 'Oh,' he said. 'I didn't mean to interrupt your lunch.'

'You are not going to interrupt my lunch, Mr Connor,' Joanna said. 'If you don't mind watching me eat. You'd better sit down.'

As she was seated at the little table, he had no alternative but to sit on her bunk. She knew he was one of two men travelling alone: they shared D Cabin. He was a young man, somewhat younger than herself, she thought, a mining engineer from South America, who had found himself in Guyana, where he had joined the ship. He was tall and well built, although thinner than be should have been; she suspected malaria at some recent stage. This had also contributed to the gauntness of his features, the somewhat yellowish-brown complexion. His eyes glowed, certainly whenever he looked at her, and his mouth had an odd twist to it, which sometimes gave him an angry expression, as if he hated the world; that made him interesting. They had not spoken more than once or twice on the voyage: she had the impression that he had not spoken to anyone, even his cabin companion, a banking executive who had joined the ship in Barbados, very often. So she gave him an encouraging smile. 'Do please feel free to complain, Mr Connor. Listening to complaints goes with being the owner.'

'Do you sail on every voyage?'

Now the smile spread to her mind. She remembered a sixteen-year-old girl asking the then owner that same question, thirteen years ago. So she made the same reply Howard had given her. 'Chance would be a fine thing, Mr Connor. I sail when I can get away. Maybe once a year.'

'Have you experienced a hurricane before?'

'No. And if things go according to plan, we're not going to experience one now.'

'You're very confident.'

'I have a good crew.'

'But an old ship.'

'You should have thought of that before booking your passage, Mr Connor. But old or not, she'll do the job.'

'I didn't come to complain, Mrs Orton. I came to tell you that I have nothing but admiration for the way you are handling this situation. That if that moron, Martin, does sue, I'll be happy to give evidence on your behalf. So will several of the others.'

'That's very kind of you, Mr Connor. Do you mean you'll be a character witness? Or that you are also an expert in marine engineering and meteorology, as well as navigation? Those are the areas where we will be challenged.'

He flushed. 'I was offering you my help.'

'And I appreciate the offer.' She drank her coffee. 'You must forgive me. I'm a little tired.' She gave him a bright smile. 'I'm going up to the bridge to see how things are going. Would you care to accompany me?'

Captain Heggie raised his eyebrows as Joanna appeared with an escort, both windblown and wet with flying spray. He had already implemented his plan to run before the storm, and the scene was startling in the extreme. In front of them the ocean dropped away in a series of rolling hills with huge valleys beyond. Seen from behind the waves hardly seemed to be breaking, but the rolling effect was even more terrifying. Joanna moved to the wing to look aft, and wished she hadn't, because behind them the rollers were indeed topped with breaking white water to a height of several feet, tumbling over, roaring almost as loudly as the engine as they sought to catch up with the ship.

They had hardly gained the bridge when the first monsters had to be encountered.

Joanna gasped, and instinctively clutched Connor's hand, both clinging to stanchions, as the bows went down into the deep trough before them, charging at the back of the water wall a hundred yards away. Heggie stood by the telegraph, and immediately he rang down for reduced speed. As promised, Bartlett responded immediately, and the ship checked, her bows only just entering the surging hillock, now so close. Even so, green water broke on the foredeck and showered aft, smothering the bridge, while from behind them the roaring increased as the wave behind them caught them up. But Heggie was already ringing down for an increase in speed, and *Caribee Queen* drove forward, scattering the wave breaking aft, driving her bows through the wave in front, to fly upwards, bows for a moment pointing at the sky, before they fell down again into the next trough, and the whole manoeuvre had to be repeated. 'How long can she stand this?' Conner shouted into Joanna's ear.

'I hope as long as we can,' she replied.

Afternoon drifted into evening. Heggie, exhausted, was relieved by Lewis, and the drill continued. Joanna was as drenched in sweat as any of them, but she did not wish to leave the bridge. Because now she knew they were winning. The seas were definitely getting smaller as they raced away from the eye of the storm, the movement was easing, and the engine continued to throb away reassuringly. But it was getting on for midnight before Captain Heggie stretched, and said, 'I reckon you can turn in now, Joanna. I'm going to resume course in an hour.'

'How late will we be?'

He made a face. 'May be twenty-four hours. But the important thing is that we'll get there.'

She stood on tiptoe to kiss him. 'You've done a great job, James. You all have. I'll congratulate you properly tomorrow.'

She staggered to the ladder, aware now of the stiffness creeping over her body, and only then remembering Connor, who was at her elbow. 'Well, now,' she said. 'You've been in at the death. Only it was the life. Did you enjoy it?'

'I enjoyed being with you,' he said. 'At the death, and then the life.'

She slid down the ladder before she replied. 'Mr Connor,' she said. 'I'm going to bed. Alone. And I suggest you do the same.' Shipboard adventures had this effect on people, as she knew only too well.

'I don't think you're going to sleep,' he said. 'I know I am not.' They had reached the foot of the ladder, where they were for a moment sheltered from the wind. He opened the bulkhead door for her and had to catch her as they almost fell through.

Perhaps he knew that shipboard had as much effect on her as anyone. And then, the still surging exhilaration-cum-fear inspired by the storm . . . She wondered how much he knew about her, about her past, or even about her present. And did it matter? She knew what she wanted at that moment. Normally she would have rejected the thought out of hand. But if Dick was really having it off with some bimbo in London . . .

Most of the passengers had retired to their bunks; they would hardly know the traumatic events that had been happening on deck. But Demont was always there. 'Mr Connor and I will have champagne, Demont,' she said.

'Of course, ma'am. Worst over, is it?'

'You could say that.'

He uncorked the bottle. 'Shall I bring it in?'

'I think we'll have it as it is,' Joanna said. Connor took the bottle, and she opened her cabin door. He followed her inside, closed the door behind him. 'I think a hot shower is in order,' she said. But she took the bottle from him first, drank from the neck. He did the same, watching her all the time. 'Do you boast of your conquests, Mr

Connor?' she asked.

'I never have.'

'I would make it a rule.' She stripped off her soaking jumper and shirt, kicked off her shoes, dropped her pants and knickers behind them. 'Another.'

He gave her the bottle, watching her all the while. She took a deep swig. The cabin was going round and round, but that could well be a combination of the movement and exhaustion, as much as the alcohol. 'I should warn you,' she said, 'that the moment my head hits that pillow, I am going to pass out.'

'Sadly, I think that's very likely to be snap.'

Yet he looked interested enough, as he undressed himself. She stepped past the glass barrier into the shower, switched it full on, turned up her face to the flow. She felt rather than heard him come in behind her. 'Did you wedge the bottle?' she asked.

'It's safe.'

'I hate wasting champagne.'

He was against her, and she could feel him. His arms went round her body, and his hands closed over her breasts, but gently, caressingly. The ship rolled and plunged, and they moved with it, to and fro. She turned into his arms and put her own arms round his neck. They kissed, savagely, while pressed against each other. And . . . 'Ooops,' she said.

'Damn,' he said. 'Damn, damn, damn. You will think me the most utter idiot.'

'Actually, I'm flattered,' she said. 'And a shower is the best place for it to happen, wouldn't you say?'

'But . . . shit! I have wanted you so badly. I have dreamed of you every night this voyage.'

She released him, finished washing him, stepped out of the shower and towelled herself dry. 'Then come and dream some more. There's always tomorrow morning.' Her hair was still wet, and she wrapped that in a towel too. It did not seem important.

She lay down with a sigh, waited for him to join her. 'Do you know,' she said, 'I don't even know your name?'

2

The Company

Peter Young was on the dock at Plymouth to greet Joanna as the *Caribee Queen* slowly nosed her way into her berth. So was all the family. Joanna had, of course, been in constant radio contact with both the office and the family since they had escaped the storm, and she had had a portent of doom. But then, she had had that before she went away; now perhaps it was compounded by guilt. She waited on board while the passengers disembarked. Connor was the last to leave. He didn't want to leave at all. 'What happens now?' he asked, having been allowed into her cabin where she was making up her face, wearing only bra and panties.

He had spent a lot of time in this cabin over the past week. He was, she supposed, a continuing moment of madness, born out of the storm and her despair at the collapse of her marriage — and the knowledge of the huge problems that lay immediately ahead. But now the moment of madness had to be ended, and the problems to be faced. 'I have some things to sort out,' she said.

'I'd like to see you again.'

'I should hope you would. But . . . ' she put away her lipstick and turned to face him. 'As I say, there are things I have to do before I can take any time off, Sean. What about Gerry?'

'Well . . . ' Sean Connor flushed. 'He knows where I've been, nights. I didn't have to tell, it was pretty obvious.'

'He's not likely to go charging off to a tabloid, is he?'

'I've sworn him to secrecy.' Sean flushed. 'It was the best I could do.'

'We'll keep our fingers crossed.'

'Would it mean a lot of trouble for you? I got the impression . . . '

'That my marriage is over? I think it probably is. But I intend to be the one who ends it, my way.'

'You're one hell of a woman, Jo. May I call you?'

She shook her head. 'Give me a number where you can be reached, and I'll call you.'

'You will call?'

'I will call. Now, I have a lot to do. Like finishing getting dressed.'

'May I kiss you goodbye?'

'Not without smudging my lipstick. But you can give me a hug and a squeeze.'

He held her against him, and his hands roamed. She did not object when he unclipped her brassiere for a last caress, or slipped his hand inside her panties. It was odd, she thought, how things had a habit of turning full circle. Howard, old enough to be her father, could have had her in this very cabin — but he had been too much of a gentleman, whatever his reputation. Hasim had taught her almost everything she knew about sex, some of which she had passed on to Sean. Dick had always been somewhat in awe of both the beauty and the wealth that had so oddly fallen into his lap. Maybe he had just been unable to grasp it. And this boy, three years younger than she . . . as she had certainly seduced him, did that mean she was no lady? She thought there might be quite a few people who would agree with that.

A last caress, and he was gone. She put the slip of paper on which he had written down a phone number into her handbag, and pulled on her blouse, before concealing her untidy hair beneath a headscarf.

* * *

Once the passengers had left, the family came on board to greet her. 'Oh, Jo!' Matilda, similarly blonde but more heavily built, her older sister, but one of her employees, was waiting to hug and kiss her. 'We were so *worried*.'

Matilda's husband, Billy Montgomery, who managed the Caribee Trust in which all her wealth was secreted, as always looked embarrassed as he in turn hugged her; he had been one of her first admirers, but had had to settle for Matilda — he had also worked for Howard Edge. 'Gosh, it's good to have you back.' Always nervous in her company, today he was more uptight than ever. Their two small children jumped up and down.

William, Joanna's brother, as fair as his sisters, the youngest of the trio but at twenty-eight powerfully built and handsome, still moved awkwardly, even if it was three years since he had stopped one of the bullets meant for Hasim. He too worked for her. 'I wish I'd been there,' he murmured into her hair.

'I'm glad you weren't.' She hugged and kissed his wife, Norma, a slender, dark and quiet young woman who never seemed quite certain that she belonged in the company of the boisterous Grain family.

'Darlings.' She hugged and squeezed Helen — Howard's child, but with her mother's crisply handsome features and fair hair — now a sturdy nine-year old, then swept seven-year-old Raisul from the deck. How like his father he looked, from his dark complexion to long upper lip.

Peter Young, tall and cadaverous in appearance, hung back until the family greetings were over, then he embraced her. When they had first met she had instinctively disliked him. Now she knew his worth and valued him as a friend, and more, an important check on her wilder flights of fancy. 'Tell me,' she whispered.

'It's not good,' he whispered back.

'Then save it for the car. Now, darlings,' she said, 'why don't you all go off home with Aunt Tilly. I'll be right behind you.'

'But Mummy,' Helen said. 'We want to be with you.'

'As I want to be with you,' Joanna assured her. 'But Uncle Peter and I have things to discuss.' She frowned, for the first time realising someone was missing. 'Where is Dick?'

'Ah . . . ' Matilda looked embarrassed.

'He's in bed with 'flu,' Billy said before anyone else could offer an explanation. 'He's at home.'

'Then I'll meet you up there.'

She ushered them to the gangway, and was joined by Captain Heggie. 'You'd better look at the damage,' she suggested to Peter.

They walked along the deck, and he bent over the length of rail that had been crumpled up as if made of matchsticks, then they went up on to the boat deck to see where the launches had been torn away. 'I've alerted the insurers,' Peter said. 'They've a man coming down this afternoon. He'll want to see the Log.'

Heggie nodded. The insurers would, of course, be eager to pounce on any suggestion of negligence or navigational incompetence. Joanna's bags had been carried ashore and loaded into the back of the company Rolls. Now she said goodbye to Heggie, and, as was her custom, to each member of the crew. 'You'll soon be shipshape again,' she told them. 'Meanwhile, have a good holiday.'

* * *

She sat in the back of the car, Young beside her, as they drove out of the city and into the Devon hills. It was odd how memory kept coming back. She had landed at Plymouth, after crossing the Atlantic in that same *Caribee Queen,* then quite a new ship, at almost this same date in 1960. Thirteen years ago! That had been her first visit to England, for despite the fact that she had English parents, she had been born and had spent her girlhood, with her brother and sister, in the then colony of British Guiana on the South American mainland. In fact, she wondered if she would ever have come to England had her father, a superintendent in the Guyanese police force, not been murdered by a man he had sought for another murder.

That had been traumatic. As had been her first thoughts about England, so different in every way to BG. Had anyone told that sixteen-year-old girl that she would one day be sitting in the back seat of a Rolls Royce about to discuss pressing business matters with her company secretary she would have said he was mad. 'Tell me,' she said.

Peter Young sighed. 'The price of oil has gone up seventy per cent. When we can get it. The Arabs are threatening a total ban on any country they consider an ally of the Israelis.'

'That will affect everyone, surely. Not just us.'

'Oh, quite. Although some companies are better able to take that kind of problem than others. Industry is in a mess. There's even talk that the PM may have to reduce the working week to conserve fuel. As for private cars, they may have to be phased out altogether.'

'Especially gas guzzlers like this one,' Joanna agreed. 'What is Andy saying?'

'Andy has been trying to get hold of you.

When I told him you were battling a hurricane in mid-Atlantic he all but blew a fuse.'

'I'll have to see him right away.' Andy Gosling was another old admirer, a one-time friend of Howard Edge's, who had come to her rescue, and that of the firm, when Prince Hasim had been murdered. The deal had been a hard one; he had insisted upon a fifty-one percent share-holding. But beggars couldn't be choosers, and he had at least guaranteed that as long as she held twenty-five per cent of the shares herself, she would remain Chairman and Managing Director. Nothing had changed there. But she had an inkling that he was going to be difficult. 'I suppose the stock market is in a tizzy as well,' she suggested.

'I'm afraid it is. There are bears crawling everywhere. Are you still going home?'

'I do have a home, Peter. We'll go to Caribee House as I promised the kids. We can call Andy from there and set up a meeting. Anyway, I feel I should visit my sick husband.'

'Mm,' Peter agreed.

Joanna glanced at him. 'You mean you don't want to be the one to tell me that he's a cheating bastard. Don't you think it's time I dealt with it?'

'It'll be nasty.'

'Perhaps I'm in the mood to be nasty.'

'Were you scared?'

'I think everyone was scared, Peter. I have never seen seas that big. But I suppose I was better off than most, because I was in charge. With Heggie, of course. He's a good man, Peter. He'll have first pick of the new ships.'

'New ships?'

'Well, *Caribee Queen* is getting old. Her engines, certainly. That's why we got into trouble. But the whole ship is old. So is *Caribee Future*.'

'I wouldn't make too many plans until you find out what Gosling has to say.'

'He'll want the ships,' Joanna said confidently.

* * *

How peaceful Caribee House looked. It was a large mansion, four storeys high, set in its own grounds in the Berkshire countryside, remote from the world save during Ascot week, when the cheers could just be heard from beyond the wood. It had been in the Edge family for two generations, even if the name was now lost, although no doubt her predecessor as Howard's wife, Alicia, was still dreaming of one day getting it back; as she had never remarried, she still called herself Alicia Edge. Alicia was an eccentric woman, to be as polite as possible in Joanna's opinion, who hated her replacement and indeed blamed Joanna for the death of her only son, shot in the same attack that had cost Hasim's life and so very nearly William's as well. Joanna had no desire ever to see her or hear of her again.

The car rolled to a stop before the portico, the dogs barked and surrounded them with wagging tails, and Cummings, the butler, and Mrs Partridge, the housekeeper, came out to greet them, along with the children. 'We only just got here,' Helen said importantly.

'Oh, Mrs Orton.' Cummings seized her hand. 'We were so worried.'

'I'm a bad penny, Cummings,' Joanna said. 'I always turn up.'

She embraced Mrs Partridge. Both Cummings and Mrs Partridge were old friends, who no doubt remembered the night Howard Edge had first brought the frightened young girl home. There had been other young girls before, but none after, and they had grown to respect and even, she thought, love her over the years. 'Are you all right?' Mrs Partridge said.

Joanna smiled. 'I've a few bruises. But

they're all fading now. How is Mr Orton?'

'He'll be the better for seeing you, I'm sure,' Mrs Partridge said, bravely; the servants were naturally aware of the gossip.

'Come along, kids, let's go see Daddy,' Joanna said. 'Mr Young will be staying for lunch, Mr Cummings.' She looked at Peter, eyebrows raised. 'And dinner too?'

He shook his head. 'I think I had better get back to town this afternoon. But I'll make that call now, if I may?'

'Of course. Use the study. Tell him I'll be up tomorrow morning.' She went up the stairs, holding the children's hands.

'Daddy has been very bad-tempered,' Helen confided. She was, of course, perfectly well aware that Dick Orton was not her father, however confused Raisul might be.

'Then we'll have to cheer him up.' Joanna opened the bedroom door. Her husband lay in bed. He had been watching television, but he switched off the set as she came in. Dick Orton was only a few inches taller than his wife, and had always been slight. Nowadays he sported a moustache, which was darker than his fair hair. His face remained as pinched as when she had first met him at secretarial college, thirteen years previously, for all the good living he had enjoyed recently.

'Home the wanderer,' he said, and blew his nose.

'I won't kiss you, if you don't mind,' Joanna said. 'I can't afford a cold right now. Wherever did you get it?'

'God knows. I hear you've been having an exciting time.'

Joanna sat down while the children roamed about the room; they didn't often come in here as Joanna maintained a separate bedroom — she liked to sleep alone, when the operative word was sleep. 'It was more terrifying than exciting,' she said.

'I can't imagine why you do it.'

'I need to live, from time to time.'

'Even if it might involve your dying, from time to time?'

'You weren't really going to die, Mummy, were you?' Helen asked.

'Of course not, darling. It was just Daddy's bad little joke. Now, I tell you what, why don't you run along and find out what there is for lunch. Take Raisul with you. I'll be down in a minute.'

The children banged the door behind them, and Dick began to look apprehensive. 'Okay,' he said. 'So it was a bad joke.'

'Certainly in front of the children. When are you getting up?'

'The quack is coming this afternoon. He

says I really should take it easy.'

'What have you been doing recently that isn't easy?'

'Holding the fort, with you away.'

'Odd. Peter Young didn't mention that to me.'

'That doesn't surprise me. He doesn't like me. None of your people do.'

'You should give them more of a chance, by letting them see you more often, at the office. You are aware that there is a crisis on?'

'Crisis, crisis, crisis. It's a bore.'

'But a bore that has to be settled. I have a meeting with Andy Gosling tomorrow morning. I'm told the share price has slipped.'

'Several points. But that goes for everything. The FT Index is down like a mineshaft,'

'It's our shares I'm worry about.' Caribee Shipping was not sufficiently large to be listed in the FT Index.

'I was meaning to talk with you about that,' Dick said.

Joanna had followed the example set her years ago by Howard Edge, and made her husband a present of a block of shares in the company as a wedding present; this was to make him reasonably independent and less of a kept man. She had in fact been far more generous than Howard had been, and had made over five percent of her twenty-nine percent holding. Nor had she regretted it, even if he had used his private income to finance at least one mistress. When it came to the crunch, that was all he was going to get — that too had been written into their marriage agreement. Until now. Now she needed at least some of those shares back, if she was going to divorce him; she had to maintain that twenty-five percent control. But there again, he was obliged to sell them to her should they ever split, again by the terms of their marriage contract. It was just a matter of which came first, the chicken or the egg. 'Forget it,' she advised. 'We've been through bad times before. We'll come back up.' She smiled at him. 'If you're bothered, I'll buy the shares back off you. Or at least some of them. At the price before I went away. Does that interest you?'

He glared at her. 'No.'

'Suit yourself. Well, I'd better get down to lunch. See you in the funnies.' He switched the television back on.

'Andy is still in an agitated state,' Peter Young told her over lunch.

'I'll cool him down,' Joanna promised. It was splendid, after so long, to preside over a family lunch, even if the chair at the far end of the table was vacant. She was her usual bright and cheerful self, engaging both the children and her siblings in conversation, telling them about the storm, while her brain was concentrating on other things. She really needed to get some of those shares back. In fact, she had to, before she dared split with Dick. So then, why split at all? He had his floozie, while she . . . she had a phone number. What an absurdly immoral situation. Or would amoral be a better word? Or maybe just modern.

She needed to talk with Matilda. When they had first come to England, Matilda had been the most amoral woman she knew; Alicia Edge had gone so far as to call her a whore. But since her marriage to Billy she had been the soul of propriety and a good mother. The ridiculous thing was that it was *she* who had insisted upon the change. 'If you're going to work for me,' she had said, 'there's to be no more sleeping around. I'm not asking you to give up sex. But choose one man and stick to him. One at a time, at any rate.'

Matilda had taken the advice to heart, chosen Billy . . . and married him. At that time, of course, Joanna would no more have considered sleeping with any man save her husband than she would have tried flying without an airplane. How times changed. But

Matilda was still her best source of advice . . . supposing she was going to carry things any further. But she had to do that. She had promised to contact Connor. If she did not, he would not have too much trouble in discovering where she lived. Besides, she wanted to see him again.

* * *

Peter Young departed after lunch to return to the office. Joanna paid Dick a courtesy call, then retired to her own bedroom, having invited Matilda to join her; the children were playing in the garden, and Billy was enjoying a siesta downstairs. 'Must feel good, to be back in your own bed,' Matilda suggested.

'It was quite an adventure. How have things been here?'

Matilda shrugged, kicked off her shoes, and lay beside her.

'What were you thinking of, specifically?'

'Dick.'

'Haven't seen much of Dick, while you were away.'

'You know he's having an affair?'

Matilda turned her head, sharply. 'You mean, you do?'

Joanna nodded, moving her head up and down the pillow. 'That's one of the reasons I went, to think about things. I had a report last month.'

'Shit!' Matilda remarked. 'You mean you had a detective on him?'

'It seemed necessary. And it was necessary.'

'What are you going to do?'

'I don't know.'

Matilda raised herself on her elbow to peer at her sister. 'You mean you're going to forgive and forget?'

'That's not my scene.'

Matilda lay down again. 'I didn't think it was,' she agreed.

'But there are complications.'

'You don't have any joint children. That's a plus.'

'I was thinking in business terms. He has too big a holding. I have to get some of it back.'

Matilda made a whistling sound. 'That was careless of you.'

'I know. I was in love. But we have a written deal. If things go bad, I can buy back the necessary to regain twenty-five percent.'

'Then what's the problem?'

'The problem is that to implement the deal, I have to make the break. You with me?'

'But if that's what you want to do . . . '

'Do I, Tilly? I mean to say, to have one husband drowned before my eyes, another shot before my eyes, and now to divorce the third . . . '

'Stuff the tabloids.'

'They penetrate through to the children. Or they will.'

'So? As I said, Dick isn't their father. And I don't reckon they're all that fond of him.'

'It'll still be nasty. And if I don't make the break, well, I have his shares supporting mine. Which is all I need.'

'Isn't that going to leave you at his mercy?'

Joanna closed her eyes. There was more to it than the children's attitude, of course. Dick, for all his vices, was her oldest living male friend — apart from William, of course. He had been one of the first boys she had met on coming to England, and they had romped together and indulged in all the excesses of the sizzling Sixties, from alcohol to coke. For her, briefly. For Dick just as briefly, he had sworn. From that degenerate scene she had been rescued by Howard Edge. Dick had gone his own way. But when they had got back together, he had been a strong, tough character, physically. He had proved that whilst defending her following Hasim's murder. Her mistake had been in supposing that physical strength and courage necessarily implied mental strength and courage as well. But still, to cast him off . . .

★ ★ ★

She had still not made up her mind when she drove into town the next morning, with Matilda, who was her PR. Secretaries and clerks gushed as she strode into Caribee Building, welcoming her back, exclaiming over the danger she had been in. Harriet, her secretary was waiting outside the lift shaft. 'Mr Gosling is upstairs,' she said.

Joanna raised her eyebrows; it was only just past nine. 'He *is* anxious,' she remarked, as they rode up.

'What are you going to do?' Matilda asked.

'Listen to what he has to say, first.' The car stopped at the fifth floor, where Peter Young was waiting for her, having been alerted by the front desk.

'Gosling is here. With Townsend.'

'So I gathered. You'd better let me see them alone, to begin with.'

He raised his eyebrows. 'Is that wise?'

'In the first instance, yes,' Joanna said. 'Don't worry, I'll buzz if I need any help. One buzz for you, Peter, two buzzes for Matilda, three buzzes for you both.'

Peter and Matilda looked at each other.

'And stop worrying,' Joanna advised. But she took a deep breath before entering the boardroom.

The two men stood as Joanna entered. Andy would be about forty now, she supposed; she had deliberately endeavoured to keep him at arm's length throughout their relationship. They had first met at a pool party in Howard's heyday, when she, on her first appearance at that kind of party, had been widely regarded as Howard's new mistress. That supposition had not then been correct, but as she had been only too well aware that it was going to happen, no matter how hard she resisted it, she had been left with a faintly defensive attitude to all the *aficionados* who had been at that party.

Principal amongst those, after Prince Hasim himself, was Andy, who had been the first to admire her bathing-suit-clad body. As he had been a friend of Howard's, he had not attempted to muscle in, but he had always been there. He had made what she had supposed to be a play following Howard's death, but on that occasion had been beaten to the post by Prince Hasim. Then he had reappeared following Hasim's death, when to her surprise, and considerable humiliation, it had turned out that he had not been after her body after all, but her company.

She had desperately needed the support following Hasim's death, thus she had accepted his offer and his plans. And in fact they had worked quite well together over the last four years. He had never overstepped the bounds of propriety, and had fulfilled his side of the bargain with meticulous honesty; his consortium had pumped sufficient funds into Caribee Shipping to keep it well afloat, and she had retained her position and authority as Chairman and Managing Director. She was puzzled as to what could have now so upset him. The situation was undoubtedly critical, but it was critical for the whole country, not just Caribee Shipping.

Now he smiled as he kissed her hand. He was a good-looking man, tall and only just beginning to run to a paunch, with distinguished grey wings to his dark hair. He dressed immaculately, and wore a carnation in his buttonhole. 'Joanna,' he said. 'You are a sight for sore eyes, as always.' He looked past her, as if expecting her to be accompanied by some of her entourage, but she had closed the door behind herself. 'You know Tom, of course.'

'I do.' Joanna shook hands with Tom Townsend, a rather raffish looking character who wore a moustache.

'So you've been trying to commit suicide,' Andy said, pleasantly.

Joanna took her chair at the head of the table, and they sat one to either side. 'If you mean I have been taking a close look at how my crews, and my ships, stand up to bad weather, that is correct.'

'You knew there was to be a hurricane?'

'We knew there was one about. We didn't anticipate actually getting involved with it.'

Andy tapped the file in front of him. 'Carton says there was an engine breakdown.'

'A burst fuel line. The fact is, Andy, *Caribee Queen*, and all her equipment, is getting too old. The same goes for *Caribee Future*. One of the subjects we need to address, as soon as possible, are replacements.' She saw the two men exchange glances. 'I said, as soon as possible. I quite understand that in the present economic climate it may not be viable. But this situation can hardly last much longer. Can it?'

'I'm afraid it not only can, but it may well do so,' Townsend said. 'The Arabs have discovered that they possess a most formidable weapon, and seem prepared to use it. Your old friend Mutil is prominent in this.'

'Well, he never did like us, anyway,' Joanna said. 'We must put our faith in the likelihood that they will start quarrelling amongst themselves. They always have in the past. And in any event, whatever the situation, whatever the costs involved, we have to live with it. The

United Kingdom cannot just shut down. So our profits may be smaller for a while. So will everyone else's. And as soon as our own oil starts to flow . . . '

'Pie in the sky,' Andy said. 'It may happen, some time in the future. We have to consider the here and now.'

'All right,' Joanna said. 'Let us do that. We have operated very successfully over the last six years, since this consortium was put together. Our profits have been good, our dividends satisfactory, our share price excellent. We have an adequate reserve fund.'

'All of which are now in deep danger,' Townsend commented. 'And that reserve fund is adequate only in what might be termed normal circumstances.'

'I repeat, we are in no different circumstances to anyone else,' Joanna insisted. 'Save that a lot of our competitors are not in such good shape. The one mistake we could make would be to give the impression we are panicking, as it appears so many other people are doing. I intend to place an order for tenders for two new ships, immediately, and to let the media know this.'

'And how do you propose to pay for these vessels?' Andy asked.

'Let's get the quotes first. Then I'll have a talk with the bank. If they can't do it, we'll talk to Miller & Sparks about a flotation. Now is the time to think big, Andy. Not small. Then when this crisis ends, we shall be in a stronger position than any of our competitors.'

'I'm afraid I don't agree with you,' Andy said.

'We feel that now is the time to pull in our horns,' Townsend said. 'Lie low, for a while. Scrap the two out-of-date ships. If, as seems likely, world trade is going to be stagnating for a while, we can operate with the two newer vessels we already have. Cut the Caribbean and the Australian sailings in half.'

'And the crews of the older vessels?'

'I'm afraid they'll have to go. Oh, we'll tell them that the moment things pick up and we can splash out on new ships they'll get their jobs back . . . ' He paused as he gazed at Joanna's expression.

'Those crews are my oldest and most trusted employees,' Joanna said.

'Well,' Andy said, 'we can mingle the best of them in with the crews of the new vessels, and let some of *them* go.'

'I have never heard such a load of rubbish in my life,' Joanna said. 'It's not even short-sighted; it's total blindness. You cut our work force, our fleet, and our delivery contracts, in half, and we'll never get them back again.'

'Once we have made sure that we can stay viable, no matter how long the crisis lasts,' Townsend said. 'Then we will be in a position to . . . well . . . ' he glanced at Andy, anxiously.

'I had dinner with Roger Petherick, a couple of nights ago,' Andy said.

'Oh, yes?' The adrenalin was starting to pump in her veins.

'Well,' Andy said. 'Naturally Petherick Shipping is feeling the crunch too. He was thinking that perhaps the time has come for some of the smaller lines to merge.' He paused, and watched Joanna's nostrils dilate.

'Makes sense to me,' Townsend ventured.

Joanna gave him a look which had him leaning back in his chair. 'And on what terms would we merge?' she asked, softly.

'He was thinking that if he and his partners bought fifty-one percent of our shares . . . ' Andy said.

'Go on.'

'Well, he is an active shipowner, unlike me. He would therefore expect to be Chairman. But I imagine he would agree to your remaining as MD, or at least, chief executive.'

'You imagine?' Joanna said.

'He would also want the name to be

Petherick Shipping,' Andy hurried on. 'Well, that again is logical, as he has more ships.'

'Six,' Townsend put in. 'All reasonably new.'

'Over my dead body,' Joanna said.

There was brief silence, while Townsend and Andy looked at each other. 'I know this is a bitter pill to swallow, Joanna,' Andy said. 'But it's not as if Caribee Shipping has been built up by your family over generations. It was founded by Howard's grandfather, brought to a viable concern by Howard's father, and began to decline under Howard. It is to your eternal credit that when Howard died you revived the company. You did wonders. But times change. And one must go with the times. I very much doubt whether in another twenty-five years there will be any small independent shipping lines about.'

'There will be, and Caribee Shipping will be one of them,' Joanna said. 'Managed by my son.'

'I think you are taking a rather limited point of view,' Andy said. 'With respect.'

'I can take any point of view I wish,' Joanna said. 'By the terms of our legally-binding agreement, I remain Chairman, Managing Director, and in complete control of this company, so long as I possess twenty-five percent of its shares. Nothing has changed.

The only decision that matters here is mine. And I am telling you that my company is not up for grabs. And just in case you have any funny ideas, gentlemen, I should remind you that, again according to our legally-binding agreement, you cannot sell your shares unless I agree to sell mine. And I am not going to do that.'

Once again the two men exchanged glances. 'I entirely agree with the situation as you have outlined it,' Andy said at last. 'But, as I say, times change. Perhaps you are unaware that you no longer own twenty-five percent of the company shares.'

Joanna tossed her head. 'Don't give me that rubbish. So I made my husband a gift of five percent when we were married. You agreed, in writing, Andy, that for the purposes of the company agreement, those shares remained in my possession, as I could buy them back from Dick whenever I chose.'

'If he still possesses them when you wish to buy,' Andy said quietly. 'If I am correct, while, as you have just reminded us, we cannot sell our shares without agreement from you as chairperson, you did not make the same stipulation with regard to your husband. I assume you did not think that was necessary But there it is.'

'You're lying,' Joanna snapped.

'My dear Joanna, that is slanderous, before a witness.'

Joanna glared at him. 'When is this supposed to have happened?'

'Two days ago.'

'Two?' While *Caribee Queen* was approaching Plymouth.

'Two days ago my husband was in bed with 'flu. He still is in bed with 'flu'

'One can buy and sell shares by telephone, Joanna.'

'But . . . why should he do that?'

'I think it may have been intimated to him, by interested parties, that you had discovered his indiscretions, and might well decide to end your marriage. In which case, again as you have reminded us, you would be entitled to demand from him the return of all his shares. I imagine he decided that the best thing to do was get rid of them before that happened.'

'You are unspeakable,' Joanna said.

'Are you suggesting it was I who told him you knew?'

'Wasn't it?'

'My dear Joanna, really! But there it is. You no longer have a controlling share in this company, and we are therefore entitled to vote for your removal from the position of Chairman and Managing Director at the next shareholders' meeting. I have put this down for next Thursday. But I felt that we should have this little private chat first, so that you would be prepared, as it were.'

Joanna looked from face to face. She was not sure she was seeing them clearly. But if there were tears in her eyes, they were tears of the sheerest outrage. They both smiled at her.

'Of course,' Townsend said, 'if you feel, in all the circumstances, that you would like to sell out, we should be happy to buy your shareholding. I'm afraid the price is a little down, and may go further, but it's still over six pounds. That would be one point two million pounds for you. Not too bad, eh?'

'Once you offered me nearly three million,' Joanna muttered.

'Ah, yes,' Andy agreed. 'But that was when you had seventy-five percent, and the price was somewhat better. Times do change, Joanna.'

'Yes,' Joanna said. 'But they haven't changed yet. Until next Thursday's meeting I am still Chairman and Managing Director. So now you can get out. Both of you. *Allons. Vamoose. Scapa.* Leave my building.'

'Well, I say . . . ' Townsend protested.

Andy jerked his head. 'I'd like a word alone with Mrs Orton, Tommy.'

Townsend swallowed, then gave Joanna a stiff little bow.

'No doubt we'll meet again on Thursday, Mrs Orton.' He left the room.

'Another offer?' Joanna demanded. She knew that at any moment she was going to explode.

'Why, yes, you could put it that way,' Andy said. 'Are you really going to divorce Dick?' He studied her for a few seconds, then went on, as she did not reply. 'If you don't, you need your head examined. You must know that he has a mistress?'

'Does all London know that?' she asked, wearily.

'I'm afraid it does. And then, he has behaved like the most utter bastard in quite literally pulling the rug from beneath your feet, in effect costing you your company.'

'Does it matter to you, now?' she asked. 'What I do?'

'It matters very much. You know how fond I have always been of you. As I have told you, I felt I couldn't compete with Howard. Not financially, but simply because you were his protege. I will admit I was bit dashed when, after Howard's death, you upped and married that wog Hasim. But he had a lot of money to spend and I suppose a girl likes to have new experiences. I can't say I wept when I saw that he'd been done down by his Arab brethren. Now, I thought . . . and damn me if you didn't go off and marry some clerk. After I had put your company back on its financial feet. That was shocking.'

'You congratulated me at my wedding, if I remember,' Joanna said.

'Well, a chap has to show the right form, don't you know. But he was a total mistake. No money, no breeding. I suppose he's good in bed. You go for men who are good in bed, don't you, Joanna? But they do need to have breeding as well.'

'You really belong crawling along a gutter,' Joanna remarked.

'I always try to be a realist, to be pragmatic, and never to lose my cool. I think you should divorce Orton and marry me. I've waited a long time for this moment. How old were you when we first met? Sixteen? You were quite enchanting. I never doubted then that you would become an even more enchanting woman. I was quite prepared to let another man break you in. But that's all done, now. And I was right. You are quite the most enchanting woman in London.'

'Listen,' she said. 'Go away. Please. Go far, away.'

'You need to think about it,' he said. 'Marry me, and you'll be richer than you have been since Hasim died. What's more, it won't just be income, it'll be capital. I'll still buy your shares for one point two, but that'll be your pin money. You'll have nothing more to worry about for the rest of your life. I will happily act the stepfather to your two children, although I will certainly hope to add to the happy home. If I say so myself, I am quite as good in bed as any of your past or present husbands. I'd be quite happy to give you a trial run, if you wish.'

Joanna pressed her buzzer, three times. Andy raised his eyebrows, then turned sharply as the door opened to admit both Peter Young and Matilda. 'This creature who masquerades as a gentleman is just leaving,' Joanna said. 'Will you kindly see him off the premises.'

'Do you really think you can throw me out?' Andy demanded.

'I know I can throw you out, Andy,' Joanna said. 'And that is what I am doing. And just in case you get any funny ideas, I should inform you that Matilda is a black belt at judo. Her real purpose in life is not to act as my PR, as is supposed, but to act as my bodyguard. Now, are you leaving, or should Matilda reveal some of her talents?' Matilda, having got the drift, began to look suitably menacing. She was, Joanna knew, an expert at both judo and karate.

'Hicks from the colonies,' Andy said disparagingly, but he got up. 'We'll meet again on Thursday, Joanna, and by then I will have destroyed you. I am going to hold a press conference to tell the world that two of your ships are barely seaworthy, that your marriage is on the rocks, and that the future of Caribee Shipping is so grim as to be unspeakable. I am going to drive the share price right through the floor, so far they'll never see daylight again.'

'But if you do that, your own shares will be worthless,' Peter protested.

'Of course. But my share-holding in Caribee Shipping, however large and valuable on paper, is only a portion of my portfolio, and besides, I'll be able to do a deal with Petherick to buy my holding at considerably above the market price. But you, dear lady, will not have two cents to rub together. Nor will you have Caribee House, or the flat, or that Rolls you keep parked outside. Think about it.' He left the room.

3

Shares

There was complete silence in the boardroom as Joanna slowly sat down. Matilda was the first to speak. 'Can he do that?' she asked.

'Probably.'

'If he's engaging in some private deal with Petherick,' Peter said. 'We'll have him in court.'

'If we could ever prove it,' Joanna said. 'Why wasn't I told that Dick had sold his shares?'

'Dick?' Peter and Matilda spoke together. They obviously didn't know what had happened.

'Your husband manages my trust company, Tilly,' Joanna said. 'You're not going to tell me he didn't know?'

'He never said anything to me,' Matilda said. 'Oh, the wretch.'

'The world is full of wretches,' Joanna said.

'Would you mind telling me just what has happened?' Peter asked. Joanna outlined her conversation with Townsend and Andy, and he gave a low whistle. 'I would say they have us by the short and curlies.'

'My short and curlies aren't for grabbing,' Joanna said, and stood up.

'But what are you going to do? What *can* you do?'

'I am going to pay a visit to my sick husband,' Joanna said.

'I would also like to have a word with your husband, Tilly.'

'He said he was flying across to Jersey today.'

'Well, get hold of him and tell him to get his ass back here, on the next plane.'

'Sorting them out isn't going to help,' Peter said gloomily.

'I know that, Peter,' Joanna said. 'But I do intend to sort them out. Then I intend to regain control of my company. Arrange a press conference for tomorrow morning.'

'What can you say to them?'

Joanna smiled. 'I'll think of something.'

* * *

'Home, Charlie,' she told her chauffeur. He was a huge, bearlike man, an old friend, who had worked for Howard Edge, and was one of those who could remember his erstwhile boss taking that pretty, innocent, teenage girl out to Caribee House. Had that pretty, innocent, teenage girl ever existed? Now he made no comment, that having driven his employer into the city, with her sister-cum-bodyguard as always at her side, she was driving out again before lunch, without her sister.

Joanna was grateful for the long drive into Berkshire, because it gave her time for her emotions to settle down. And they were settling in the direction she wanted, a white heat of fury at the people who had betrayed her. How she could ever have supposed herself in love with that creep Richard Orton? But he was only a blip compared with what he had done. What she would now have to do. She had no option.

Cummings was as usual on the doorstep to greet her. 'Is anything the matter, madam?'

'A lot, Cummings. But we'll sort it out.' The thought that she might have to leave this house, her home for thirteen years, and people like Cummings and Mrs Partridge, her most faithful supporters in everything she had ever set out to do . . . it only hardened her resolve. She went upstairs, opened the door of Dick's bedroom.

'Well, hello, sweetheart,' he said. 'That was a quick trip. No problems, I hope.'

Joanna advanced to the bedside. 'Get up,' she said.

'My dear Jo, I'm sick, I have a temperature.'

'I don't give a damn if you have galloping pneumonia. Get up, get dressed, and get out.'

'You can't throw me out. I'm your husband.'

'Not any more, you're not. I am filing for divorce, this morning.'

'Now, Jo . . . '

'You have fifteen minutes to be off my premises,' she said. 'Or I will have you dumped on the street.'

He swung his legs out of bed. 'You've found out about the shares!'

'I have found out about everything,' she said.

'Listen. I can explain.'

'Who did you sell the shares to?'

His face tightened. 'I don't think I can tell you that.'

'No matter. I will find out from Billy. But if you won't tell me, then you cannot explain. Anything.' She slammed the door behind herself and went downstairs, grateful that the children would both be at school.

Mrs Partridge appeared. 'Is there anything needs to be done, Mrs Orton?'

'Yes,' Joanna said. 'Don't ever call me Mrs Orton again.' She went into the study, dialled her solicitor.

‘Joanna?’ John Giffard was another avuncular figure; the city, all London, was full of avuncular figures as regards her — she wondered how many of them she could trust? ‘I’m told you’ve been risking death on the high seas.’

‘John, I wish you to prepare papers for the divorce of myself and Dick.’ There was a moment’s silence. ‘I wish them filed today,’ Joanna said.

‘You wouldn’t like us to meet and talk about it first?’

‘There is nothing to talk about.’

‘There are, you know. Grounds — ’

‘I have proof of adultery.’

‘Ah. Yes. Messy. Now, a separation, followed by — ’

‘Adultery,’ Joanna said.

‘Ah. Right. Now, settlement . . . ’

‘No settlement,’ Joanna said.

‘My dear Joanna . . . ’

‘As I am sure you remember, John, when we married,’ Joanna said, ‘I settled fifty thousand shares of Caribee Shipping on Dick. They were then worth roughly a quarter of a million pounds, which was more money than he had ever had in his life before. He accepted that that was in full and final settlement of any claim he might have if we split.’

'I don't think they're quite worth that now,' Giffard ventured.

'He also accepted that the value of the shares would be subject to market fluctuation, and that if we split I would buy the shares back at the original price, or the present price, whichever was higher.'

'And is that what you are proposing to do?'

'I can't,' Joanna said. 'He's already sold them.'

Giffard was silent for a few seconds. Then he said, 'But, now that I do remember the marriage contract, it was stated that he could not sell his shares without your permission. Did you give permission?'

'No I did not.'

'Well, then . . . '

'What do you want me to do, John? Sue my husband for the money? He's probably already spent it. Anyway, I don't give a damn about the money. It's the shares that were important, and they're gone.'

'Does that mean you lose control of the company?'

'Over my dead body,' Joanna said. 'Just prepare those papers and file them.'

'I'll get on to it right away. Thank God there are no mutual children to complicate matters. But there is one more thing: co-habitation.'

'Dick is leaving Caribee House, today,' Joanna said.

* * *

He stood in the doorway, fully dressed, his expression a mixture of anger and apprehension. 'You're not going to get away with this,' he said.

'Watch me. Where are your suitcases?'

'I haven't had time to pack. I'll send for my things.'

'Make it soon. And don't come yourself.'

'Jo . . .' he came into the room. 'Can't we sit down and talk this over? I mean to say, I'm your oldest friend. Remember the good times we had when we were kids? And I saved your life from the Qadiri assassin. Remember?'

'I do remember, Dick,' she said. 'And I was, and am, eternally grateful. But now you may have cost me my company, Raisul's inheritance. And you did it in an underhand way. You have also found a sexual interest apart from me. I hate you for both of those things. Now please leave.'

'Where am I supposed to go?' he asked, plaintively.

'Doesn't your girlfriend have a home?' He glared at her for several seconds, then left the room. Joanna discovered she was shivering.

* * *

There was so much to be done, so much of it really unpleasant. There was only one source from which she could obtain the shares to regain control of the company. The deal had been that Andy and his associates had bought enough of her stock to give them a fifty-one per cent shareholding. They had then bought out all of the remaining shareholders, save one, and their actual holding was sixty-three percent. Of the remaining thirty-seven percent, she held twenty-nine, five of which she had given to Dick and was now apparently lost to her, reducing her holding to twenty-four percent, one per cent below the figure required to give her perpetual control of the company. But there remained eight per cent, a matter of a hundred thousand shares held by Alicia Edge, Howard's first wife. Even half of those hundred thousand shares would put her back in control, by the terms of the original agreement. Andy had presumably not considered them important, because he knew that she and Alicia hated each other, that indeed the last time they had met Alicia had physically attacked her; it had been Andy himself who had separated them.

So, whatever now needed doing, had to be done. And it had to be done before Andy reflected long enough to realise that there could just be a chink in his armour. She called Cummings.

'Is Charlie still here?'

'Of course, madam.'

'Very good. I am going out, possibly for several hours. I don't think I shall be back for lunch.'

'Of course, madam. Should anyone call . . .'

'Just tell them I'm out, and you don't know where.'

'Of course, Madam.'

Joanna telephoned her bank, was put through to Barry Andrews, the Area Manager. Like almost everyone else in the business world, Andrews had regarded her with acute distrust when as a twenty-year-old widow she had told him she intended to take charge of Caribee Shipping herself, and would need a good deal of financing to do so. His immediate rejection had been dissipated by the backing of Prince Hasim, and since then he had come to accept, and indeed, admire her, as a woman who meant what she said and who invariably got what she wanted. But today even his voice was worried. 'Half a million, Joanna? This is a bad time.'

'For everyone. I'm not going to buy a yacht, Barry. I need to buy some shares, and they are going to be expensive. You know I'm good for it. And you can have the new shares as additional security as soon as they're mine.'

'Well, of course, Joanna, we'll back you,' he agreed.

'You're a dear. I'll be in touch the moment I've actually written the cheque.'

Joanna put on her mink, went out to the car. Charlie had already been alerted, and hastily stubbed out his cigarette. 'Where to, Mrs Orton?'

'From now on I would like you to call me Mrs Edge again,' Joanna said.

'Yes, madam.'

'So let's go call on the other Mrs Edge. You know the address, I should think?' Charlie gulped.

* * *

It was a long drive. Alicia lived with her daughter Victoria on the south coast, just outside the Hampshire town of Lymington, in a small house which had views out over the harbour, principally a yacht haven and ferry terminus, covered with gleaming water at high tide and glutinous mud at low, with a glimpse of the Isle of Wight in the background. There was a small drive and a garage to the right of the building. Neighbours parted curtains to stare as the Rolls turned in, crunching the gravel, and stopped outside the door. 'I don't know how long I'm going to be, Charlie,' Joanna said.

'No problem, Mrs Or . . . Mrs Edge.'

Joanna rang the bell, and after a moment it was answered by a maid. Alicia had not given up all of her creature comforts. 'Is Mrs Edge in?' Joanna asked, pleasantly.

'Who shall I say is calling, madam?'

'What are *you* doing here?' Alicia was coming down the stairs; clearly she had seen the car from an upstairs window.

'A social call, my dear,' Joanna said. 'You're looking well.'

Alicia was some ten years older than herself, and was a very well-preserved forty. She was a small woman, her pretty features somewhat tight, who wore her fair hair short, and had a compact figure. She wore a trouser suit, and as always several expensive rings. 'So do you,' she remarked, grudgingly.

'May I come in?' Joanna asked, as the maid stood by helplessly. The meeting was not getting off to a flying start.

'As you're here.' Alicia came down to the foot of the stairs and held out a limp hand. Joanna gave it a quick squeeze. Alicia led her into a comfortable lounge. 'Coffee? Oh, I forgot: you always drink champagne at twelve in the morning.'

'I think coffee would be best, today,' Joanna said.

'Coffee, Joanna,' Alicia called, and smiled. 'Her name isn't actually Joanna, but I call her that.' Joanna sat down; this is simply not going to work, she told herself. But she had to try. Alicia sat opposite her. 'So, what brings you down to this little neck of the woods.'

'A business matter,' Joanna said. Alicia raised her eyebrows. 'I'm attempting to dot some i's and cross some t's,' Joanna explained. 'And I was wondering . . . how would you like to sell some of your shares in the company?'

Alicia's smile this time was more genuine. 'You are attempting to be a smarty-pants, as always, Joanna. You are looking for a bargain while the price is down.'

'Well,' Joanna said, and waited while the maid served coffee and withdrew. 'There is some talk that the price may not recover for a while. However, I don't want to do you down, my dear Alicia. I will pay the price the shares were before the Arab-Israeli War began. I think it was about eight. If you were to sell me half your shares at that price, you would realise four hundred thousand pounds.'

'You have that kind of money to splash around?'

'I do.'

'And it doesn't occur to you that if I needed, or wanted, that much cash, I would have already sold the shares?'

'You're not going to tell me you have?'

'No, I have not. That is my stake in Howard's company, and I intend to keep it.'

'Selling half, you would still retain a considerable holding.'

'And you would be increasing yours. You'll have to tell me why you want my shares.'

Joanna drank some coffee while she got her thoughts in order. There was more than one way to play this, but Alicia had just indicated the most promising. She gave an elaborate sigh. 'You may as well know the truth. Dick has stabbed me in the back. He has sold his shares, illegally, and left me with only a twenty-four per cent interest.'

'Aha!' Alicia said. 'So you have lost control.'

'Not yet. The shareholders' meeting is next Thursday.'

'I haven't been advised.'

'I'm sure the advice is in the post. Andy is in a hurry.'

'Well, well,' Alicia said, all manner of expressions passing over her face as she considered the power she had just acquired. 'And then you're out on your ass.'

'Not quite,' Joanna said. 'I still have my twenty-four per cent.'

'But no control. I suppose Andy intends to run the company himself. He should have done that long ago.'

'Andy,' Joanna said, 'intends to liquidate the company, by selling it to Petherick.'

Alicia frowned at her. 'He can't do that.'

'I'm afraid, if I am no longer Chairman and Managing Director, he can and he intends to, by the simple process of selling all his holding to Petherick. The deal has already been drawn up, I understand. The Caribee flag, the Caribee logo, will disppear, the Caribee ships will be absorbed into the Petherick line, and you and I, and Howard, of course, will be history. Forgotten history within five years.'

Alicia continued to stare at her. 'How do I know this is true?'

'You can ring Peter Young.'

Another long stare. 'I think I'd rather ring Andy.'

'Oh, but . . . ' Joanna bit her lip.

'You wouldn't like that, would you?'

'No, I would not like that,' Joanna snapped. 'My object is to save Howard's company. I thought you might feel the same way. Once

Andy finds out I intend to fight him, he . . . well . . . '

'He'll come down here and make me a better offer.' Alicia got up and began to walk around the room. 'One thing I have always admired about you, Joanna, is your unmitigated gall. Howard and I were perfectly happily married when you appeared. You inveigle yourself into his life, make him think he is in love with you, get him to rewrite his will in your favour, and then carry him off to the wilds of South America to drown him in some rapids.'

'Listen,' Joanna said. 'If there were a single other person present I'd have you in court for slander.'

'Ha!' Alicia commented.

'You know as well as I that your marriage was over long before I ever met Howard. He was taking girls to the flat on a virtually nightly basis. He went for me because I wouldn't play.'

'The oldest trick in the world,' Alicia sneered.

'It happened to be genuine. I only ever moved in with him after you had left. I never asked him either to marry me or change his will in my favour. Those were his decisions, just as it was his decision to shoot those rapids. I begged him not to.'

'Ha,' Alicia commented again. 'The fact remains, you had no right to the company, to Caribee House, to the flat, to that Rolls outside. By rights they were all mine. And young Howie's. Now, thanks to you and your Arab prince, my Howie is dead. I hate you for that. And now that you've gone in over your head you have the cheek to come here and ask me to bail you out.'

'I have made you a perfectly fair offer,' Joanna said, now also standing. 'Most people would say it is a generous offer. More than generous, in the present circumstances. I am doing it to keep control of the company. Because that is what Howard wanted. If you can't appreciate that, you are a vicious, twisted woman.' They glared at each other. Because she is, a vicious, twisted woman, Joanna thought. 'Well,' she said, 'as I seem to have made a wasted journey, I'll say goodbye.' She picked up her handbag. 'Thanks for the coffee.'

'What are you going to do?' Alicia asked. Suddenly she was genuinely curious.

Joanna shrugged. 'Whatever I can.'

'There's nothing you can do,' Alicia said, 'without my support.'

'So, have a good gloat. In time you'll merely feel ashamed to have let Howard down.'

'If I agreed to support you,' Alicia said, 'there are things I would require.'

Joanna, almost at the door, checked. But there couldn't be any misapprehensions. 'Your support is no good to me, Alicia,' she said. 'Merely having your shares voting with mine at the meeting won't matter a damn. We don't have enough. The only way we can save the company is for me to regain control as stipulated in my agreement with Andy. I have to have twenty-five per cent of the shares, in my name, by next Thursday.'

'I wish the use of the flat. When you are not occupying it, of course.'

Was it going to happen? Joanna felt a sudden glow of both confidence and energy, whereas five minutes before she had been absolutely drained of both. 'I have no objection to that.'

'I wish a seat on the board.'

Joanna's jaw dropped. 'You? You have never had a seat on the board.'

'That was because Howard wouldn't let me. But you are going to let me, aren't you, Joanna? I think it would be a good thing for there to be two women on the board.'

Joanna sighed. But having Alicia making stupid suggestions and raising irrelevant points, as would certainly be the case, would be nothing more than an irritation, compared with losing the company. 'All right,' she said.

'And for Stephen.'

'Who?'

Alicia flushed. 'So you don't know everything, after all. There is a man called Stephen Maddox, who I wish to have a seat on the board of Caribee Shipping.'

Joanna sat down. 'I'm surely entitled to ask who this man is? What are his qualifications?'

'Oh, he knows about boards and things. He's my financial adviser.'

'You have a lover?' Joanna was astounded.

'What's so remarkable about that?' Alicia demanded, flushing more deeply.

'Nothing. I apologise.'

Alicia sniffed. 'You mean you are surprised that I, unlike you, remained loyal to Howard's memory for so long. But a woman needs love.' Clearly, she meant sex.

'Absolutely,' Joanna agreed. But the idea of having some toy-boy on the board . . . On the other hand, she had always worked on the principal of selecting priorities, and sticking to them absolutely. Priority number one was the company. If she didn't control it, it wouldn't matter to her who sat on the board. If she did control the company, well, she had always controlled the board as well.

'Well?' Alicia demanded.

'If that's what you want, my dear,' Joanna

said. 'So, will you now telephone your broker and authorise him to sell half of your shareholding in Caribee Shipping to me, at the price quoted last November, and I will telephone my broker and tell him to complete the deal.'

'Now?'

'Before I leave,' Joanna said, and gave one of her bright smiles. 'I wouldn't be able to digest my lunch if I thought you might be having seconds thoughts.'

* * *

'Find me a nice pub, and join me for lunch, Charlie,' Joanna said. It was past one, and she was hungry.

'It will be a pleasure, Mrs Edge,' Charlie said, and obliged almost immediately. 'I would say your meeting with the other Mrs Edge went well,' he ventured as they sat together, drinking beer and eating cold meat sandwiches.

'As well as I could have hoped,' Joanna said.

'So . . . all is well, then?'

She glanced at him. Charlie had been Howard's chauffeur before she had inherited him, and he had served her faithfully and well for the ten years since Howard's death. She had more than a suspicion that when Howard *had* died, Charlie had had a few ideas about taking advantage of the situation, but he had soon realised that Joanna was not the loose woman Alicia made her out to be. He was now over forty, she supposed, and delighted in their very real, but very chaste, intimacy; he knew nearly all of her secrets. 'The water is still a little choppy,' she told him. 'But nothing the ship can't ride.'

'I am very glad about that, Mrs Edge.'

'You're a dear, Charlie. Now let's get home. There's still a lot to do.'

* * *

Because a triumph like this morning always left her feeling randy, she needed to get home . . . and use that telephone number?

It was three before they reached Caribee House. 'Mr Montgomery is here, madam,' Cummings said.

Joanna had recognised the car parked in the drive. She went into the lounge, where Billy and Matilda were waiting, both looking anxious. 'I came right back,' Billy said.

'Thank you. When did you find out that Dick had sold his shares?'

'Well, I was advised when it happened, of course.'

'That was two days ago. The day I got back.'

'Well . . . yes, it was.'

'But you didn't think to tell me?'

'Well, Jo, I meant to, but what with all the excitement of your homecoming, I'm afraid I forgot.'

'You forgot to tell me something which might have jeopardised the company? What about yesterday?'

'There was so much going on . . . '

'Where is Dick, by the way?' Matilda asked. 'Still in bed upstairs?'

'Dick has left.'

'Just like that? I thought he had 'flu.'

'He probably has raging pneumonia by now. But I no longer consider it my business.'

Matilda goggled at her. 'You threw him out? But . . . he's your husband!'

'The divorce papers are being filed now.'

'Good lord.' Matilda sat down.

'I'm most terribly sorry,' Billy said. 'Matilda has put me in the picture. What a mess. I can't help feeling that telling you two days ago wouldn't have changed anything. It would only have spoiled your homecoming.'

'It would have saved me from being utterly humiliated by Andy and that creep Townsend,' Joanna pointed out.

'Yes. As I say, I am most terribly sorry, but

there was nothing I could do about it.'

'Wasn't there? Those shares were held in trust. You are the manager of my trust company. Those shares could not be sold without our joint authority, in writing. Do you have such authority?'

'Well . . . no.' He was flushing. 'But Dick was your husband, and you weren't here . . . '

'You knew I was arriving, that very day.'

'I . . . I was confused, I suppose.'

'I am sure you were confused,' Joanna agreed. 'Who actually runs the trust company?'

'Jimmy Haddon. He's very good. I don't think you can blame him for what happened.'

'I have no intention of blaming him for what happened, Billy. I am blaming you. I therefore wish you to get in touch with Mr Haddon, immediately, and inform him that he is now manager of the Trust Company.'

'But . . . what about me?'

'You are fired,' Joanna said.

There was a moment's silence. 'You can't fire Billy,' Matilda protested.

'I have just done so.' Joanna went to her desk picked up the phone, dialled.

'He's your brother-in-law,' Matilda shouted.

'Give me Mr Young,' Joanna said into the phone.

'He's my husband!' Matilda shrieked.

‘Peter? I am sorry to disturb you. This call is to inform you that Mr Montgomery is no longer in the employ of Caribee Shipping, or me personally. Will you please arrange for him to receive the correct amount of severance pay?’

She could hear Peter gulping on the far end of the phone.

‘You are a bitch!’ Matilda screamed. ‘Bitch, bitch, bitch!’

‘Jimmy Haddon will be taking over the Trust Company. Would you please inform him?’

‘Is this an act of vengeance?’

‘I’m sorry you should think that, Peter,’ Joanna said. ‘I am firing someone who has proved himself to be incompetent and uninterested in the real interests of my company.’

‘Do you still have a company, Joanna?’

‘Yes,’ Joanna said. ‘I, we, still have a company, Peter. Did you arrange that press conference for me?’

‘They’re coming in at nine tomorrow morning.’

‘I’ll be there.’ She hung up, gazed at Matilda, who had advanced to stand on the far side of the desk

‘You are a bitch,’ Matilda said again. ‘I ought to break every bone in your body.’

'Then you'd better begin with my neck. Because if you lay one finger on me and I survive, I will have you, and him, sent to prison for a very long time,' Joanna said, keeping her voice low and even.

Matilda burst into tears; she entirely lacked her sister's strength of character. 'He made a mistake,' she said. 'One mistake. It was just an oversight. It was — '

'One oversight too many. I am sorry.'

'We'd better go,' Billy muttered.

'I will never speak to you again,' Matilda said. 'Never, never, never.'

'That is entirely up to you.'

Matilda glared at her a last time, then turned and marched for the door. Billy followed without looking at Joanna, who sat down with a thump and rang the bell absently. 'Madam?' Cummings appeared in the doorway.

'Bollinger.'

'Ah . . . ' Cummings only just prevented his gaze from drifting to the clock on the mantelpiece. 'Yes, madam.'

Howard had always drunk champagne in moments of crisis. But she did look at the clock. It was half-past three, and Helen and Raisul would be in from school at any moment. She did not feel up to seeing them. She went into the study, called the bank. 'The shares are being transferred now,' she said. 'I imagine the call will come through from Miller & Sparks tomorrow morning. I've told them you'll be sending across the papers making them security.' She hung up, went into the hall, encountered Cummings, armed with tray, bottle and glass. 'Upstairs, please, Cummings,' she said.

He followed her up the stairs. At the top, Mrs Partridge waited. 'Are you all right, madam?'

'No,' Joanna said. 'But there is nothing the matter with me a rest won't cure.' She opened her bedroom door. 'Just put the tray down, Cummings.'

Cummings obeyed, and left the room. Mrs Partridge hesitated. 'Is there anything I can get you, madam?'

'I have everything I want, thank you, Mrs Partridge. I don't want to be disturbed, please. Not even when the children come in.'

'I'll tell Mrs Winshaw,' Mrs Partridge said, and closed the door.

They had both, of course, heard Matilda shouting, Joanna supposed. She reckoned she was an endless source of gossip in the servants' hall. But they remained utterly faithful to her . . . or at least Cummings and Mrs Partridge did. She poured herself a glass of champagne, drank half of it, undressed, went into the bathroom and had a shower; she was wet through with perspiration. She towelled herself dry, finished the glass, refilled it, and sat on the edge of the bed.

Presumably she had now quite destroyed the family. She had no sympathy for Billy. He had been in at the very beginning, regarding himself as Howard's right-hand man, whereas Howard had always referred to him, and regarded him, as 'my man'. He had been another who had tried to muscle in when Howard had died; he had even, she recalled with savage amusement, envisaged himself as the new Chairman of the company! And when she had politely informed him that was not on, and married Prince Hasim, he had married Matilda. It did not matter that Matilda had undoubtedly made the first move; Billy had seized the opportunity to stay close to the seat of power. Tilly, now . . . Tilly would come round, perhaps. If Billy would let her. She was given to strong statements and strong stances, without the strength of mind to carry either through. But they could never be close again. There was a shame. Joanna smiled as she recalled some of the escapades they had got up to in their youth. The time Howard had taken them to his London flat — her flat now — after Tilly had been arrested for go-go dancing in the nude,

Howard had bought her an entire outfit from Harrods to replace the clothes she didn't have.

But even then, it had been *her* he had wanted, not big sister. She wondered if Matilda had always been jealous of that; it would have been against human nature for her not to be.

She drank some champagne. And William would have to choose sides, at least in the short term. She lay back, the glass held between her breasts, gazing at the ceiling. And as if she had used mental telepathy, the phone rang.

She stretched out her hand and lifted the receiver, just as Cummings answered from downstairs. 'Jo?'

'Cummings here, Mr William. The mistress is resting.'

'I'm awake, Cummings,' Joanna said.

'Ah, yes, madam.' Cummings replaced the phone.

'Jo? What the hell is going on?'

'Not a lot, save that I am trying to get some rest.'

'I've had Matilda on the phone.'

'I thought you might.'

'Is it true you have fired her?'

'No, it is not true. I think she may have resigned. She didn't actually put it in as many words, but that was the gist of it.'

'You can joke about it?'

'What am I supposed to do, cry?'

'You did fire Billy.'

'Yes, for total incompetence and disloyalty. And I suspect a smack of dishonesty, although I can't prove it.'

'Jo, these are your own flesh and blood.'

'Billy isn't. God forbid.'

'Jo, look, maybe I can sort things out.'

'Did Tilly ask you to do that?'

'Well . . . not exactly. But I know she'd like to make it up. She really is in a bad way, Jo. She was crying, on the phone.'

'I would give it a little while,' Joanna said.

'Jo! This is family. Can we come down tonight?'

'Who?'

'Norma and I, of course. And we could bring Tilly. There'd be no need for Billy to come, if you didn't wish to see him.'

'Not tonight,' Joanna said. 'I have had a pretty traumatic day. I have sacked one husband, one brother-in-law, and one sister. I have had virtually to crawl on my hands and knees to regain control of the company. Tonight I want to do my own thing, all right?'

There was a brief silence. 'I'm not sure what that means,' he said, apprehensively. 'What are you doing?'

'Right now, I'm drinking champagne. Then I am going to have a nap. And when I wake up . . . I'll decide that when I wake up.'

'But you don't want to see us?'

'Definitely not. Call me tomorrow.'

Another hesitation. Then he said. 'Well, take care.'

'Oh, I shall do that,' she said, and hung up.

But she had already decided what she wanted to do when she woke up. She got out of bed, refilled her glass, then opened her handbag and took out the slip of paper Connor had given her on board the *Caribee Queen*.

4

The Crime

Joanna slept heavily, then got up and had a tub. She knew she was more nervous than she had been for a long time, but it was important not to allow anyone to see that. Equally, she had to recreate the atmosphere of the ship. That was going to be difficult. There was no storm raging outside, although it was threatening to snow. The important thing was to recreate her aura of total command. She hoped Sean wouldn't turn out to be a wimp like Dick, and require that aura always. But she felt it was important on this first occasion when they would meet in her natural habitat, as it were.

So she dressed in a pale blue evening gown with a deep *décolletage*, wore a choker of pearls and the huge ruby embedded between diamonds Howard had given her as an engagement present, and put her hair up — she could always let it down if the evening went as she hoped. The children were astounded. 'Mummy, are you going to a ball?' Helen inquired.

'You look lovely,' Raisul confided.

'Why, thank you, darling. No, I am not going to a ball; I'm expecting a guest for dinner.'

'Oooh. May we stay up?' Helen asked.

'Not for dinner. But you may stay up and say good-night,' Joanna said.

* * *

She had given Cook her instructions, as well as Cummings, and the huge refectory dining table was laid for two, a setting at each end, which meant that they would be separated by some fifteen feet of wood. She supposed she was being somewhat childish, wishing to awe him to such an extent, but she felt it was important to preserve their respective positions, at least in the beginning. But she was intensely nervous as seven-thirty arrived. He had said he would have no difficulty in getting to her, or in finding the house. As she heard headlights in the drive, and the crunching of gravel, Joanna remained sitting in front of the open fireplace, watching the flickering flames. The house was centrally heated, but she did like an open fire. The double doors opened. 'Mr Connor, madam,' Cummings said.

Joanna stood up, stared at him. He was

better looking than she remembered, but he wore an open-necked shirt and a wind-cheater. On the other hand, she reminded herself, she had not asked him to dress. He was staring at her, in turn. 'Sorry,' he said.

'Why? Cummings?' Cummings served champagne. Joanna raised her glass. 'Welcome.'

'It's great to be here. Some place you have.' Connor came into the room, and Cummings left, having placed the bottle on the sideboard in its bucket, closing the doors behind him. 'I'm not sure of the drill,' he confessed.

'I think we could kiss each other,' Joanna suggested.

He held her in his arms, reaching past her to put his glass on the mantelpiece, then sliding his hands down the side of her gown to hold her buttocks. She didn't resist him; she felt the same way. He kissed her mouth for several seconds, then pulled his head back. 'I was beginning to wonder if that ship wasn't a dream.'

'Your first hurricane?'

'And yours, I seem to remember. But I gather you're still in one.'

She released him, topped up their glasses. 'You've been reading the newspapers.'

'And some. Anything I can do to help?'

'You?' She smiled. 'Oh, indeed. Just by

being here. The papers don't know everything, you see.'

She sat on the settee, and he sat beside her. 'You mean things are worse than they appear?'

'That's a point of view. I'm divorcing my husband.'

Just for a moment his eyes narrowed. 'Why?'

'Oh, don't worry, it has nothing to do with you. I went away to get myself sorted out, attitudes and that sort of thing. And when I came back, I found my mind was made up.'

'But I had nothing to do with your decision?'

'Nothing at all. Does that bother you?' She gazed at him.

'I was actually wondering if I could be of help in the business.'

She smiled. 'Thanks, but no, really. I've sorted that out as well.'

'You've had a busy few days. So why am I here?'

He was definitely put out, and therefore aggressive. She rested her hand on his. 'You are here because I wish you to be. I promised to call, remember?'

'I never thought you would.'

'I always keep my word. Now you must meet the children.' The door opened, and

Helen and Raisul filed in, wearing their nightclothes and dressing gowns. Mrs Winshaw remained in the doorway. 'This is Mr Connor,' Joanna explained.

Helen held out her hand. 'Hello, Mr Connor.' Connor looked bemused.

Raisul took his sister's place. 'Hello, Mr Connor.' Connor shook hands.

'Say good-night,' Joanna commanded.

'Good-night, Mr Connor,' they chorused, and turned to Joanna to be hugged and kissed.

'I love your dress, Mummy,' Helen confided, and then scampered to join her brother. Mrs Winshaw closed the doors.

'So you don't dress for dinner every night,' Connor remarked.

'Only when I feel like it,' Joanna said. 'I do most things when I feel like it.' She was being deliberately provocative, but the evening was not going as she had intended; she could sense waves of hostility beaming at her. But he had come, however resentfully, at her summons. 'Will you fill our glasses?'

He obeyed, then sat beside her again 'I had no idea you had children.'

'Helen is nine, and Raisul is seven. They are by different fathers, but both fathers were my husband at the time. Raisul, in a perfect world, would be the present Emir of Qadir.

No, I take that back. That would be a most imperfect world. He's better off where he is, the future Chairman of Caribee Shipping.'

'You think very positively.'

'I have found that necessary, from time to time.'

'So . . . ' he put down his glass. 'What happens next?'

'Isn't that up to you?'

He shook his head. 'Not in these surroundings. You're the boss lady. But then, you always are, aren't you?'

She considered him for several seconds. 'I try to be,' she said at last. 'But tonight, I would like to surrender, absolutely. Just tell me what you would like to do.'

She was remembering the little nibbles and sucks from on board the ship, so titillating. But those had been to the accompaniment of the howling wind and the gigantic slaps of the sea. In this drawing room there was no sound at all apart from the guttering of the flames.

'Anything?' he asked.

She raised her eyebrows. 'Are you trying to frighten me?'

'I've an idea that might be difficult. I'd like to possess you, for one short hour.'

'There's a pessimistic point of view. Your wish is granted, sir.'

'Now?'

'Dinner is in half-an-hour. But after that the night is yours.'

'You know how to turn a man on.'

'Don't sound so disparaging. It's what women were put on earth to do.'

'There's a refreshing point of view in this bra-burning age. That butler fellow, is he likely to come back?'

'Cummings will knock on the door at eight o'clock to tell me that dinner is served. He won't come back before then, unless I ring.'

'Then will you take off your gown?' Joanna stood up, released the zip, allowed the silk to settle about her ankles. She wore only panties underneath. 'You are divine,' he said. 'All that beauty — and a brain as well.' He himself slid the pants down, and she stepped out of both them and the dress.

'Do I keep my shoes?' she asked.

'I think we could do without them.'

She kicked them off. 'And my jewellery?'

'Oh, no, keep the jewellery. That makes you more exciting.'

'And what about you?'

He undressed in turn. 'I have always wanted to make love on a hearthrug in front of a roaring fire.'

'Snap,' Joanna said. 'You mean you have never done it before?'

He grinned. 'Not with a beautiful millionairess wearing all her rocks.' He released her hair.

She could remember his caresses from on board the ship; they were divine. At the same time, she was realising that she didn't actually like him, or at least, the image he was presenting. On the other hand, as far as sexual therapy went, he was perfection. She did not object when, having brought her close to a climax by stroking her front, he rolled her on her stomach. He was kissing her neck as he did so, while his hands still roamed, then suddenly she realised something was wrong.

She had been so relaxed it took her a few seconds to understand what was happening, as he parted her cheeks and let his fingers roam between.

'We need a lubricant,' he whispered. 'What did they use in *Last Tango in Paris?* Butter, right. We need some butter.'

'No.' She tried to twist, and was suddenly held firm by his hand placed firmly between her shoulder-blades, pressing her to the carpet. 'I'm not into that,' she gasped.

'But I am. Possession. That's the name of the game. That's what you said you wanted.' His face was close to her neck. 'And this is the ultimate possession.'

'You . . . ' she tried to push herself up, but she was no match for him in strength, and was driven down again, face bumping against the floor.

'Hey,' he said. 'You promised I could do whatever I liked.'

'So long as I liked it too,' she gasped. 'Let me up, you bastard.'

'Well,' he said, 'without butter, this may hurt.'

My God, she thought, I've got myself in the hands of a satyr. She felt him against her flesh, and still his hand was on her back, pressing her down. Desperately she flung out her own hand, found it virtually in the fire, touched a lump of burning wood, screamed with the pain of it, but still held it, and brought it back, stabbing it into his side. He gave a shout of anguish and rolled off her and away from her. Joanna rolled as well, dropping the piece of wood and rising to her knees as she gazed in horror at the smoke rising from her hand, the black mark across the palm.

That distracted her, and gave Connor time to recover and hurl himself at her. Instinctively she brought up her hands, still only aware of the searing pain shooting from her hand into her wrist and up the entire length of her right arm, for a moment knocked senseless by the swinging blow that caught her on the side of the jaw and sent her rolling across the carpet. Why aren't I being helped? she asked herself. I am in a house full of servants, who are *my* servants, who will do anything for me . . . but she had trained them all, most of all Cummings, never to interfere unless called for.

She had to reach the bell, before this madman destroyed her. Because she could no longer doubt Conner was mad, at least temporarily, with a mixture of pain and desire. He was at her again, kneeling above her, rolling her over as he wanted her to be. 'Bitch,' he growled. 'Mistress of everything. Mistress of mine, too, bitch.'

Joanna swung her arms, to and fro, behind her, and was rewarded with a grunt, then they were caught and forced down. But he needed at least one hand to hold her while he made his entry. She gasped for breath and waited for one of her wrists to be released, then swung again, connected with his head, sent him one way and herself the other, realised that her choker had burst and the floor was covered in pearls. On which his knees slipped as he came at her again, sending him thudding to the floor. Joanna reached her own knees, scattering pearls, clasped her hands together, and swung them against the side of his face. Her left hand was uppermost, the knuckles with the diamond and ruby ring exposed. The stones swung into his cheek, and as he shrieked and tried to pull away, they continued to bite and opened up a jagged cut down to his jaw, from which blood poured. 'Aaaagh!' he screamed again, falling back to the floor, rolling on to his back on top of the scattered pearls, holding his face while blood seeped through his fingers.

Joanna reached her feet, panting and crying, and again he grabbed at her ankle. She freed it with a kick, and then jumped on him with both feet, landing on his lower abdomen. This time he gave a choking gasp and she was free. She stumbled and staggered across the pearls and through the mist clouding her mind, and pressed the bell. Then she fell to her knees, coughing and choking. The door burst open. 'Madam!' Cummings clearly could not believe what he was seeing.

'Help,' Joanna gasped. 'You'll need help.'

Because Connor was starting to recover; he was sitting up, still holding his face, moaning but also muttering curses. Blood still dribbled from his cut cheek, and she thought some was coming from his mouth as well — he must have cut his lips.

'Charlie!' Cummings bellowed, at the same time running across the room to arm himself with the poker. Joanna also ran across the room, to reach her discarded gown. Connor reached his feet, staggering to and fro. 'Now, sir,' Cummings said.'Nothing foolish.'

'Get dressed,' Joanna told him, stepping into her gown. 'And get out of here.'

'Bitch!' Connor lunged forward, and Cummings stepped in front of his mistress, the poker thrust forward. 'Listen, old man,' Connor said, spitting blood. 'I'm going to break your fucking head open.'

Charlie appeared in the doorway. Connor checked, looking from the diminutive figure of Cummings to the very large and athletic chauffeur. 'Get him out of here,' Joanna panted, zipping up her dress.

'You,' Charlie said. 'Out!'

'Yeah?' Connor asked, and ran at him. His feet slipped on the pearls, but he wouldn't have stood a chance anyway. Charlie cupped his hands together and brought them up in a huge uppercut as Connor reached him. Connor arced backwards and struck the floor with a tremendous crash.

Charlie stood above him, and looked at Joanna. 'Out,' Joanna said.

Connor struggled to his knees. 'I have to dress,' he mumbled, pawing at the blood on his face, augmented now by the cut on his chin.

'He can dress outside,' Joanna said.

Charlie seized him by the shoulder and threw him through the door. Connor landed on his hands and knees in the hall. Cummings gathered up the discarded clothing. 'The gentleman may well catch cold, madam,' he suggested.

'One catches cold from germs, not temperature,' Joanna said. 'And he's as much a germ as anything out there.'

By now the rest of the household had been aroused. Cook stood at the far end of the corridor, Mrs Partridge and Mrs Winshaw at the head of the stairs, watching as Charlie grasped Connor's shoulders, heaved him to his feet, and thrust him at the front door, which Cummings, still grasping Connor's clothes, was thoughtfully holding open. The air outside was icy. 'You can't do this!' Connor shouted. 'I'll have the law on you.' He tried to wriggle free to face Joanna, and Charlie pushed him through the door. Cummings threw his clothes behind him, and the door was shut.

Joanna found that she was sitting on the settee, knees pressed together, shoulders hunched. Mistress of all she surveyed, he had called her. She had been proud of that. But once again her relationship with men had turned out disastrously. That could never be allowed to happen again. 'Madam?' Mrs Partridge sat beside her. 'Are you all right?'

No, Joanna thought. I *am never going to be all right again*. But she nodded. 'I'm all right, Mrs Partridge. Thank you.'

'But . . . all this blood.'

'His blood, Mrs Partridge.'

Cummings appeared. 'Will you dine, madam?'

Joanna shook her head. 'I couldn't eat a thing. Apologise to cook for me, Mr Cummings.'

'You must take something,' Mrs Partridge said, severely.

'A cup of soup. I'll have a cup of soup, in bed. And a glass of brandy.' Joanna got to her feet, unsteadily, and Mrs Partridge held her arm to help her across the room. 'Charlie,' she said, 'you'd better collect up these pearls.'

Charlie dropped to his hands and knees. Mrs Partridge help Joanna up the stairs and into her bedroom, helped her off with her gown and got her beneath the sheets. 'The children didn't wake up, did they?' she asked.

'I don't think so, madam.'

'Thank God for that.' Joanna sighed, and closed her eyes. But Mrs Partridge had seen her right hand. 'Oh, dear me, madam. I must get something for that.' She bustled off, and hurried back with antiseptic cream, gently coated the hand. 'I won't bind it up,' she said. 'It's better to let the air get to it.'

'Thank you, Mrs Partridge,' Joanna muttered. The hand was actually quite painful.

'Did you know the gentleman very well, madam?' Mrs Partridge asked.

Joanna opened her eyes. 'Know him? No, I don't think I knew him at all. We met on the ship, and I had hoped to know him better.'

'I see, madam. It's just that, did you notice? He was driving a very expensive car. What do they call them? Italian. A Ferrari.'

He probably stole it, Joanna thought, as she drifted off after her soup and brandy. But she didn't sleep well, her brain tormented with images and memories, her body with the very real bruises she had accumulated, and her hand intensely painful. How could she have been so stupid? No, she realised, not stupid, merely arrogant. Which was, of course, another word for stupid. She had been on a high, because she had again triumphed, had regained control of her company, had taken on the world and beaten it, so of course she could point an imperious finger, as perhaps Cleopatra had done when in the mood, and said, you, I will have you. But even Cleopatra had fallen on her face, or was it her asp, at the end?

'What was all that noise, Mummy, last

night?' Helen asked at breakfast.

'Noise, darling? Oh, I am sorry. I must have had the television on too loud.'

'Did that Mr Connor come here to watch television, Mummy?' Raisul asked.

'Yes, but I don't think he liked my choice of programmes; he left early.' She watched Cummings pouring coffee, with never a change of expression.

* * *

'Was Mr Connor really driving a Ferrari?' Joanna asked, as Charlie drove her into town.

'Yes, madam.'

'Where do you suppose he got it?'

'I can find out, madam. I made a note of the number.'

'Thank you, Charlie. I'd be most grateful.'

'I have all those pearls gathered up, madam. What shall I do with them?'

'Oh, when you have dropped me, take them to Garrard's and have them re-strung.'

'Of course, madam.' Like Cummings, Charlie was a master at maintaining a po-face, even at the thought of driving round London with several thousand pounds' worth of pearls in his pocket.

Peter Young was so agitated that Joanna

almost suspected he knew about last night. 'Joanna!'

'Peter? What new crisis?'

'Haven't you heard the news?'

'I'm afraid I haven't listened to the news this morning, Peter.'

'The Prime Minister has declared a three-day week.'

Joanna blinked at him. 'You mean he's taken away four days? I'm not sure he can do that. Or anyone.'

'No, no,' Peter said. 'He hasn't reduced the number of days in the week; he's reduced the number of days people can work. Offices can open, ships can do business. That sort of thing.'

Joanna frowned at him. 'Is that legal?'

'The government makes the laws. It's to save fuel while this crisis lasts.'

'For heaven's sake, the crisis could last for months.'

'I know. It's pretty grim.'

'Has he thought of the unemployment that could result?'

'He, or his advisers, must have taken into account every possibility.'

'You have more faith in advisers than I have,' Joanna growled, and sat behind her desk. 'When do we have to close?'

'Starting tomorrow.'

'And suppose one of our overseas customers wants to get in touch?'

'I've arranged for any calls to be transferred to my flat. I'll handle them.'

'You really are a dear.' Joanna squeezed his hand. 'What about Thursday's shareholders meeting? Is that an off day, or an on day?'

'Well, it would appear to be an off day, for us. But I'm sure we can hold the meeting somewhere not on the premises.'

'Yes,' she said. 'We will. We'll hold it at Caribee House. That ought to be fun.'

⋆ ⋆ ⋆

William came in to see her, peered at her. 'Are you all right?'

'In a manner of speaking.'

He studied her for several seconds, uncertain how to take her remark. 'You look kind of uptight.'

'I have a lot on my mind. Doesn't everyone?'

He peered at her hand. 'What happened?'

'I rather stupidly picked a burning brand out of the fire. It'll be all right.'

'Does it hurt?'

'Of course it hurts. Like hell.'

'And what's that mark on your chin?'

She touched the bruise and winced. She

had covered it with powder, but the make-up had worn off. 'I fell out of bed, if it's any concern of yours.'

He sat before her desk. 'How does this three day week thing affect us?'

'Here in London? The same as everybody else. Overseas it doesn't affect us at all. We can't tell our ships to stop sailing every other day. Again, loading, or unloading, here in London or down in Plymouth may cause some problems. But rice and sugar aren't that perishable, and neither are washing machines or dishwashers.'

'Crazy,' he commented. 'But not funny. Obviously, jobs are going to be at a premium.'

'I think they probably are, in the short term.'

'Billy may find it difficult.' Joanna gazed at him. 'They didn't ask me to say that,' William added hurriedly. 'But I know they really would like to make it up. They're very upset. So is Norma.'

'May I ask what she has to do with it?'

'She's part of the family, now.'

Joanna considered. Never had she felt so lonely, so vulnerable. Not that surrounding herself with family would really help; she had tried that before in times of crisis, with no great amount of success. She needed a man. Not necessarily for sex, although that helped.

But she wanted someone strong and resolute, anxious to help her move forward. Howard had been like that. So had Hasim. Only Dick had lowered the level of the relationship she sought. But she dared not involve the family in her quest for a replacement for the two men who had made her what she was, neither of whom, she realised, she had really loved.

Was she the world's most selfish woman? Or the most unfortunate? That was a laugh. She had everything, beauty, money, power, perfect health . . . if she was feeling sorry for herself, if she had exceeded the bounds of good taste and morality in her search for private gratification, it was she who was the wimp, not any of the men in her life. She squared her shoulders. 'Come out and have dinner, tonight.'

'Who?'

'Oh, all of you. Even Billy.'

'Gosh,' William said. 'I knew you'd come round. Thanks a million, sis. Tilly will be overwhelmed.'

'Now let's get some work done, while we can,' Joanna suggested.

* * *

She had barely delved into the contents of her in-tray when Harriet came in.

'I'm sorry to bother you, Mrs Orton, but there is a policeman outside.'

Joanna raised her eyebrows. 'Come to see we're not breaking the law? According to Mr Young, we don't have to close until tomorrow.'

'This man wishes to speak with you personally, madam. There are two of them.'

Joanna leaned back in her chair. 'Then, you'd better show them in.'

Her intercom buzzed. 'Do you need me, Joanna?' Peter asked.

'I am going to find out what it's all about, and let you know,' Joanna promised.

'You don't want me in there with you?'

'Not unless they've come to arrest me for something,' Joanna said. 'Then I'll buzz, and you come running.'

She watched the door open, did not get up. Harriet was looking agitated. 'Sergeant Welcom, and Detective Constable Woolley, Mrs Orton.'

'Thank you, Harriet.' Harriet hesitated, then closed the door. The sergeant advanced to stand before the desk; the constable remained by the door. Both men looked acutely embarrassed. 'Well?' Joanna asked. But she pressed the button on the intercom, just in case.

'Mrs Joanna Orton?'

'That is my name. At present.'

'At present? Do you mean that is an alias?'

'It is my present married name, sergeant. But I am in the process of divorcing my husband. Would you care to sit down?' Joanna invited.

'I will stand, Mrs Orton. Are you the owner of this company?'

'I am the Chairman,' Joanna said. 'And Managing Director.'

Almost, she thought he was going to remove his hat and scratch his head. 'What is going on?' Peter Young bustled in.

'These gentleman are police officers,' Joanna explained.

'Doing what?'

'They haven't told me that, yet.'

Sergeant Welcom pulled himself together, visibly. 'May I ask your name, sir?'

'My name is Peter Young.'

'And you are . . . ?' he looked from one to the other.

'I am Company Secretary.'

'Ah. Right, sir. This is a personal, not a company matter. So . . . '

'I would like Mr Young to stay,' Joanna said.

'Very good, madam. I need to ask you one or two questions. Are you acquainted with a man named . . . ' he took his notebook from his pocket and opened it. 'Sean Connor?'

Joanna sat up straight, frowning. 'Yes.'

'Did you entertain Mr Connor to dinner at your house last night?'

'I did.'

'Thank you, madam. I have a warrant here for your arrest for assault and battery, and grievous bodily harm, committed by you upon the person of Mr Connor.'

'Are you out of your mind?' Peter shouted.

'That little bastard,' Joanna muttered.

'Please understand, Mrs Orton,' Sergeant Welcom went on, 'that you need not say anything in answer to this charge, at this moment. But if you do say anything, we shall take it down and it may be given in evidence.' Detective-Constable Woolley also produced a notebook, together with a biro.

'This is outrageous,' Peter declared. 'Joanna . . . ?'

Joanna stood up. Her brain was spinning. 'Am I allowed to telephone my solicitor?'

'From the station, madam.'

Joanna turned to Peter. 'You do it.' She turned back to the policemen. 'Am I to be handcuffed?'

'Good heavens, no, Mrs Orton. You're not going to make a run for it, are you?'

'Not in high-heeled shoes, sergeant.'

Harriet was waiting with her mink. 'What

shall I do?' she whispered.

'Mr Young is handling everything,' Joanna said.

They rode down in the lift, past floors of amazed clerks, and emerged in the lobby. Charlie, as usual, was seated behind the front desk with the receptionist, and hurried forward. 'Madam?' He looked quite capable of dispersing the policemen.

'Just relax, Charlie,' Joanna said. 'Mr Young will tell you what to do.'

William burst through an open door on the left. 'Jo!'

'Ah,' Joanna said. 'Dinner. I imagine I'll make it. But don't tell Tilly until then, William. My brother,' she explained to the bewildered sergeant.

This was the first time Joanna had ever driven in a police car. In her extreme youth, on the one and only time she had been involved in a drugs bust, with Dick, she recalled, they had been thrust into the back of a Black Maria. And from that horrible misadventure she had been rescued by Howard — her knight in shining armour. Now she had to rely on Peter Young and John Giffard. But she knew she could. At the station she was ushered past a host of curious eyes, both officers and clients, into a windowless office. 'One would suppose I was a murderess,' she remarked.

'GBH can be a very serious offence, madam,' Sergeant Welcome remarked. 'Would you like a cup of coffee?'

'Not really. I'd prefer a glass of water.'

Welcom nodded to his constable, who hurried off, and returned with the water at the same time as another plain-clothes officer entered the room.

'Mrs Orton? I'm Inspector Langridge. Do sit down.' Joanna sat down and crossed her knees; she was still wearing her mink, and the room was rather warm. 'You understand the charge?' Langridge asked. 'And you have been cautioned?' Joanna nodded. 'We will have to ask you some questions. Would you like to telephone your solicitor?'

'He's on his way,' Joanna said, and a moment later John Giffard, looking extremely hot and bothered, was shown into the office.

'Joanna!' He kissed her. 'I hope you know what you're doing, Inspector?'

'Are you prepared to let your client answer questions, Mr Giffard?'

Giffard looked at Joanna. 'I am quite happy to answer the inspector's questions,' Joanna said.

'Thank you, Mrs Orton.' Langridge nodded to the waiting constable, who switched on a tape recorder, gave the time, date, and the names of the people present. 'Now, Mrs Orton,' Langridge said. 'Did you have dinner with Mr Connor last night? At your home in Berkshire?'

'Yes.'

'This was at your invitation?'

'Yes.'

'And after dinner, did you assault Mr Connor, and cause him severe facial injuries with a sharp instrument, as well as bodily injuries with a blunt instrument? These injuries including burning him? Following which you stamped on him?'

'Don't answer that, Joanna,' Giffard advised.

'I cut his face with my ring,' Joanna said, and took off her left-hand glove. 'This one. And I seem to remember stamping on him, at some stage. And yes, I tried to drive him off me with a piece of wood I took from the fire.' She took off her right-hand glove, showed him the scorch mark. Giffard sighed.

'You are aware that Mr Connor had to receive several stitches, and may well be scarred for life?'

'I was not aware of that. But I can believe it.'

'And that he may have received internal injuries?'

'I am not aware of that.'

'Will you tell me why you assaulted him?'

'I did not assault him,' Joanna said. 'I was defending myself against rape.' Giffard's head came up with a jerk.

'You are accusing Mr Connor of attempting to rape you?' asked the inspector. 'In your own living room, into which you had invited him?'

'Is that supposed to represent an invitation to have sex?' Joanna demanded.

The inspector flushed. 'Forgive me for asking this, Mrs Orton, but it will come out: had you ever had sex with Mr Connor before last night?'

'Don't answer that,' Giffard said again, his tone indicating that he had not the least hope of his advice being taken.

'Yes, I had had sex with Mr Connor before last night,' Joanna said.

The inspector looked down at his notes. 'Can you remember where and when this was?'

'It was on board one of my ships, the *Caribee Queen*, while we were on our way back from the West Indies.'

'You have known Mr Connor for a long time, then?'

'Not at all. We met for the first time just over a fortnight ago. When he boarded the ship.'

'And you first had sex with him . . . ?'

'It would have been ten days ago, I think,' Joanna said.

'Four days after you had met him for the first time?'

'More like six, I should think.'

'Six days.' Langridge glanced at the constable, to make sure the the tape recorder was working. 'Very good. You took a liking to Mr Connor, is that it?'

'If you weren't a policeman,' Joanna said, 'and I wasn't in your custody, I'd slap your face. The *Caribee Queen*, and that means both Mr Connor and myself, had just survived a hurricane. We were perhaps a little hysterical. So one thing led to another.'

'But you had sex with Mr Connor on most of the remaining days of the voyage, right?'

Joanna sighed. 'Yes, we slept together several times during the rest of the voyage.'

'Then you will not deny that he — how shall I put it, Mrs Orton? — turned you on?'

'Yes, Inspector, he turned me on.'

'But when, a few days later, he came to have dinner with you, at your invitation, and attempted to resume relations with you, the relations he had enjoyed on your ship, you scarred his face and stamped on his body, and burned him with a piece of wood. Mrs Orton, I must put it to you straight: did you or did you not invite Mr Connor to have dinner with you for the purposes of sex?'

'Joanna . . . 'Giffard said.

'Whatever reason I had for inviting Mr Connor to have dinner with me, Inspector,' Joanna said. 'The decision as to what we did either before, during, or after dinner, was surely mine.'

'You do not accept that, after what had happened on board your ship, he was entitled to believe that you had in mind a continuation of that relationship?'

'He was entitled to believe whatever he liked. That does not alter the fact that the decision had to be mine.'

Langridge looked at his notes. 'Mr Connor has said, in his statement, that you invited him to have sex again, on your drawing-room floor. Is that true?'

Giffard looked about to tear his hair out by the roots. 'That is true, yes,' Joanna said.

'But you suddenly changed your mind and scratched his face with your diamond ring.'

'I changed my mind when he wished to sodomise me, Inspector.'

There was complete silence in the room for several seconds. Langridge was the first to recover. 'You are saying that Mr Connor tried to . . . '

'Bugger me,' Joanna snapped.

Another brief silence. Giffard might have fainted. 'Mr Connor makes no mention of this in his deposition,' Langridge said.

'Would you have expected him to?'

'Well . . . Can you prove that he attempted such an assault upon your person?'

'No.'

'Would you like to be medically examined by a police doctor? I can arrange it immediately.'

'It would serve no purpose for me to have a medical examination, Inspector. Mr Connor did not succeed in his endeavours. I hit him first.'

Once again a brief silence; the tape recorder whirred gently.

Again Langridge recovered. 'You would be prepared to swear that this assault did happen.'

'Yes, because it did happen.'

'I am sure you can appreciate, Inspector, that it comes down to a simple matter of Mr Connor's word against Mrs Orton's,' Giffard said. 'I am sure you also appreciate that this case, should it come to court, has certain aspects which will appeal to the tabloid press.'

'It is not my business to give an opinion upon that, sir,' Langridge said. 'I am required to deal with facts. And the facts are that Mr Connor was invited to dinner by a lady who he had every reason to believe was content to be his mistress, and when he endeavoured to continue their relationship, was very badly hurt.'

'You did not expect my client to defend herself, against a perverted attack?'

'As to whether the attack was perverted, that remains to be proved. Mrs Orton has acknowledged that she cannot prove it. I entirely agree that she was entitled to change her mind about continuing her relationship with Mr Connor, but in that case, surely all she had to do was ring the bell for her servants, of whom, I understand, there were several in the house that night.'

'I did ring for my servants,' Joanna said.

'After having inflicted a most grievous wound upon Mr Connor.'

'Therefore you intend to bring my client into court,' Giffard said.

'I am afraid, sir, that will be necessary.'

'Very well. Then I apply for police bail. Immediately.'

'I'm afraid bail in this case is a matter for the magistrate, Mr Giffard. Tomorrow morning.'

'You intend to lock my client up overnight?'

'That is the normal procedure, yes, sir.'

'That is outrageous,' Giffard declared.

'I am sorry, sir. Madam.'

'I don't think you like me,' Joanna remarked.

Part Two

Catastrophe

'All punishment is mischief;
all punishment in itself is evil.'

Jeremy Bentham

5

The Aftermath

At least Joanna was given a cell to herself. 'You'll be comfortable here, Mrs Orton,' said the WPC. 'And it's just for the one night.'

Joanna supposed it was not all that more confined than a cabin on board ship, save that in a cabin the toilet compartment was separate — and one could leave the cabin whenever one felt like it. It was, in any event, at the end of a humiliating half-hour, during which she had been photographed from every angle, and been required to give her fingerprints.

But it really was absurd that she should be locked up when she was totally innocent . . . but was she? The police clearly did not think so. Quite apart from their desire to make an issue of so well-known a personality, who had now, in their eyes, gone way out on a limb. What a field-day the media were going to have. As for the family . . . they were coming down for dinner tonight. She had forgotten to tell John Giffard that. He had promised to let Peter Young know exactly what had happened, he had promised to send in some things for her, but she had forgotten to tell him of her domestic arrangements. The constable was peering at her. 'Are you all right, dear?'

Joanna's head jerked. 'Eh? Oh, yes, I'm all right. Just thinking.'

'I know,' the young woman said sympathetically. 'I'm sorry, but I have to search you.'

'Whatever for?'

'A concealed weapon. Not that we imagine you'd try to break out, but if you did have one . . . and I have to take certain items. Some people get taken all queer when they're locked up.'

'If you think I'm going to commit suicide, forget it.'

'I'm sorry, Mrs Orton, but rules are rules.' Joanna knew it was no use feeling resentful towards this poor young woman, who was only doing her job, and was very embarrassed by the whole thing. She submitted to the search, watched the belt being drawn out of her skirt. 'I'm terribly sorry,' the constable said, 'but I have to have the bra as well.' Her blouse was already open, Joanna took it right off, removed the brassiere. 'And the stockings.' Joanna sat down, rolled down her stockings. 'You're being very co-operative,' the constable said. 'Some women, well, they get quite abusive.'

'I am feeling quite abusive,' Joanna assured her, buttoning her blouse. 'But not towards you.'

'It'll all turn out all right.'

'Will it?'

'Well . . . of course, dearie. You just have a rest.' The door closed and the key jangled as the lock was turned. For a moment Joanna was quite overwhelmed with the immensity of all the forces that were pressing upon her. That hurricane! Everything dated back to that hurricane. Because of the mood she had been in when the engine had failed, and the even greater mood she had been in when she had realised she, and her crew, and her passengers and ship, were safe. For a moment she must have been mad.

But the madness had continued for the rest of the voyage. Because she had wanted . . . not sex, so much, as the feeling of strength that a man's arms could provide. Dick's arms had never really provided that. And the two men who had provided that had both died, violently. She shuddered.

But at the end, she realised she had been brought down by her own arrogance. She was Joanna Grain/Edge/Princess Hasim/

Orton. She had been faced with disaster so often before, and had squared her shoulders and told the world, fuck off! And won! So she had supposed she could do anything she liked, and still win. She had to prove that all over again. But she thanked God she had got those shares from Alicia before this happened!

* * *

WPC Dearson brought in a bag of toiletries, nightclothes, and a change of day clothes with lunch. 'Where did you get these?' Joanna asked.

'Your sister.'

'Matilda has been here?'

'Mrs Montgomery. Yes. She asked to see you, but it's against the rules.' But she was staking a place in the gratitude stakes, Joanna thought.

* * *

She was awakened just after dawn. Actually, she had appreciated the rest, the inability to do anything more than lie on her somewhat narrow bed and stare at the ceiling. She had been on the go since that storm. Now the world had to be faced. She put on the clean clothes, which included brassiere, belt and stockings, watched by Dearson, did the best she could with her hair, had breakfast, and was then escorted outside to the waiting Black Maria, in which there were three other women. She didn't think they had been as well-treated as herself; they looked scruffy and bad-tempered. But perhaps they always looked scruffy and bad-tempered. She was relieved that two policewomen got in to the back with them.

'Why ain't she cuffed?' asked one of the women. 'She's on GBH. I'm on soliciting. How come she ain't cuffed and I am?'

'Just mind your own business,' said one of the constables.

But the other leaned towards Joanna. 'We will have to cuff you to take you in, Mrs Orton. It'll only be for a few minutes.'

Joanna said nothing; she could not imagine the day could possibly get any worse. And then realised she was wrong; as the van stopped outside the doors of the magistrate's court, it was surrounded by the media, men and women, screaming questions, flash-bulbs exploding. 'Would you like a blanket?' asked the constable, affixing handcuffs to Joanna's wrists.

Joanna hesitated, then tossed her head. 'They know what I look like.'

'Hey,' asked one of the prostitutes. 'You famous, then, darling?'

'Very,' Joanna told her.

The rear doors were opened, and she was assisted down by the two constables. The driver and his mate had got out and were trying to push the media back, but it was an impossible task.

'Joanna! Look this way!'

'Joanna, show us the ring!'

'Joanna, how's the bum?'

'Well, really,' commented one of the policewomen, pushing her forward.

'Joanna! Give us a smile!'

'Joanna, is it true you bit him where it hurts?' Then they were inside, and the doors were closing.

'Now I think I know what it feels like to be lynched,' Joanna gasped. They had come close enough to touch her, and she felt quite breathless.

'Did you really bite him where it hurts?' the woman constable asked.

'I never had the chance,' Joanna said, regretfully.

Then the cuffs were taken off, and she was with John Giffard.

* * *

The hearing lasted one minute, and she was required to state only her name and address. What was more embarrassing was having to sit there while the prostitutes were heard, and fined; they happened to be first on the case sheet. Then John applied for bail, which was immediately granted, in her own cognisance of a thousand pounds.

Joanna wasn't sure whether to be pleased or sorry that Connor was not in court. But she had been committed for trial, on his say so. The bastard. William and Norma, Matilda and Billy, and of course Peter, were waiting for her as she was escorted through an inner room to a back door. 'I'll come out tomorrow, Joanna,' Giffard said. 'And we'll talk things over.'

'Not tomorrow,' Joanna told him. 'I have a board meeting.'

He glanced at Peter, eyebrows arched.

Peter shrugged. 'You know Jo, John.'

'Where do you want to go?' William asked.

'Home,' Joanna told him.

* * *

'I should've hit that character harder,' Charlie commented, as they threaded their way through the traffic.

'Then you'd have been in the dock beside

me,' Joanna commented, 'What about the children?' she asked William, who was seated in the back beside her, together with Norma. Matilda was in the front beside Charlie. Billy had sensibly decided now was the moment to keep a low profile — no one was sure of Joanna's mood.

'Well,' William said, 'because it all happened yesterday morning, it's in all the papers today. And it was on the TV news last night.'

'I told Mrs Winshaw to keep them home from school today,' Matilda said.

'Why did you do that?' Joanna demanded.

'Well . . . ' Matilda stared through the front window; her ears were pink.

'She did it on my recommendation,' William said quietly.

Joanna turned her head, but he met her gaze. She had no means of telling whether or not he was lying.

'They could have been put through an unthinkable ordeal,' he said.

She sighed. 'I suppose you're right.'

'You know what I think?' Matilda asked brightly, at last turning round as she felt sure of her brother's support. 'The case doesn't come up for a couple of months. I think you should take a holiday, away from it all.'

'But she can't leave the country,' William

objected. 'Those are the terms of the bail. They've taken her passport.'

'Well, she can go to some remote island, off Scotland, or the Channel Islands. You don't need a passport to go there. Just to lie low.'

'While my children take all the flak and my company collapses,' Joanna mused. 'Forget it.'

* * *

'Mummy!' Helen was in her arms. 'Oh, Mummy! Were you really arrested?'

'It's something everyone should experience,' Joanna told her. Not, she remembered, that it had been the first time she had been arrested. But before there had been Howard, waiting to rescue her.

'Did that man really attack you?'

'Yes,' Joanna said. Fortunately, the fact that it had been a sexual attack did not seem to have penetrated the girl's awareness.

'I'd like to kill him,' Raisul said.

Joanna hugged him in turn and ruffled his hair. 'Next time he comes to visit I'll let you.'

'Oh, madam.' Cummings looked ready to burst into tears, as did Mrs Partridge. 'Shall I . . . ?'

'Oh, indeed, Cummings. Bollinger.'

'Is it going to be all right, madam?' Mrs Partridge asked.

'Of course it is.' But she couldn't be sure.

* * *

Next morning she was at the office early. Harriet had bought every newspaper, and the headlines made some pretty ghastly reading, varying as they did from the sedate; 'COMPANY DIRECTOR AND CITY WHIZ WOMAN COMMITTED FOR TRIAL ON GRIEVOUS BODILY HARM' of *The Times*, to 'HE TRIED TO BUGGER ME, SAYS GLAMOUR-GIRL, JOANNA ORTON' of the tabloids. Presumably Dick would be having a quiet chuckle. 'Mrs Edge is here,' Harriet said.

'You'd better show her in.'

'She has someone with her.'

'Her toy-boy. Yes. I'll see them both.'

'Joanna!' Alicia announced. 'You are absolutely impossible!'

'I find a lot of people impossible,' Joanna said.

'Ha! This is Stephen Maddox.'

It had to be. Stephen Maddox had a moustache and glowing dark eyes, but he also had good shoulders and a powerful body, which presumably was what Alicia was after.

She shook hands. 'May I say that we are entirely on your side, Mrs Orton,' Maddox gushed. 'The fellow should be castrated.'

'My own feelings entirely. Shall we talk a little business?' She gestured them to chairs in front of her desk. 'I have been looking up the company rules, and it is not possible for anyone to have a seat on the board who does not have shares, so . . . '

'That's all right,' Alicia said. 'I have sold Stephen one percent of my holding.'

'Ah. Right. Well, brace yourselves for a battle. I want your full support.'

'And we'll have yours.'

'Agreed. But there is still going to be a battle.'

* * *

Andy and Townsend arived with their partner, a man called Amalia, who was Greek, who Joanna hardly knew at all. They had also brought their solicitor, but Joanna would not accept him in the boardroom. 'You can nip out and talk to him whenever you wish,' she said. 'If he comes in, I'll have to get hold of John Giffard, which will not only be time-wasting but even more tedious when he gets here, as the two of them will spend the morning arguing.'

'Quite on top of the world, aren't we?' Andy asked. 'You do understand that we intend to turf you out?'

Joanna smiled sweetly. 'I know that's what you wish to do, Andy.'

'What's it feel like to be raped?' Townsend asked.

'Being raped feels slightly more attractive than talking to you two,' Joanna said. 'Shall we get to business, then we can maybe have some fresh air in here. Alicia, you know. This is Stephen Maddox.'

'Who?' Andy inquired.

'He's a shareholder,' Alicia snapped.

Andy frowned, and glanced from Alicia to Joanna, for the first time realising that he might have a united opposition. 'Yes,' he said, 'let's get to business.'

Joanna sat at the head of the table, Peter Young sat at the bottom. The five other shareholders seated themselves, but before Joanna could invite Peter to read the minutes, there was a knock on the door. 'A Mr Holroyd, Mrs Orton,' Harriet said. 'Says he's a shareholder.'

Joanna looked at the man coming through the door. He was massive, with shaggy hair that badly needed cutting, and heavy features; he made her think of a bull mastiff. 'You'll be Joanna,' he said. 'Sorry to barge in like this.

No one notified me of this meeting.'

He looked around the staring faces.

'Just who are you?' Joanna asked.

'James Holroyd. I bought your husband's shares.'

'Good lord!' Joanna commented. 'You and I need to have a chat.'

'Can you prove you hold those shares?' Peter inquired.

'I can, sir. I have the certificates with me.'

'Well, we knew Dick sold his holding to someone,' Andy said expansively. 'You'd better sit down, Mr Holroyd. Can we get on?'

'Of course.' Joanna nodded, and Peter read the minutes. Joanna signed them, and leaned back as she looked at the itinerary.

'This was drawn up at the request of the majority shareholder,' Peter explained. 'Mr Gosling. I tried to get it to you yesterday, Joanna, but . . . well . . . '

'She was all tied up,' Townsend said. 'Haw haw haw.'

'Item number one, the position of chairman to be resolved,' Joanna read, and looked up. 'I have no objection to that. Although I am not sure what is to be resolved.'

'Now, Joanna,' Andy said, 'prevaricating is not going to help. We all know the situation. Or . . . ' he looked at Maddox and Holroyd, 'perhaps we do not. Just to put you gentlemen in the picture, when the company was restructured a few years ago, while I became the majority shareholder, I agreed, with my partners, here, that Mrs Orton should remain Chairman and in complete control of the Company for as long as she owned twenty-five per cent of the shares. As it happened, Mrs Orton wished to alter that agreement very shortly, when she married Mr Orton. She wished to make him a present of a percentage of her shares, which would reduce her holding below the twenty-five percent we had agreed, but which she claimed would actually remain hers because she had the contractual right to buy the shares back whenever she wished. I was quite happy to agree with this; I and my associates have always had the greatest confidence in Mrs Orton's handling of the company, till now.

'Now things have changed. Mrs Orton's plans are, in the present economic circumstances, unacceptable. As Chairman she might be able to push these plans through, but now it also turns out that Mr Orton has sold his shares. Apparently to you, Mr Holroyd. The sale was illegal, I suspect, but that is a matter between Mrs Orton, her husband, and you, sir. The fact is that Mrs Orton no longer possesses twenty-five percent of the company shares, and therefore has no right to remain as Chairman. Now, my associates and I might have been willing to continue our present arrangement, providing Mrs Orton would agree to certain proposals put forward by us. This she flatly refuses to do. In these circumstances therefore, I propose, indeed I and my associates insist, that Mrs Orton be removed from her position as Chairman and a new chairman be installed.' He paused for breath.

'Thank you so much for that succinct appraisal of the situation, Andy,' Joanna said. 'There is just one small error in your summing up. You have just said that you have no right to remove me as chairman as long as I hold twenty-five percent of the shares.' She picked up the phone and held it out. 'I suggest you ring Jersey, speak with James Haddon of my Trust Company, and ascertain my exact shareholding.'

He guessed immediately what had happened, looked at Alicia, who smiled at him. 'You wretched woman,' he said. 'You sold out.'

Alicia sniffed. 'I did what I felt was right. I am Howard's wife. I have no intention of seeing the company disappear.' Andy's mouth opened and shut.

'I imagine you have already informed

Roger Petherick what would be the outcome of this meeting,' Joanna said. 'Well, I suggest you give *him* a ring, and inform him that nothing has changed, that Caribee Shipping is not for sale, under any circumstances, and that I look forward to not hearing from him again. Now, ladies and gentlemen, shall we move on to more important matters: the ordering of two new ships for the company, to take us through the seventies and hopefully into the eighties.'

⋆ ⋆ ⋆

'Champagne, I think,' Joanna said.

'It's on ice.' Harriet hastily fetched a bottle from the fridge.

Joanna smiled at her new associates: Alicia and Maddox had joined herself and Peter in her office; Holroyd had indicated he would like to stay, but she was not in the mood for recriminations at this moment — she'd agreed to a meeting the following day. 'You were so calm,' Alicia said. 'While that thug was trying to destroy you.'

'Well, it's easy to be calm when you know exactly what the opposition is doing, and when you know you hold the last trump,' Joanna pointed out.

'I think you were brilliant,' Maddox said

admiringly. Alicia gave him a dirty look.

'They'll still be fighting,' Peter reminded them.

'What with?'

'Well, this court case . . . '

'Is a straightforward business of self defence,' Joanna said.

'We may leave that with John Giffard.'

'What exactly happened?' Alicia asked. 'The papers said this man Connor was a friend of yours.'

'The operative word is was,' Joanna told her. 'He attacked me. It is as simple as that.'

She had no intention of going into the gory details. 'Now, I feel quite exhausted, and I have the family coming out for dinner. Peter, I'd like those tenders put out immediately.'

'I shall do that. I suppose you have taken financing into consideration?'

'Actually, I haven't,' Joanna said. 'I simply have not had the time. Get some figures together, and we'll have a meeting with Prim and Barry Andrews.'

'It could be tight.'

'Whenever wasn't it tight? Alicia, thanks a million for your support. Maybe we could get together for a meal some time. With Stephen, of course.'

'Of course,' Alicia said, and squeezed

Stephen's hand. 'Don't look so frightened, darling; her bark is worse than her bite.'

'Well . . . ' Joanna stood up, and her buzzer went.

'I have Mr Giffard on the line, Mrs Orton. He says it's urgent.'

Joanna sat down again, picked up her private phone. 'John?'

There was a kind of gulp on the end of the line. 'Joanna, I'm afraid I have some bad news. Sean Connor died in hospital, an hour ago.'

He had been speaking as quietly as he could, and Joanna was quite sure no one else in the room had heard what he had said. For a moment she couldn't think what to say, remained with the phone held to her ear. 'Joanna?' he asked. 'Are you all right?'

'Yes,' she said. 'I'm all right.'

'I think we need to talk. Are you available this afternoon?'

'Yes. But not here. I'm going out to the house. Can you come out?'

'I'll be there . . . ' a brief hesitation while he checked his diary. 'About five. And Joanna, please don't discuss this with anyone until we've spoken.'

'I understand that.' She replaced the phone, smiled brightly at the people seated in front of her.

But Peter was frowning. 'Nothing wrong?'

'Oh, no,' she said. 'But I really must be getting home. You're in charge, Peter.'

'Of course. Will you be in tomorrow?'

'Of course,' she said. She kissed them all, then went down to Charlie and the waiting car.

'All well?' Charlie asked, as he threaded his way through the midday traffic.

No, Joanna wanted to scream. *All is not well. Nothing is well*. 'Everything is fine, thank you, Charlie,' she said.

I have killed a man, she thought. But so have you, Charlie, on my instructions. He had not been charged with assaulting Sean Connor, because Connor had only brought charges against her. Now Connor was dead . . . had he had time to add Charlie, and perhaps Cummings, to the list? And did that matter beside the fact that Connor was dead, dead, dead? She had been too closely associated with death, too often, in her life. And it hadn't been all that long a life.

And now? What was John Giffard going to tell her? The police had intimated that they felt she had gone over the top in her response to Connor's assault. She had denied that. Now the police had a great deal of ammunition to support their claim. My God, she thought: I could lose the case. And then what? But they couldn't possibly send her to gaol, for defending herself against an attempted rape?

Her hands were clammy inside her gloves, and she took the kid off to rub her fingers together. Just when she had again triumphed, when she was again in command, of the company and of her destiny. Had she ever been in command of her destiny?

'You sure you're all right?' Charlie asked, studying her in the rearview mirror as they began to leave the traffic behind. 'You don't look so good.'

'I feel sick,' she said. Charlie pulled over to the side of the road and stopped. 'Must be something I ate,' she said.

'For breakfast?'

She hadn't realised the time; just coming up to twelve. She smiled. 'Must be something I need to eat. Just pour me a glass of brandy and get me home, Charlie.'

* * *

Caribee House was quiet; the children lunched at school. But Cummings was every bit as observant as Charlie, even though Harriet had telephoned to tell them the mistress was on her way. 'Is everything all right, madam?' he asked.

'Everything is fine, Cummings,' she assured him.

'Cook has prepared lunch. And if you'd like a word about the dinner menu . . . ?'

'I'm sure it's perfect, Cummings. As for lunch, I think I'll skip it. I just want to lie down.'

'Of course, madam.' His gaze drifted past her, and she knew Charlie was signalling in the background. But neither would press her too hard.

Mrs Partridge was at the top of the stairs. 'Is everything — '

'Everything is fine, Mrs Partridge,' Joanna lied. 'I'm just exhausted.'

'Of course, madam. Would you like me to cancel dinner?'

'No, no,' Joanna said. 'I'll be all right if I have a few hours' sleep.'

'Of course, madam.'

She stumbled into her bedroom, stripped off her mink and her sweat-wet clothing, had a hot shower, and fell across the bed. Oil shortage or no oil shortage, the central heating was maintained at seventy degrees Fahrenheit in the house. She closed her eyes, and saw Connor's face in front of her. The Connor from the ship, who had seemed a kind and caring person. Although even then she had recognised in him a streak of almost vicious anger. At her? Or the world? Or just at his own desires? Had what he wanted been so terrible? Had she over-reacted? Or had her reaction been caused by the underlying sense of shame and guilt, that she, Joanna Orton, should have had to send out for a man?

She wasn't going to sleep. So, pill, or drink? She thought a pill would be safer and took two. Then it seemed only a moment later that she was awake, sitting up and pulling hair from her face, as she listened to the gentle knocking on the door. She got out of bed, pulled on her dressing gown, opened it. 'I'm sorry to disturb you, madam,' Mrs Partridge said, 'but Mr Giffard is here. He seems sort of agitated.'

'I knew he was coming. I should have told you. God, is it five o'clock already? Tell him I'll be right down. And ask Cummings to bring some tea.' Her mouth tasted like a sewer. She had another shower, cleaned her teeth, pulled on jeans and a loose blouse and thrust her feet into slippers, went downstairs. Giffard stood looking out of the French windows at the traces of snow on the croquet lawn. 'Well?' she asked.

He turned, came towards her, held out his hands. She took them. 'There's to be a post mortem, of course. Either tonight or first thing tomorrow morning. At the moment, it seems he died of pneumonia.'

'Because I had him thrown out into the snow?'

'Not entirely. Everyone dies of pneumonia, Joanna. It's a condition which overtakes one as the heart ceases to beat; the lungs collapse. But the bleeding suggests that he had a serious internal injury.'

'Which I am supposed to have caused?'

'That is something that will be determined after the post mortem. The hospital recognised the symptoms of an internal injury right away, but initially they were more concerned about the gash in his face, which appears to have been quite considerable. Then Connor's general condition was so poor they were hoping to improve it somewhat before operating. In the event, he didn't improve. And, sadly, the police have it on tape that you admit jumping on his stomach with all your weight.'

'God, what a mess. I didn't mean to hurt him, John. Not badly enough to cause internal injuries. You know that.'

'Of course I know that. You were acting in self defence. That's our defence. But the police claim, as they have done all along, that you over-reacted, and kept over-reacting until Connor was a hospital case, and then just threw him out.'

'Okay, so I went over the top. I was frightened, I was disgusted, and I was angry. You get enough women on the jury and they'll know exactly how I felt.'

'Of course. Unfortunately, you see, this is no longer a case of grievous bodily harm.'

'I know. It's manslaughter. That doesn't alter the facts, does it? That Connor tried to rape me, and that I defended myself. Perhaps a shade too vigorously.'

Still holding her hands, Giffard guided her to the settee and made her sit. He sat beside her. 'I had a visit from Inspector Langridge just after I'd spoken with you this morning. You remember him? He was handling the investigation.'

'I don't think he likes me.'

'Possibly not. But that's neither here nor there. He's on his way down here now.'

'Here? I don't want to see him here.'

'I'm afraid you will have to. You see, the police have decided not to charge you with manslaughter; they're going for murder instead.'

6

The Prosecution

Joanna knew her fingers were tightening into claws; she could tell by Giffard's expression that her nails were biting into his flesh. 'But . . . that's not possible,' she whispered. 'Murder . . . that implies pre-meditation. I invited Connor here to sleep with him. That was all. I had no idea he was going to turn out to be a satyr.'

'The police think they can prove otherwise. You see, they obtained an order to search Connor's digs, as they were entitled to do. They found it filled with cuttings of you since your return to England. They also found various notes he had made, including items regarding money, indicating that he intended demanding some off you. They reckon he was doing that when he came here. And that you knew what he was planning, and were prepared for it.' Slowly Joanna released him to clasp both hands round her neck. 'Their theory,' Giffard went on, speaking slowly, 'is that you and he had an affair on board the ship, as you say, but that it was strictly a shipboard romance, as these things so often are, and that you had every intention of ending it the moment you reached dry land, again as so often happens in these affairs. And you thought you had done that. But Connor by then knew all about you, how wealthy you were and where you lived, and he contacted you and demanded to see you again, or he would take the story to the papers. The police reckon you agreed to see him, with every intention of ending the affair for good. And that that is what you did. They reckon the story of the attempted rape, and attempted, ah, bestial assault, is all make-believe.'

'That is ludicrous,' Joanna shouted. 'He never mentioned a word about blackmail. He even offered to help in the company's difficulties, if he could.'

'Can you prove that?'

'Of course I can't.'

'There's our problem. The police do have proof that he was planning blackmail. Or so they claim.'

'For God's sake, John, if I had intended to kill him, wouldn't I have had a gun or a knife or some poison? Would I seriously have assaulted him with my bare hands? I'm a woman, not an all-in wrestler.'

'They reckon you were too smart for that. They reckon you invited him down here, provoked him into attacking you, preempted the situation, and then had your staff beat him insensible and throw him into the snow to die. There are warrants out for Charlie and Cummings as well; they will be served this afternoon.'

'Oh, my God! Oh, Jesus! They were only doing what I told them to do.'

'Joanna, please don't ever say that again, not even to me.'

'I can't let them take the blame for my decisions. Listen!' She held his hands. 'They say Connor demanded to see me to extort money. But he didn't know where I lived. I invited him down, John.'

'Can you prove *that*?'

'When we left the ship, he gave me his address and telephone number, so that I could contact him if I felt like, well . . . seeing him again. He wrote it down. He did. Surely the police can match up the writing.'

'I would imagine so. Let me see the piece of paper.'

'Oh, gosh! I've just remembered. After I'd called him, I threw it away.' Giffard sighed. Joanna held his hands again. 'John! How much trouble am I in?'

'It's not good. But, as you said the other day, we have to see how many women we can get on the jury.'

* * *

The new hearing lasted no longer than the first, only this time there was an increased grimness about the proceedings, and bail went up to twenty-five thousand pounds. Joanna went straight from the court to Caribee Shipping, where Peter Young had, as she had requested, set up a meeting with Jonathan Prim, the senior partner at Joanna's stockbrokers, Miller & Smart, and Barry Andrews. 'Good of you to come,' she told them. 'Do sit down. Harriet, coffee.'

'Was it very wearing?' Andrews asked. They had all known her for a long time, watched her climb to stardom in the city. But with them, too, she sensed a certain grimness.

'Not really,' she said. 'The wearing part comes later. But we're not here to discuss my personal problems. As you may imagine, we need some financing.'

'So does everybody,' Andrews pointed out.

'Then surely old and loyal customers come first.'

'Of course. What are we talking about, apart from the half million last week?'

'That was to regain complete control of the company. The shares are your security.'

'Yes.' His tone was doubtful. 'They are dropping. Quite fast.'

'That is the problem I wish to address. We have to show the world that we are totally confident, not only in *the* future but in *our* future. We had a bad press because of that mid-Atlantic breakdown. But we brought the ship home, which must count for something. However, the breakdown was caused by age, and the same goes for *Caribee Future*. So the first thing we need to do is order, and let the world know we have ordered, two new, modern vessels. You put out for those tenders, Peter?'

'Yes, I did. Early days yet, of course. But . . . ' he looked as if he would have continued, but changed his mind.

'How much were you thinking of spending?' Andrews asked again.

Joanna looked at Peter. 'To get what we want, ten million.'

Prim gave a low whistle.

Andrews sighed. 'Not on, I'm afraid, Joanna. Certainly not at this time.'

'Well, then . . . ' Joanna looked at Prim.

He shook his head. 'It won't work, right now, Joanna. For several reasons. We are about to enter a period of extreme recession, if not worse. I also believe we are about to enter a period of extreme inflation as well. To have both depression and inflation at the same time may sound absurd, and it may well turn out to be catastrophic. But the fact is that the price of oil has already gone through the roof and is going to go higher. And almost everything the civilised world does, makes, sells or consumes is based on oil. So, the economic outlook is grim in the extreme. People are not in the mood to take up substantial share issues. Add to that, well . . . you don't wish to discuss your personal problems, and I respect that, but they are there. People are asking just who will be running Caribee Shipping in a month or two.'

'I shall be, Jonathan.'

'I sincerely hope you will be, Joanna. But it needs to be proved to the public, and especially the institutions who we need to take up substantial parts of any issue.'

Joanna looked from face to face. 'Just what are you telling me?'

'That you just have to be patient,' Andrews said. 'Sit it out.'

'We are about to start losing money, Barry.'

'You have a reserve fund. Use it. This situation can't last very long, it's too serious. Another few months.' He looked at Prim.

'After your trial, when you are clear of all charges, people will be back on your side.'

'Meaning they are not on my side now?'

'Now, Joanna, you know what I mean.'

'And suppose, just suppose, I am *not*

cleared of all the charges against me?'

Again Prim and Andrews exchanged glances. 'That's impossible, surely,' Andrews said.

Joanna and Peter, left alone, gazed at each other across the boardroom table. 'What a mess,' he commented.

'Can we go on as we are, for a few months?'

'A few months, yes. As Andrews said, we can dip into our reserves, but they are not going to last forever. Our share price is dropping. So of course is everyone else's, but ours is travelling a bit faster. That has to do with, well . . .'

'My being charged with murder.'

'I'm afraid so. But again, as Andrews and Prim said, once that is out of the way . . .' he paused, looking at her face. 'Are you scared?'

'Yes,' Joanna said. 'I'm scared.' It was the first time in her life that she had made such an admission.

* * *

'I can't tell you how sorry I am about this,' Joanna told Charlie and Cummings. Both had been charged as accessories, and released, like herself, on bail; she had stood the bail.

'It's you we worry about, madam,' Cummings said, while Charlie merely looked embarrassed.

'In my evidence, I shall of course entirely exonerate you both.'

'There is no need for that, madam,' Charlie protested. 'The bastard, begging your pardon, deserved everything he got.'

'But whatever you did, it was because I told you to do it,' Joanna insisted. 'I do promise you that neither of you is going to jail.' Even if I go myself? she wondered. But that was impossible. Whatever theories the police might dream up, she had acted in self defence. But she was still frightened. 'Give it to me straight, John,' she told Giffard, when he came down to see her. 'The very worst.'

'Well . . . ' he sipped his champagne. 'As you know, I have already asked the charge to be reduced, from murder to manslaughter, and the magistrates have refused. I shall make the same request of the judge, when we come to trial. Hopefully he will show more sense.'

'I want to know what happens if he doesn't.'

'Well, then, I'm afraid we are going to have to go through the whole business of your relationship with Connor. I have people working on his background, which appears to be rather mysterious. It would seem that he is, or was, fairly well connected.'

'The Ferrari.'

'Yes. He actually did own it. Now that is odd for a mining engineer who has been invalided home. Where did he get the money to buy, apparently outright, a car like that? As I say, I have people working on it, but at the present time it looks rather as if he might have been a remittance man.'

'Say again?'

'A remittance man. That is, the scion, probably a child of a wealthy family, who decided to get rid of him by sending him to the 'colonies' as they would consider it. The question is to find the family, as he does not seem to have confided in any friends as to his real background, or even his real name, supposing Connor is not it. In fact, he doesn't seem to have had any friends at all.'

'Isn't that something in our favour?'

'Well, slightly. The fact that a man does not have many, or any, friends, does not necessarily make him a criminal. It just suggests that there may have been something abnormal in his personality.'

'Well? Can't we use that?'

'We can and we will. But merely getting too close to someone with a personality disorder is not a reason for killing him. No, I'm afraid if the worst comes to the worst, I am going to have to put you in the witness box and take you through your relationship, step by step. And when I have done that, the prosecution will do it all over again, only from a more hostile point of view.'

'Every word of which will be reported in the papers for my children to read.'

'Sadly. The prosecution are going to set out to prove, from the various episodes in your life, that you are an immoral woman who, when for the first time in her life was threatened with blackmail for her immoral activities, reacted like a vicious animal and murdered the would-be blackmailer.'

'Sounds terrific,' Joanna muttered.

'Our only defence is going to accept that you have behaved immorally from time to time in your life, but that you have never revealed the slightest vicious streak, or indeed engaged in the slightest physical violence. That is, of course, not quite true, but on both the previous occasions you were the attacked rather than the attacker. I shall also, of course, make a great deal of the point you raised earlier, that there is simply no evidence that you had made any preparations for killing Connor, if that is what you had in mind. There was no trace of a weapon, unless your ring can be so called, your servants will testify that they responded to your call for help and had not been briefed in any way as to what to expect.'

'What about Charlie and Cummings?'

'Their fate really depends on yours. You will be tried first. If you are acquitted, then the cases against them will be dropped. If you were to be convicted, their trials will go ahead. But their positions are infinitely less serious than yours, if you do not require them to say anything more than that they were called upon for help and told what to do.'

'Which happens to be the truth.'

'Yes,' he said pessimistically. 'However . . . ' he brightened. 'I think you will do very well in the witness box. I am expecting an acquittal. It's just a pity that at the very minute you are being tried for murder, you are also divorcing your husband. I don't suppose . . . ?'

'No,' she said. 'Absolutely not.'

'Well, we'll have to see if that cannot be somehow used to our advantage.' His tone indicated that he didn't quite see how.

'I want to know what happens if there is not an acquittal, John.'

'Well . . . ' he finished his drink. 'If that were to happen, you would have to be condemned and sentenced. But it can't possibly happen.'

'Condemned and sentenced to what?'

'Well . . . ' he looked longingly at the bottle, and she refilled his glass.

'I assume I can't be hanged.'

'Oh, good lord, no. That went out years ago. But there would probably be a custodial sentence. A few years . . . '

'A few *years*?'

'Joanna, you simply have to get it through your head that, were you to be found guilty, it would be of murder. Now, of course, we should appeal, but . . . ' He shrugged.

Joanna refilled her own glass.

* * *

'What are you going to do?' William asked.

He was dining alone with his sister. Norma had understood there were matters to be discussed with which she had no business. Matilda would have liked to be present but William had talked her out of it; Joanna had shown no sign of wishing to re-employ Billy. 'There is nothing I can do, save wait. It's all in John Giffard's hands now.'

'You're taking it very well.'

'I'm not, really. I'm a gibbering wreck, inside.'

'You can't possibly be convicted. Can you?'

'I can, Willy. I'm claiming self-defence, but I am the only surviving witness to what actually happened that night. Just as I am the only witness to what I had in mind. So it's going to come down to whether or not the jury believe me. That jury is going to be composed of twelve men, and hopefully women, who are going to be given an image of me, if they didn't already have one. The women may be sympathetic towards a rape victim, but was I a rape victim? They're going to be told how I was Howard Edge's mistress for a year, and then, when he finally married me, I mysteriously inherited his entire business empire only a fortnight later. They're going to be told how I married Prince Hassim for his money. I can't deny that. Telling them that I grew to admire and respect and love him afterwards isn't going to do all that much good. They'll be told how I am in the process of divorcing my third husband. They'll be told how I fired my own brother-in-law. They'll be told how I had an affair with Sean Connor on board my ship. I can't deny any of those things. At the end of it all, they're going to be told how I planned his murder, because he was getting in my way. That's the only thing I can deny, and having been depicted as an utterly ruthless woman who will do anything to get her own way, that denial isn't going to sound very convincing, is it?'

'You're being too pessimistic,' William

argued. 'The prosecution can't bring in anything about your previous life,, surely.'

'Yes, they can, once I take the stand. And I have to take the stand, because I'm my only witness. Right?'

'What a fucking awful mess.'

'What about afterwards? Assuming the worst. I may have to go to prison, for a while.'

'You can say it, that calmly? Have you any idea?'

'What are you trying to do, send me into a nervous breakdown? Yes, I have an idea what it may be like. It's something I have to accept. But I'll be back, soon enough. Someone will have to hold the fort until then. It has to be somebody I can trust, absolutely. Can you do it?'

'Well . . . ' he flushed. 'What about Tilly?'

'I can't trust Tilly, and you know that. She's entirely at the mercy of Billy, and I wouldn't trust him to sell my clapped-out washing machine for the best possible price and give me all he got for it. I want you to come in and sit on the board next week. It's grim, I know. The money people tell me we can't have any new ships right now. But we simply have to have the new ships just as soon as it is possible. You have to keep pressing. Peter Young will give you maximum support, I know.'

William licked his lips in a mixture of anticipation and uncertainty.

'You'll also have control of all my personal finances, including the trust company. I'll make out all the necessary authorities. But I don't want to come out of prison worth a penny less than I am now. Right?'

'I'll do my best. But Jo, it isn't really going to happen, is it?'

'Of course it isn't,' Joanna assured him.

* * *

'Did you really kill Mr Connor, Mummy?' Helen asked.

'Of course she did,' Raisul said. 'It says so in the papers.'

Joanna regarded them across the breakfast table. 'You don't want to believe everything you read in the newspapers, darling. I didn't kill Mr Connor. Not intentionally. It seems I may have hit him a little too hard, and he died.'

'Will you be hanged?' Helen asked. 'One of the girls at school said you will be hanged.'

'No, darling, I won't be hanged,' Joanna said. 'They don't hang people any more.'

'But you'll be locked up, for ever and ever and ever,' Raisul said. 'One of the boys at school said you would be.'

'And I'm sure he knows best,' Joanna agreed. 'Charlie's waiting.'

They kissed her and scampered off. They didn't really understand what was going on, she supposed. But . . . she looked at Cummings, standing by the sideboard.

'Should I keep them home, Cummings?'

'I think you are doing entirely the right thing, madam,' Cummings said, as loyal as ever.

But she needed more than loyalty. She summoned Mrs Partridge to her bedroom. 'You understand that I may have to go away for a while,' she said.

'Oh, no, madam. I will never believe that,' Mrs Partridge declared.

'I don't believe it either,' Joanna said. 'But it is a possibility that we have to face. Now, in that eventuality, I do not wish anything to change here.' Mrs Partridge looked terrified. 'My brother will be handling all of my affairs, with full powers of attorney,' Joanna said. 'He will therefore be handling all the expenses of Caribee House, together with all staff salaries, of course. Including yours, naturally, Mrs Partridge. But yours will be doubled.'

'Madam?' Now she looked about to faint.

'Because I am going to appoint you legal guardian of the children until I return. Don't look so alarmed, it will only be for a few years, at the very worst.'

'But, madam, the children . . . ?'

'Adore you, Mrs Partridge.'

'Yes, but . . . Mrs Montgomery . . . '

'Mrs Montgomery has her own children to worry about,' Joanna pointed out. 'I know I can rely on you, and trust you, Mrs Partridge.' She gave a brief smile. 'Molly.'

It was the first time she had ever used the housekeeper's first name.

'Oh, madam!' Mrs Partridge burst into tears.

* * *

'Well!' Matilda declared. 'Of all the ways to treat your own sister.'

'I'm sure you have enough to do with your own two, Tilly,' Joanna said.

'You think I'm irresponsible,' Matilda declared.

'Well, since you have raised the subject, I do not think you are a hundred percent reliable,' Joanna acknowledged. 'What I wish, should the very worst happen, is that my children be brought up, until I can come back to them, in the most sane and uneventful manner possible. God knows, should I lose my case, they will be subjected to enough pressure, both at school and from the media.

They need always to be able to return here to an atmosphere of the utmost safety and tranquillity. I believe that Mrs Partridge and Mr Cummings are the people most able to provide that safety and tranquillity.'

'This is all because of Billy,' Matilda stormed. 'You hate him.'

'I do not hate him,' Joanna said, keeping her own temper with difficulty. 'But I certainly do not intend to allow him any say in the upbringing of my children.'

'You can talk like that,' Matilda snapped. 'What kind of a mother have you been? Swanning about the world, marrying and remarrying, and now, inviting some layabout to come here and spend the night, and then killing him . . . you're not fit to be a mother.'

'My dear Tilly,' Joanna said, 'You are sounding just as I expect the prosecution to.'

* * *

'It's strange how things turn out.' Alicia, as she always did when visiting Caribee House, moved restlessly about the drawing room, checking for dust here, straightening a picture frame there, as if she still owned the place, Joanna thought. Or as if she intends to own it again.

'I'm sure you're right,' she said politely. She

had not asked Alicia to call, could only wait to discover what was on her mind.

'I mean, when you came down to see me . . .'

'I had not yet killed Sean Connor, Alicia.'

'Of course I know that. But you were already setting up to meet him.' She gazed at her rival, eyebrows arched.

'I was already setting up to do nothing,' Joanna said. 'The reason I got in touch with Connor that night was because I was feeling on top of the world, after seeing you.'

'Those shares.' Alicia sat down. 'I'll buy them back from you, if you like.'

'Why on earth should you want to do that?'

'Well . . .' she gave a little smile. 'You're going to have no use for them where you're going.'

'All cut and dried, is it? Alicia, even if I am sent to prison, which everyone agrees is highly unlikely, I will still be Chairman and Managing Director of Caribee Shipping.'

'That's absurd. How can you run a company from prison?'

'Someone will run it for me, pending my return. The only necessary requirement is that I retain my controlling interest.'

'Ha,' Alicia commented. 'And who *is* going to run the company, pending your return?'

'My brother, William. He is already a director.'

'That boy? What does he know about running a shipping company? Do you suppose Andy Gosling will put up with that?'

'He'll have to.'

'Ha,' Alicia said again. 'I really don't want to quarrel with you, Joanna, but it would make far more sense for someone more experienced to act for you.'

'I see. Someone like your Stephen, for instance.'

'Well, he's been in the City all his life.'

'What as? Someone's messenger?'

Alicia stood up. 'I did not come here to be insulted.'

'Then I apologise. I have a lot on my mind. But I have made all the necessary arrangements for the conduct of the company during my absence. Just as I would have done had I been told that I needed a serious operation that would keep me out of circulation for some time. This is exactly the same thing.'

'It is not at all the same thing,' Alicia said. 'Going into hospital for an operation is an honourable thing, whereas going to prison . . . '

'I think you had better leave,' Joanna suggested.

Alicia got up again. 'You don't have so

many friends that you can afford to throw them away.'

'Are you my friend?' Joanna enquired. 'I never knew.'

Alicia snorted, and left the room.

⋆ ⋆ ⋆

'Appearance is very important,' said Jeanette Corder. She was one of John Giffard's juniors, and the senior woman in his partnership. She was somewhat older than Joanna, very smart and handsome in an efficient sort of way. 'May I look?' she asked.

Joanna waved her hand at the wardrobe, and Jeanette opened the doors. 'Their idea will be to convince the jury that you are a brazen hussy,' she said over her shoulder. 'We must present you as what you are, a hard-working, talented businesswoman. This is ideal.' She took out a grey wool suit, and then frowned. 'Oh dear. Trousers. Don't you have a skirt for it?'

'I'm afraid not. Won't trousers do?'

'Definitely not. The trial judge is old Crowther. That's bad in any event. He's the sort of old-fashioned MCP who doesn't believe there is such a thing as rape in the first place. Trousers on women are definitely a guarantee that she is loose.'

'But that's outrageous,' Joanna said. 'I mean, his point of view. Can't we get him changed?'

'It happens to be his turn on that particular bench. But it's not all down. If, in his misogynistic fervour, he misdirects the jury, or even shows extreme prejudice, it could be grounds for an appeal against your conviction . . . supposing you are convicted, of course.' She paused to give a bright, and quite unconvincing, smile. 'Here's what we want.'

It was a blue suit, with skirt, and a thin white pin-stripe. 'Wear this with a white blouse, buttoned right up, plain stockings, court shoes, and a modicum of jewellery — just a pearl necklace and your wedding and engagement rings.'

'I don't have an engagement ring, at the moment. It's exhibit A.'

'Ah. Right. Then just your wedding ring. That's probably better, anyway. Now, hair . . . you should put it up. I mean, that hair, worn loose it'll have every man in court dreaming of being in bed with you, and that can be a short step from believing that they could be, if you are the sort of woman depicted by the prosecution. Do you always wear it loose?'

'Not when I'm in a business meeting.'

'Regard this as a business meeting. I

assume you have your own hairdresser?'

'Of course.'

'Not everyone does, you know. I want you to have it put up in a tight bun. That'll serve two purposes. One, it will again lessen the allure. Two, you have superb bone structure. With no hair about that will heighten the suggestion of total innocence. Right?'

'Right,' Joanna said. 'I never realised presentation was so important.'

'Presentation is everything, Mrs Orton. The prosecution are going to do their damndest to present you as a guilty woman. We are going to do our damndest to present you as an innocent woman. And you are going to do your damndest to help us do that. Right?'

'Right,' Joanna said.

* * *

'Brandy, madam?' Cummings asked.

'Why, not, Cummings?' Joanna asked. The children had been put to bed, and the servants had disappeared into their quarters. All but faithful old Cummings. Because in precisely twelve hours she would be standing in the dock at the Old Bailey accused of murder. Tomorrow, tomorrow, tomorrow, she thought. Cummings brought the drink, waited for any further orders. 'Go to bed, Cummings,' she told him. He looked doubtful. 'I will switch off the lights.'

'Yes, madam.' He sounded more doubtful still, and she presumed that when she finally went upstairs he would immediately reappear to check that everything was in order.

Now she waited for his footsteps to die away along the hall before standing up, glass in hand. She kicked off her shoes, walked through the double doors into the hall, then across the hall into the billiards room. A room that had hardly been used since Howard's death. It was on that table that his coffin had been laid, after their return from the West Indies, as it had been here that the funeral had commenced and the wake had followed.

She went on, into the dining room, with its huge refectory table and its row of chairs. Again, a room seldom used since Howard's death. Hasim had preferred to entertain in his London flat, had used this house as a weekend getaway. Dick had not really been up to a great deal of entertaining.

She had, she supposed, never used this house sufficiently. She had camped here, for thirteen years. Was she now going to have to move out? Nobody would tell her. She went upstairs, prowled through the bedrooms, the Blue Room, where she had first surrendered to Howard, the other guest rooms, and then the master bedroom, where she had slept in solitary splendour since her honeymoon. Even then she had not really enjoyed sharing a bed with Dick. All behind her, now.

* * *

She slept heavily, waking with a start as the telephone jangled. She picked it up, but Cummings had already answered, downstairs. 'Madam is asleep, sir,' he was saying. 'I do not think — '

'I'm awake, Cummings,' she said.

'It's Mr Orton, Madam.'

'Jo! Listen! I have to see you.'

'Why?' she asked.

'I've been subpoenaed. By the prosecution.'

'Then to see me would be incorrect. I'm not sure it wouldn't be illegal.'

'Stuff that. Listen, they'll want to ask about, well . . . your character, I suppose.'

'Tell them the truth.'

'If they were to manage to bring out something about that drugs bust . . . '

'Tell the truth,' Joanna said again. 'I was totally innocent, and you know it.'

'Of course I do, but they could still manage to make it look bad.'

'So?'

'Well . . . I could deny it.'

'It's a matter of police record, Dick. Your denying it would only get you charged with perjury.'

'I'm trying to help you, Jo. I will help you, if . . . '

'If what?'

'If you'd drop all this stupid divorce thing. That isn't helping you much, either, you know. If we were to show a united front . . . '

'It would have so many cracks in it we'd both fall flat on our faces. I won't thank you for the offer, Dick, because I don't think you really had me in mind.'

'Bitch!' he said. 'I hope they — ' She hung up.

* * *

She had not expected the court to be so crowded. But, of course, not only was the case sensational in itself, it promised to be salacious as well. She stood in the dock, flanked by two policewomen, and although John Giffard and Jeanette Corder both smiled at her encouragingly, she felt more lonely than ever before in her life. Grahame Long, seated in front of them, did not look at her at all. When would British courts become civilised and allow the defendant to sit at a table with his, or her, lawyers? After all, she was supposed to be innocent until she was found guilty. Standing isolated in the dock, surrounded by policewomen, was an indication of guilt.

It all came down to Grahame Long. The best man in the business, John Giffard had assured her. She could only hope he was right. At least he looked like a lawyer, and a successful man, medium height, somewhat stout, with a sharp nose, reeking of good tobacco and wearing a Savile Row suit. They had had three meetings, and he had clearly studied the evidence very carefully. He had asked her various questions about her past life and previous marriages, noted the answers, and made no comment. So she had asked him. 'Well?'

'On the evidence that I have been shown, Mrs Orton, both for and against, there should be an acquittal. I say should rather than will. The jury system requires that, even in a case in which all the odds are stacked on your side, you still have to convince them that you acted only as any decent woman would have done.' At last he had smiled at her. 'Just be yourself.'

She had been so reassured. 'What about this terrible judge we have?'

'If the jury believe you are innocent of

murder, Mrs Orton, Crowther can foam at the mouth, but there is nothing he can do about it.'

* * *

Total reassurance, however, was prevented by the media, who were not a hundred per cent for her. In fact, they seemed pretty well divided. And the division was simply along the lines of whether or not she had indeed acted in her own self-defence, as any decent woman might have done. The newspapers, and television, were pretty well agreed that she had proved herself to be a hard, and ruthless businesswoman over the past thirteen years.

* * *

The prosecution case was a simple one, and it was exactly as Long had suggested it would be. 'The Crown will prove,' said Mr Horton-Smith, QC, 'that on a voyage home from England, in November of last year, Mrs Orton, Managing Director of Caribee Shipping, travelling in one of her own vessels, had an affair with the deceased, Sean Connor. The Crown will contend that when the voyage ended, Mrs Orton assumed that this romance had also ended, as shipboard romances are wont to do. However, the Crown will prove that Mr Connor did not see it that way, that he wanted to see Mrs Orton again, and that, having discovered that she was a wealthy woman, he intended to blackmail her by threatening to reveal their affair to the press. With this purpose in mind, he visited her at her home on the night of sixteenth December, last. He had informed Mrs Orton that he was coming, and she was waiting for him.

'The Crown will prove that she sent her children to bed and told her servants that she was not to be interrupted unless she called for them, so that she could be alone with him. But after only a little while, Mrs Orton attacked Mr Connor, so viciously that he received extensive injuries. She then called her servants and had the injured man thrown out into the snow. The Crown will show that despite his injuries, Mr Connor managed to regain his car and drive away, but that he collapsed before he could reach his home. He was taken to hospital, where, forty-eight hours later, and after making a statement to the police, he died of the internal injuries he had received, aggravated by the extreme cold to which he had been subjected when ejected from Mrs Orton's house.'

The jury listened intently, and Joanna was disturbed that they seldom looked at her; she had been told this was a bad sign. She was also disappointed that despite Long's efforts, there were only three women, and none of these looked particularly sympathetic, either. She preferred not to look at the judge, a large, red-faced man who seemed to glower at her.

Long's riposte was savage. 'The prosecution's case,' he told the jury, 'is entirely built upon supposition and circumstantial evidence. The defence will not deny that Mrs Orton had a shipboard romance with Mr Connor. But she did not wish it to end when the voyage was over. Rather, she wished it to continue. It was she who contacted Mr Connor and invited him to her home for dinner. When he arrived, he was introduced to her children before they went to bed; we have the evidence of the children's nanny, Mrs Winshaw, to prove this. Hardly, you might say, the procedure of a woman who is about to carry out a brutal murder.

'The defence will not, it cannot, pretend that Mrs Orton is a woman of great moral stature; she is, however, as is well known, a highly successful businesswoman who must be given credit for her clear-sightedness and determination. We thus again ask you to consider whether such a woman would plan a murder in her own home, virtually in the presence of her children, when there would be no hope of concealing the crime.

'We will admit freely that she invited Connor to visit her with a continuation of their relationship in mind. She only turned against him when he wished to indulge in sex of the most perverted kind. When she requested him to stop, he refused to do so. She therefore defended herself, as would any woman in those circumstances. As a result of her spirited defence of her person, Mr Connor was injured. The prosecution have contended that it was from those injuries, and the way he was manhandled by Mrs Orton's servants, that he died. Sadly, this may well be so. But there is not the slightest indication that Mrs Orton pre-meditated or planned this tragedy. She acted in self defence, and we shall prove this to your satisfaction.'

The prosecution evidence was mercifully brief. They were biding their time. After the various routine evidences of arrest had been given, Demont the steward was called and, clearly very embarrassed — he kept glancing apologetically at Joanna — established that he had served drinks and coffee to Mrs Orton and Mr Connor, in her stateroom, not only on the night of the storm but on several occasions afterwards. In view of the fact that the defence had conceded that Joanna and Connor had had a shipboard romance, this seemed a rather unnecessary crossing of t's and dotting of i's to Joanna, especially when Demont was followed by Connor's cabin mate, Gerald Aston. But Mr Smith-Horton had his reasons. Aston could only testify that Connor had never again slept in their cabin after the night of the storm, and that Connor had said he was sleeping with Mrs Orton. The Boss, he called her. But then Mr Smith-Horton asked him: 'When the ship had docked in Plymouth, Mr Aston,' he said. 'What happened then?'

'We cleared customs and immigration on board, and then we went ashore,' Aston said. He had not looked at Joanna at all.

'You and Mr Connor went ashore together?'

'No, sir. Mr Connor hung behind. He said he had to say goodbye to the boss.'

'And when did he come ashore?'

'About fifteen minutes later.'

'And what did he say to you?'

'He said that she was the most exciting woman he had ever known.'

'And what else did he say?'

'He said that he was going to have a lot more of her.'

The spectators gave the required gasp of

appreciation, Judge Crowther the required tap of his gavel.

'He did not specify what he meant by that statement?' Smith-Horton asked.

'No, sir.'

Smith-Horton did not call for speculation on the part of the witness, which would have led to an objection. Long did what he could. 'In his conversation with you, Mr Connor did not mention that he had given Mrs Orton his phone number, and expected her to call him?'

'No, sir,' Aston said.

There were various police officers to testify that they had searched Sean Connor's room and found a good deal of material to indicate that he was planning to blackmail Joanna. This material was produced as evidence. There was also the medical evidence, outlining Connor's various injuries. The doctor described the beating as severe, and concluded that Connor had died of a ruptured peritoneum caused by being stamped upon with extreme force, and that he had then been subjected to exposure that had gravely weakened his condition.

'How healthy was Connor when he visited Mrs Orton?' Long asked in cross-examination.

'I would say perfectly healthy. He had had a bout of malaria a few months previously, but had made a complete recovery.'

'You are saying that there was no trace of any existing stomach problem before sixteenth December last, or any other internal complaint?'

'None at all,' the doctor said, with total certainty.

Then the prosecution got down to its real business. Captain Heggie was called. 'For how long have you worked for Mrs Orton?' Smith-Horton asked.

'Ever since Mr Edge died sir. Thirteen years, now.'

'Has she been a good boss?'

'Oh, yes, sir.'

'Would you describe her as firm?'

'Oh, yes, sir.'

Grahame Long began to frown at the ceiling.

'No doubt during those thirteen years there have been many crises?'

'Well, sir, that's the nature of the shipping business.'

'Through all of which Mrs Orton has triumphed. By her firmness? Her determination? Her courage?'

'Absolutely, sir.'

'Her ruthlessness, would you say? In letting nothing stand in the way of her gaining her objective?'

'Objection, m'lud,' Long said. 'The introduction of this witness has no bearing on this case, which is a matter of facts, not opinions.' He allowed himself an important smile. 'However favourable.'

'With respect, m'lud,' Smith-Horton argued. 'The only fact we possess about this case is that Mr Connor is dead, as a result of an assault upon him by Mrs Orton. It is the prosecution's contention that this attack was pre-meditated and planned. Mrs Orton denies this. Thus the case hinges upon what was actually in Mrs Orton's mind at the time. She is unlikely to tell us the truth about this. It seems to me, therefore, that learning about her state of mind, on various previous occasions of a critical nature, is very relevant indeed.'

'That is preposterous,' Long said.

'I will see you gentlemen in chambers,' Lord Crowther decided. 'Court is adjourned.'

* * *

Long was furious when he joined Joanna and Giffard for lunch. 'He's going to admit the evidence. And anything else that may indicate your ability to make critical and perhaps ambiguous decisions. Well, that is grounds for an appeal, for a start. And I have told him I will object to every one.'

'What did he say?' Giffard asked.

'He said that was my privilege.' Long squeezed Joanna's hand. 'Don't worry, my dear. They are playing entirely into our hands.'

* * *

'Mr Montgomery,' Smith-Horton said. 'For how long have you worked for Mrs Orton?'

'Ever since Howard . . . Mr Edge . . . died. Thirteen years.'

'And before then you worked for Mr Edge?'

'For eight years, sir.'

'I believe you were in a position of some responsibility?'

'Mr Edge had a trust company in Jersey which I managed. Mrs Orton inherited that, and I continued to manage it for her.'

'I believe you are related to Mrs Orton?'

'I am her brother-in-law, sir.'

'And do you still work for her?'

'No, sir. I have been fired.'

'How sad. When did this misfortune take place?'

'In December of last year. Right after she returned from her Caribbean voyage.'

'May we ask why you were dismissed?'

'Well . . . ' for the first time Billy looked at the dock, his cheeks pink. 'She intimated that she was not happy with the way I was running her company.'

'Just like that? After twenty-one years in the employ of Mrs Orton and her late husband, she sacked you?'

'I'm afraid she's like that,' Billy conceded.

'You mean she acted in a totally ruthless manner, because you had, perhaps, failed her in one small direction. Did you suspect that she might have acted as she did because she had another grave matter on her mind?'

'Objection,' Long said, wearily.

* * *

'How long have you been married to Mrs Orton?' Smith-Horton asked Dick.

'Four years.'

'But you have known her longer than that?'

'Oh, yes. I knew her since she came to England, thirteen years ago.'

'You were friends. Close friends?'

'I thought so.'

'But your friendship was interrupted. How did that happen?'

Dick shrugged. 'She took up with this wealthy guy, Edge.'

'Were you upset by this?'

'Very.'

'But you understood that Mrs Orton, or Miss Grain as she then was, would always go for the main chance, with a ruthless disregard of whoever might get hurt in the process.'

'Objection.'

'Now, Mr Orton, I understand that you and Mrs Orton are in the process of getting divorced.'

'She has filed for divorce against me, yes,' Dick said, choosing his words carefully, as he had no doubt been coached to do.

'Do we take it that you not wish for this divorce?'

'Heavens, no,' Dick said. 'She's my wife. I love her.' The court smiled.

'But Mrs Orton is determined to divorce you. Why?'

'She found out that I had had an affair.'

'Did she ask you for an explanation? Or perhaps even a promise that it would not happen again?'

'Joanna isn't like that.'

'You mean she just announced she was divorcing you?'

'She threw me out of the house,' Dick said.

'This being a day or so after her return from the Caribbean?'

This time there was no need for an objection.

'Mr Orton,' Long said, 'is not the real reason Mrs Orton is divorcing you is because you sold a block of shares in her company, held by you, and which, by the terms of your marriage agreement, you were not entitled to sell without her permission?'

'That may have had something to do with it.'

Joanna felt her barrister might have made a tactical error, as that was just another example of her presumed ruthlessness.

But there remained Alicia. 'When did you first meet Mrs Orton, Mrs Edge?'

'I have no idea. It was some time in nineteen sixty-four.'

'You were, at that time, married to Mr Edge?'

'Yes, I was.'

'And Mrs Orton, or Miss Grain as she then was?'

'Was one of his floozies. Or so I thought. I soon realised my mistake when he moved her into Caribee House.'

'You had, of course, moved out?'

'Of course.'

'And Mr Edge then divorced you to marry Miss Grain?'

'Yes.'

'Did you wish to divorce Mr Edge?'

'Of course I did not. But when that woman

gets her claws into someone — '

'Strike that remark,' said Lord Crowther. 'Please confine yourself to answering the questions, Mrs Edge.' But he smiled at her as he spoke.

Smith-Horton was happy enough. 'I do not suppose you have seen a great deal of Mrs Orton since your mutual husband died?'

'Not a lot,' Alicia said. 'She attempted to be friends, but I found it difficult.'

'Quite. Will you tell the court when last you met up with Mrs Orton?'

'Well, we've seen quite a lot of each other over the past few weeks.'

'This was after Mrs Orton called on you at your home, on the morning of . . . ' he checked his notes, 'sixteenth December last.'

'Yes.'

'Why did she visit you?'

'She wanted to buy some of my shares.'

'Did she tell you why?'

'She needed my shares to replace those sold by her husband. So that she could retain control of the company.'

'And you agreed to this?'

'Well . . . ' Alicia glanced at Joanna. 'She made me an attractive offer. She offered both myself and a friend of mine seats on the board of Caribee Shipping if we would agree to sell her the shares.'

'Would it therefore be correct to say that Mrs Orton was going to allow nothing, absolutely nothing, to stand in the way of her retaining control of the company?'

Again Long did not even bother to object. Then the prosecution case was closed.

* * *

For only the second time in their acquaintance, Joanna saw Grahame Long smile. 'I am amazed that they have had the effrontery to put up such a case,' he said. 'We, you and I, dear lady, will utterly destroy them.'

'They've painted the picture they wanted,' Joanna pointed out.

'In many ways it is a flattering one,' Long said. 'They have depicted you as a strong-willed and determined businesswoman. All right, so they may have got across the idea that you are also a ruthless woman. That doesn't make you a murderess. Rather does it make you a woman who would in no way jeopardize her company, and her place within that company. All you have to do is be yourself and tell the absolute truth when I put you on the stand, and we will have nothing to worry about.'

* * *

Joanna wished she could be as certain. William and Norma came down for dinner, but it was a sombre occasion. 'How are the children taking it?' Norma asked.

'They think it's great fun,' Joanna said. 'Mummy against the world.'

'And Mummy always wins,' William said. Joanna made a face at him.

Cummings appeared. 'There is a phone call, madam.'

'If it's another reporter, tell him to take a running jump.'

'The gentleman does not claim to be a reporter, Madam. He merely says that he would like to speak with you on an important matter.'

'I have no wish to speak to anyone tonight, Cummings,' Joanna said. 'You may tell him so.'

'Yes, madam.' Cummings withdrew.

'Don't you think you could at least have found out his name?' William asked.

'His name is irrelevant. Nothing is relevant, William, until after tomorrow.' Norma squeezed her hand.

* * *

Grahame Long had a fairly full quiver even before he got to her. Mr Cummings was very embarrassed. 'Yes, sir,' he agreed with Long's question. 'There are several telephones in the house, but only the one number. I normally answer the telephone downstairs. If it is for Madam, and she is not downstairs, I can switch it to her bedroom.'

'But you cannot remember Mr Connor telephoning Mrs Orton?' Long asked.

'No, sir, I cannot.'

'Well, then, will you tell the court when you first were informed that Mr Connor was coming down to dinner.'

'That very evening, sir.'

'Did you usually receive such short notice about providing for a dinner guest?'

'Well, sir, yes and no. There is always plenty of food in the house. All we, Cook and I, need is the necessary notice to prepare it.'

'But on this occasion the notice was something like two hours.'

'Yes, sir.'

Charlie was even more helpful. 'No, sir,' he said. 'I had received no instructions for that evening at all.'

'But you were still in the house at eight o'clock,' Long said.

'Yes, sir, I often stayed late, had a bit of supper with Cook and Mr Cummings and Mrs Partridge, before going off.'

'Had you ever seen or heard of Mr Connor

before that night?'

'No, sir.'

'So, what actually happened, as far as you were concerned?'

'Well, sir . . . ' Charlie gave Joanna a quick glance. 'I was with Mr Cummings and Mrs Partridge, and we heard Mrs Orton calling for help. Mr Cummings and I ran along to the drawing room, and we found Mrs Orton and Mr Connor fighting. And Mrs Orton told us to throw him out, which we did.'

But Smith-Horton had a telling response available. 'Mr Hatch, you said you found Mrs Orton and Mr Connor fighting. Will you describe what you actually saw?'

'Well, sir . . . ' Charlie hesitated. 'Connor was lying on the floor, like.'

'And Mrs Orton?'

'Was standing over him.'

'What was she wearing?'

'Well, sir . . . ' now Charlie's checks were pink. 'She wasn't wearing anything.'

'You mean she was naked.'

Charlie licked his lips. 'Yes, sir.'

'And she told you to throw Mr Connor out. Was he moving, did he resist you in any way?'

'He tried, sir.'

'What did you do?'

'I hit him, sir.'

'You knocked him down?'

'I knocked him out, sir.'

'You mean, as far as you could see, he was unconscious.'

'He wasn't moving, sir.'

'Then tell us exactly what you did?'

'We . . . Mr Cummings and I, took him down the front steps and across the courtyard to his car.'

'Took him? You have just testified that he was unconscious?'

'Yes, sir — we dragged him.'

'I see. You dragged him across the courtyard to his car. But you didn't actually put him in it?'

'No, sir. We didn't have the keys.'

'Where do you suppose the keys were?'

'In his pocket, I suppose, sir.'

'But you made no effort to take them out. You dragged an unconscious man across the courtyard to his car, and then you . . . what exactly *did* you do?'

'We left him there.'

'Was it snowing?'

'Yes, sir, it might have been snowing.'

'You dragged an unconscious, bleeding man across the courtyard to his car, and you left him, lying in the snow. Did it occur to you to call for an ambulance?'

'Well . . . no, sir. But he really was all right.

After a few seconds he got up and got into the car and drove away.'

'You saw this?'

'Oh, yes, sir.'

'Where from? Were you still standing beside the car?'

'No, sir. We had gone back to the porch.'

'So, having dropped Mr Connor beside his car, literally, in the snow, you retired to the porch to watch. And after some time . . . '

'A few seconds, sir.'

'How many seconds?'

'Well, sir . . . '

'Five, ten, twenty . . . a minute?'

'Oh, it was less than a minute, sir.'

'What was Mrs Orton doing while you were watching Mr Connor drive away?'

'I don't know, sir.'

'What was she doing when at last you went inside?'

'She was standing in the drawing room. She told me to pick up the pearls; Mr Connor had broken her necklace.'

'How do you know?'

'Sir?'

'How do you know that Mr Connor had broken Mrs Orton's necklace?'

'Well, sir, she told me he had.'

'Quite. Just two more questions, Mr Hatch.

When you returned inside, was Mrs Orton still, ah, naked?'

'Oh, no, sir. She had put on her dress.'

'Of course. Tell us about the dress.'

'Sir?'

'Was it torn? Damaged in any way? You have just testified that Mrs Orton told you to gather up the pearls scattered about the floor as a result of Mr Connor having torn the necklace from her neck. I imagine you, or I, could have burst a pearl necklace, and 'torn' it from Mrs Orton's neck, without very much difficulty. But removing her dress, against her will, would have been a somewhat more difficult matter. If the pearl necklace had been snapped, as Mrs Orton resisted the alleged rape, the dress would almost certainly have been torn. Did you notice any tear, or rent, in the dress Mrs Orton had put on?'

Charlie gulped, started to look at Joanna again, and changed his mind. 'No, sir.'

'Thank you, Mr Hatch.'

Lord Crowther looked at Long.

'I will now ask the defendant to take the stand, m'lud.'

There was a stir around the court. This was the moment for which they had all been waiting.

7

The Defence

'Joanna,' Long said. 'The prosecution has made a determined effort to depict you as a hard and ruthless woman, who would do anything to maintain her position. Is that how you see yourself?'

'I was given a hand to play,' Joanna said. 'And I felt it my duty to play it to the best of my ability.'

'This has to do with your first marriage. Will you tell us exactly what happened?'

'Howard Edge asked me to marry him,' Joanna said. 'His first marriage had broken down. I accepted his proposal. I had known him for several years, and I was in love with him. I was twenty years old and I had no vision of the future other than as his wife. But he died on our honeymoon, and to my astonishment I learned that he had willed his entire stake, a controlling stake, in Caribee Shipping, to me. I was pregnant with his daughter. I felt it was my duty to maintain and use that controlling stake in the company for the sake of his memory and my unborn child.'

Long looked pleased. This was jury convincing stuff. 'And this is what you have done?'

'To the best of my ability, yes.'

'Did this have any influence upon your second marriage?'

'I suppose it must have done. I approached Prince Hasim, whom I knew was an old and valued friend of Howard's, and asked him to back me while I got the company back on its feet. He agreed to do this. I was totally surprised when, some time later, he proposed marriage.'

'Why were you so surprised?'

'Because it entailed such a great sacrifice on his part. He was heir to the Emirate of Qadir. He had to renounce this if he was going to marry a woman who was both a foreigner and a Christian. I asked him to consider the matter most carefully, but he insisted.'

'And it cost him his life. What was your reaction to that?'

'I was totally shattered.'

'And then you married for a third time. Did this have anything to do with the preservation of your stake in your company?'

'No. Dick was an old and treasured friend. I thought we were in love.'

'And then you found out that he was having an affair, and you reacted as I suspect most women would have done. But then you had an affair yourself. May I ask, was this your first extra-marital affair?'

'Yes,' Joanna said.

'And was it undertaken in a spirit of revenge against your husband?'

'Not really. There had been a severe storm. We were perhaps lucky to have survived it. I think we were all on a high when we realised we were safe, and Mr Connor and I just got together. Perhaps having made up my mind to divorce my husband made it easier for me.'

'This affair with Connor was therefore entirely fortuitous. But you wished to continue it.'

'Well . . . ' Joanna gave the jury a surreptitious glance. 'He seemed a nice man. And I was very lonely.'

'So, you invited him to spend the night with you at your home.'

'I invited him to dinner,' Joanna said. 'I was going to let the evening take care of itself.'

'Had you any idea that he might be going to blackmail you?'

'The thought never crossed my mind,' Joanna said.

'He gave no indication of it?'

'None at all.'

'But you found it necessary to attack him?'

'I found it necessary to defend myself,' Joanna said in a low voice.

'This man was already your lover, but on this occasion you found it necessary to reject his advances. Violently. Why?'

Joanna licked her lips. 'He . . . attempted to perform a perverted act.'

'He wished to sodomise you.' There was a rustle of comment around the court, and Lord Crowther used his gavel. 'And this assault you would not permit.'

'No, I would not,' Joanna said.

'You asked him to stop, but he attempted to persist, and you defended yourself. Tell the court exactly what happened.'

'I hit him. I had forgotten I was wearing my ring. It cut open his face and he went berserk, and came at me again. I managed to knock him down, and I jumped on him with both feet. I was trying to stop him from attacking me again.'

'Of course. And then?'

'I rang for my servants and told them to throw him out.'

'Did you realise he might be badly hurt?'

'No, I did not. I was too upset.'

'Was he bleeding?'

'There was blood on his face, where my

ring had cut him. And there was some on his mouth.'

'What did you suppose caused that?'

'I thought he must have cut his lips.'

'You had no idea that he might have been bleeding internally?'

'No, I did not.'

'So you had him thrown out. What did you do then?'

'When I had recovered a little, I asked my servants what had happened to him, and they told me he had driven away.'

'What did you do then?'

'I went to bed.'

'Joanna, you are under oath. Did you, at any time that evening, or at any time before that evening, plan, or even contemplate, killing Sean Connor?'

'I did not.'

'Did you, at any time that evening, or at any time before that evening, plan, or even contemplate, seriously injuring Sean Connor? Or injuring him at all?'

'I did not.'

'Your attack on him was an instinctive, violent reaction to the perverted attack he was attempting to inflict upon you?'

'It was.'

'Thank you, Joanna,' Long said.

'I'm afraid I do not feel able to call you

'Joanna',' Mr Smith-Horton said, 'because I do not know you as well as my learned friend. But I am afraid I must go over the ground that counsel for the defence covered so carefully, but yet, I suspect, not carefully enough. You have stated, under oath, that the only extra-marital affair you have ever had was with Sean Connor. Will you deny that, when you were plain Joanna Grain, you were the late Howard Edge's mistress for a year before your marriage?'

'I was Howard's mistress,' Joanna said. 'I became his mistress when he asked me to marry him. The year's delay was caused by the divorce proceedings against his first wife. As we were not yet married, that can hardly be classed as an extra-marital affair.' The court smiled.

But Smith-Horton was not put out. 'No doubt. However, you moved into Caribee House as if you were his wife, a year before your marriage. And a fortnight after your marriage, Mr Edge was killed in a boating accident, following which you discovered, almost equally by accident, that you were heiress to his entire fortune. Is that correct?'

'Yes,' Joanna said in a low voice. 'That is correct.'

'Now you have testified . . . ' Smith-Horton ruffled his notes as if he did not know by heart what was in them, 'that having inherited Mr Edge's estate, and his controlling interest in Caribee Shipping, you discovered that the firm's finances were in a bad way, and so you applied to an old friend of Mr Edge, Prince Hasim of Qadir, for help. Am I right?'

'Yes.'

'And Prince Hasim most generously gave you this help. A noble fellow. I'm afraid I must ask you this, Mrs Orton, or Mrs Edge as you had by then become, were any favours offered to Prince Hasim for this remarkable act of generosity on his part?'

Joanna bit her lip. 'We were old friends.'

'How charming. Mrs Orton, you are under oath: did you or did not not have sex with Prince Hasim in return for his investment in your firm?'

'I . . . it was not for a year after his investment.' She looked at the jury. 'I was pregnant.' This time they did not smile.

'However,' Smith-Horton continued, relentlessly. 'You did have sex with Prince Hasim before your marriage. But of course, as you were by then a widow, this was not an extra-marital affair either. And obviously you had sex with him after your marriage. What a silly question. You bore him a son! And then, following Prince Hasim's tragic murder, you married your old friend Richard Orton, and have now decided to divorce him.' He looked at the jury. He would not dare put into words the obvious implication, that to be married to Joanna Grain did not imply longevity as a husband, but he was inviting them to read his thoughts.

'Following which,' he went on, 'you had an affair with Sean Connor. One of these romantic shipboard events. One which, you have testified, you wished to continue. But one which, you have also testified, could not stand any attempt at perversion. This shocked you to such an extent that you attacked Mr Connor with, if I may so put it, tooth and claw. Now, Mrs Orton, I hate to be indelicate, but I'm afraid I must probe the secrets of your marriage bed. I find it difficult to comprehend how a woman who has admitted to having shared that bed, in and out of marriage, with several men, should suddenly react so violently to an attempt to, shall we say, extend the bounds of lovemaking.'

'I did not wish it to happen,' Joanna insisted.

'And it was not something that had ever happened to you before?'

'Of course not.' Long snapped his pencil in two; he had suddenly realised where Smith-Horton was heading.

'Mrs Orton, you are under oath. You were

mistress and then wife to an Arab gentleman over a period of some four years. Once again, I hate to be indelicate, but . . . well . . . '

'Prince Hasim was the most perfect gentleman I have ever known,' Joanna snapped.

'And his sexual habits were those of a gentleman. But also those of an Arab.'

'Of course. But he would never do anything I did not wish.'

'He never attempted to, ah, enter you from the rear?'

'If this noise does not cease,' remarked Lord Crowther, 'I shall clear the court. I am not sure in any event that this evidence should not be heard in camera, Mr Smith-Horton. Is there much more of it?'

'I think just two more questions, m'lud, if Mrs Orton will answer the last.'

'Very well. Mrs Orton?'

Joanna had had the time to recover. 'Yes, he did.'

'But you did not consider this an ungentlemanly act, between man and mistress, or husband and wife.'

'It is not an ungentlemanly act,' Joanna said. 'It is the way many people suppose we are intended to have sex.'

'No doubt it is. And you were happy to humour your husband, or even your would-be husband. Now, will you answer the court this: supposing your husband had elected to use yet another method, the method attempted by Sean Connor, would you have resisted him?' The court was absolutely quiet as Joanna stared at him. 'Would you have turned on Prince Hasim like a tigress? Would you have split open his face with your ring? Would you have stamped on his stomach, rupturing his peritoneum? Would you have called your servants and had the prince thrown out into the snow?'

Joanna licked her lips. 'You are under oath,' Smith-Horton reminded her.

'It would have been different,' Joanna muttered. But her defence was in ruins, and everyone in the court knew it.

Not that Grahame Long intended to lower his flag without a fight. 'The prosecution case,' he told the jury, 'rests upon two very debatable points. The first point is that Sean Connor intended to blackmail Mrs Orton, and that she killed him to prevent that happening. We cannot deny that it seems to have been in Mr Connor's mind to blackmail the defendant. But we do deny that Mrs Orton ever knew of it, or that she in any way planned Mr Connor's death. Her assault was that of a woman defending her body from the most foul kind of rape.

'Which brings us to the second point upon which the prosecution has based its case. Mrs Orton was defending herself against sodomy. No one is arguing about that. The prosecution has seized upon the fact that she may, or may not, have endured this from one of her previous husbands. Ladies and gentlemen, this is irrelevant. A woman's relations with her husband do not imply that she is bound to accept such relations from any other man, against her will. That is rape. The prosecution have implied that as Mrs Orton and Mr Connor were lovers, he was in the position of a husband. But that is not so and cannot be so. When a woman marries, it is implicit that she has taken on certain obligations towards her husband, including that of sharing and giving comfort in the marriage bed. This does not apply to an affair. For a woman to have an affair may be morally reprehensible, but it does not bestow upon the lover any of the rights of a husband, or upon the woman any of the obligations to submit to his requirements that may be the case in a marriage.

'Mrs Orton was defending herself against rape. That she defended herself too successfully is a tragic misfortune. But under no circumstances can she be found guilty of premeditated murder.' But he was not happy.

The jury were looking uncommonly grim-faced.

'I do not think anyone can truly deny that Mrs Orton, née the Princess Hasim, née Mrs Howard Edge, née Joanna Grain, has lived a very full life,' Mr Smith-Horton told the jury. 'She has had, one might say, a singular penchant for marrying both well, and fortunately. She lived with Howard Edge for over a year until he finally married her, divorcing his own wife to do so. She inherited his considerable wealth, but when she discovered that the company which was the foundation of that wealth was in financial difficulties, she promptly married again, to an even more wealthy man, with whose assistance she was able to put Caribee Shipping back on its feet. Again, this marriage took place approximately a year after Prince Hasim first guaranteed Mrs Edge's, as she then was, finances. Then, when Prince Hasim was assassinated, she married again. This time she did not marry for money; perhaps she had enough of it, by then. She married for what she hoped would be love, but when that did not materialise, without the slightest hesitation she sacked her third husband, as she might have sacked a clerk in her office. Of course she was, is, entitled to do this; Mr Orton has admitted adultery. But it is a measure of the woman's character that, having landed in England from her adventurous voyage to the Caribbean, on fourteenth December last, the very next day she gave Mr Orton his marching orders. Mrs Orton is clearly a lady of great decision.

'By then she had embarked on an affair, which might have been intended, she says it was so intended, to progress. Let us not forget that Mrs Orton has testified, almost proudly, that she never slept with a man she did not then marry. Was Mr Connor to be the fourth in line? But she very rapidly found out that he was perhaps not a suitable husband. I think we are entitled to ask ourselves why. One may confidently assume, as Mr Connor spent eight consecutive nights in Mrs Orton's cabin on board the *Caribee Queen*, that it was not a matter of sexual inadequacy or sexual delinquency. We do know that Caribee Shipping is again in financial difficulties. Possibly Mrs Orton had discovered that Mr Connor had no money. She says she still wanted the affair to continue. But the evidence suggests otherwise.

'We have proof that Mr Connor intended to blackmail her, and this proof has been presented to you. When he visited Mrs Orton with the intention of implementing the blackmail threat, he was beaten so badly that he died from his injuries. The fact that he drove his car away from Mrs Orton's home in no way alters that fact. It may be a testimony to Mr Connor's strength of both body and mind, but the fact remains that even as he carried out this act of will, he was dying, of the injuries he had received at the hands and feet of Mrs Orton, and of Mrs Orton's servants, as instructed by her.

'Ladies and gentlemen, Mrs Orton has said she attacked Connor in self-defence while resisting an attempted rape. This with a man with whom she had spent eight presumably blissful nights, on board her ship. Had there been anything distasteful about any of those nights she had merely to end the affair there and then, without any recourse to violence. They were on her ship, surrounded by her most faithful and obedient employees. But she did not wish to end it. Yet, surprisingly, she did wish to end it as soon as Mr Connor visited her at her home. She says this was because he attempted to commit an unnatural act. Ladies and gentlemen, we need to keep a sense of perspective about this. Any woman is entitled to defend herself against rape. She is not entitled to kill to do so, unless her own life is in danger. Could Mrs Orton really have supposed that a man with whom she had spent eight blissful nights was about to murder her?

'She further claims that she did not intend to resist having sex with him. She wanted that. That actually rules out any consideration of rape. But she refused to accept the unnatural act. Ladies and gentlemen, are we to believe that this woman, who, as I say, has lived a very full life, in and out of bed, and who in the course of that life has married outside of what might be called the English norm, with apparently total contentment, is going to react so viciously to an attempted unnatural act as to kill her lover? I think not.

'Ladies and gentlemen, we have before us a bold, determined, mentally brilliant woman. The facts of her life speak for themselves. She is regarded by many in the city as the ultimate entrepreneur. She has used her beauty, and her brains, and her charm, and her determination, to succeed in business. She has never let anything stand in her way. Anything! Her first husband died at the beginning of December, nineteen sixty-three. He died in South America, and his widow brought his body home by ship. A matter of ten days. Then he had to be buried, and she had to pick up the pieces of his business. Yet at the beginning of January nineteen sixty-four, less than a month after Howard Edge's tragic death, Prince Hasim was guaranteeing her borrowing with her bank. Prince Hasim himself died in December, nineteen sixty-nine. Again, less than a month later a consortium of businessmen was injecting capital into Caribee Shipping to make sure it stayed afloat.

'Mrs Orton returned from her Caribbean voyage in December of last year, her mind made up to divorce her husband, with all the trauma that was going to involve. Within two days she was negotiating to buy shares from Mrs Alicia Edge. If there is one thing of which we can be certain with regard to Mrs Orton it is this: if the centre of London were to be blown up tomorrow, the day after she would be opening an office for her company in Birmingham or Bristol. We cannot help but admire a woman of such single-minded determination to succeed.

'But let me ask you to consider this: what then would be the reaction of such a woman when an itinerant lover with whom she has had a few enjoyable nights informs her that he is going to blackmail her? I have to say that we also have to admire Mr Connor's courage in taking such a risk. But then, perhaps he did not know her as well as we now do. Sean Connor is dead. He was killed in a vicious, and we believe we have proved to your satisfaction, a pre-meditated attack, planned and carried out by the defendant. I thank you.'

* * *

'It's so unfair,' Joanna said at dinner. 'That attack upon Hasim's character, simply because he was an Arab. How could they *do* that?'

'Because he's dead,' John Giffard pointed out. 'If he were alive, we could have called him in evidence.'

'If he were alive,' William pointed out, 'this situation could never have arisen.'

'If only he *were* alive,' Joanna muttered. 'What's going to happen, John?'

'I very much fear that will depend a great deal upon Crowther's summing up,' Giffard said.

* * *

'The task before you,' Lord Crowther told the jury the next morning, 'is one of the most difficult with which a jury, any jury, has to cope. Only the defendant knows the truth of what happened that night last December. Only she knows what was in her heart when she launched that vicious attack upon Sean Connor. She claims it was an instinctive reply to being attacked in a perverted and obscene fashion. The prosecution claims it was a carefully planned and meticulously carried out murder. You have to decide whether or not the defendant is telling the truth, or whether, as a continuation of that carefully planned and meticulously carried out murder, she is now defending herself with that brilliance to which both sides have attested.' Joanna, sitting in the dock, stared at him in consternation, while icy hands closed on her heart and stomach.

'In most murder cases,' Lord Crowther went on, 'there are at least one or two points of evidence which are incontrovertible. And there are just a few points of evidence which you may care to consider here. Firstly, it is incontrovertible, accepted by both sides, that Mrs Orton and Sean Connor were lovers. It is for you to determine whether a woman could so viciously attack a man with whom she has shared her all, and with whom there does not appear to have been any differences, either of a sexual or a social nature, before that dreadful night, unless there was some ulterior motive preying on her mind. Secondly, it is incontrovertible that the police found evidence in Sean Connor's lodgings that he was planning to blackmail Mrs Orton. Thirdly, it is incontrovertible that Mr Connor visited Mrs Orton on the night of sixteenth December last year, that she sent away her servants with instructions not to return unless called, and that within half an hour of their being alone together, Sean Connor was attacked. These are the only facts we possess. It is your duty to interpret them and determine whether or not Mrs Orton is guilty of murder, or of involuntary killing — manslaughter — in self-defence.

'In arriving at your verdict, there are several points you need to consider very carefully. One is the relationship between Mrs Orton and her lover that I have already mentioned. Then you need to consider the various facets of Mrs Orton's life that have been revealed to you in this court. You need to determine just how susceptible this woman, this enormously successful, experienced, and sophisticated woman, was to an event which might, or might not, have been outside of her previous experience. You need to consider the events of that night. The defence have made much of the fact that it was Mrs Orton who telephoned Mr Connor, and not the other way around. But Mrs Orton has made no secret of the fact that she wished to continue the affair. Therefore why should she not have made the first move to ensure that continuance? It was what was said on that telephone call, and more importantly, what was said after Mr Connor had arrived at Caribee House and the servants had been sent away, that you need to consider. Mrs Orton has denied that anything was said about blackmail. It is your duty to determine whether she is telling the truth, or not.

'But it is also your duty to consider the behaviour of the defendant *after* the event. You may wish to consider the analogy of a hit and run driver. If a man driving a car knocks down a pedestrian, and kills him, he is guilty of involuntary manslaughter. If he then stops his car, renders what assistance he can to his victim, calls for help, accepts his error of judgement, we may sympathise with his misfortune, and although evidence must be taken as to how fast he was driving, and whether or not he had been drinking alcohol, he remains an object of some sympathy. If, however, instead of stopping, he drives away and leaves his victim, perhaps dead, perhaps dying, perhaps able to recover from his injuries if given sufficient help soon enough, then he is guilty of a crime. You may wish to consider why Mrs Orton, if her attack upon Mr Connor was totally unpremeditated, did nothing to offer him any assistance, even when supported by two of her servants, which would surely have prevented any risk of a further attack. She has said she did not know how badly he was hurt. But she could certainly see that his face was split open. She could also see that he was only half conscious. Yet she had her servants throw him out into the snow. I should remind you that a few minutes later she asked what had happened to him. And on being told that he had managed to get into his car and drive away, Mrs Orton went to bed. As she had earlier dismissed her husband from her house, so now she calmly dismissed her lover. You may wish to consider all these points.'

* * *

'That old buzzard virtually directed them to find you guilty,' Grahame Long said as they sipped coffee in the small office just off the courtroom, under the watchful eye of a woman police constable.

'Well, you said he wouldn't like me,' Joanna reminded him.

'I can tell you . . . ' his head turned as the door opened.

'Ready for you, Mrs Orton.'

'Gosh, that was quick,' William said.

'Is that good?' Joanna asked.

'Ah . . . not really,' John Giffard said. 'Keep your fingers crossed.'

Joanna was led away from them, down beneath the courtroom, and up the steps into the dock. For the last time, she thought. She was curiously calm. She had accepted the fact that she would be found guilty. It was a matter of bracing herself for what came after that. She hardly heard what they were saying, as the forewoman handed over the piece of paper on which she had written the verdict, and it was passed up to Lord Crowther, who peered at them as he read it. 'The verdict is unanimous?'

'It is.'

The woman police constable standing beside Joanna gave her a little nudge, and she came to attention, at the very edge of the box, the panel eating into her waist. 'Joanna Orton, you have been found guilty of the pre-meditated murder of Sean Connor on the night of sixteenth December last,' Lord Crowther said. 'Have you anything to say before I pass sentence?'

For a moment Joanna couldn't speak; even though she had guessed what was coming, her tongue still seemed to be stuck to the roof of her mouth. Desperately she found some saliva. 'I did not mean to kill him,' she said.

Lord Crowther waited, to see if she would add anything, but as she didn't, after a few seconds he continued. 'You have been found guilty of the crime of murdering your lover. We do not know, because you will not tell us, whether it was because he was trying to blackmail you, or whether it was simply that you had grown tired of him. The fact remains that you determined on his death, and you carried out the crime with an efficiency which only those who have no knowledge of your business methods would consider unusually ruthless.

'You are a woman who has spent her adult life reaching for goals which many might suppose unattainable, but in which you have always attained your objective by a single-minded determination to succeed, and a willingness to take extreme risks to achieve that success. Perhaps it was inevitable that such a life, a life that has been, more than once, touched by violence and death, should culminate in a determination to be rid of a man who had become, at the very least, a nuisance and, at the worst, a positive danger. However, those that take the law into their own hands must be prepared to suffer the severity of the law when they are found out. Joanna Orton, it is my decision that you will go to prison for twenty-five years. Take her down.'

8

The Prison

There was a moment's total silence in the courtroom, then Matilda, seated in the public gallery, screamed, 'Oh, my God!'

Her comment was caught up in the swell of noise from the body of the court itself, against which Lord Crowther banged his gavel in vain in an attempt to gain the silence necessary to discharge the jury. 'Let's go,' said the woman constable, holding Joanna's arm.

Joanna felt about to faint. Twenty-five years! Giffard had said a few years. She had anticipated ten, which with remission might mean she was out in no more than six. Twenty-five years! Even with remission she'd be past forty! An unimaginable age! Giffard was waiting for her downstairs. 'We'll appeal, of course.' Joanna stared at him. Did he really exist?

'Come along, dear,' said the woman constable.

'No, wait,' Joanna said. 'There are people I have to see. My company secretary . . . my accountant . . . my children, for God's sake!'

'I'm afraid that isn't possible, right now,' the woman said. 'It'll all be arranged later. Now you must go to prison.'

Joanna turned to Giffard, her eyes suddenly opaque as they filled with tears. 'I'll see to everything,' he promised her. 'Joanna, we'll appeal. Don't give up.'

Joanna was hurried along the corridor and down a flight of steps to where a Black Maria waited. The rear doors were opened, but to her enormous relief there was no one else inside. She stepped up, and was followed by two women constables. The van drove off, into a crowd of reporters who had assembled outside the gates. 'Parasitic swine,' remarked one of the policewomen.

'Where am I going?' Joanna asked.

'Liddleton.'

'Where is that?'

'Just outside London. It's not too bad. Overcrowded. But then, where isn't, nowadays?'

'Overcrowded? I won't have to share a cell?'

'I'm afraid you will, dear. At least for a while.'

Joanna licked her lips. She had always been such a private person. Even in her marriages, she had slept alone when sex wasn't involved. My God! When sex wasn't involved! 'Can't

I . . . well, I'd be willing to pay . . .'

'Hush, dearie. You want to forget that you used to buy everything you wanted. Find your feet, first.'

Joanna hunched her shoulders. This can't be happening, she thought. It just can't. I have to wake up some time soon and discover it's all a nightmare.

'You all right, dear?' asked the policewoman.

'My head hurts.'

'Try to relax. When you go to prison, you have to take each day as it comes. You start thinking about the future, you'll go bonkers. Same thing if you start thinking about the past. Live each day as it comes, minute by minute.'

'For twenty-five years?' Joanna shouted.

The woman sniffed. 'Just trying to help, dear. You did kill a man, you know.'

Joanna hunched her shoulders and closed her eyes. Live each day, each minute, as it comes. God, she should be driving back to Caribee House, sitting in the back of the Rolls behind Charlie, looking forward to a glass of champagne and a romp with the children . . . would she ever see them again? Right that minute, if she had a knife or a gun or a bottle of poison, she thought she would cheerfully end it all.

Liddleton might only have been just outside London, but the drive took a couple of hours. In the back of the van, Joanna couldn't see out to gain any idea of where they were or where they were going. But at last the van stopped, and she heard voices. Then they drove beneath an archway into a yard surrounded by high walls in which there were small windows. It looked just like every prison film set she had ever seen. But this was real. 'Here we are, dearie,' said the policewoman, as the doors were opened.

Now the policewomen were replaced by female guards, large, strapping women with jangling keys hanging from their belts. They did not look particularly aggressive, merely frighteningly efficient and cold-spirited. 'Joanna Orton,' one said, reading from her clipboard. 'Murder.' She raised her eyes to gaze at Joanna, who was little more than half her size. 'Mrs Anstey is waiting to see you. That way.'

Joanna glanced at the policewomen, wondering if she should say goodbye, but they had already got back into the Black Maria, and were lighting cigarettes. I'm a non person, she thought. Joanna Orton, murderess. I'm a statistic. She followed the wardress through a door set in the wall, and along a corridor. Another wardress followed.

Presumably I'm dangerous, she thought. Murderesses are dangerous.

Around them were the sounds of people; hundreds of people. All women. All criminals. To whose ranks she now belonged. They climbed several flights of stairs, marched along a corridor. Now the sounds were muted, as they were left behind. They reached a door, and the wardress knocked. 'Come,' a quiet voice said.

The door was opened, and Joanna was ushered into a large office, cosy with book-lined walls. The only chair was behind the desk, and it was occupied by a small, gray-haired, quiet-looking woman who wore her hair in a tight bun. Her face was a trifle pinched, but was not unkind. 'Orton, ma'am,' said the wardress.

Mrs Anstey leaned back, and gazed at Joanna, who realised that her eyes were colder than they had first appeared. 'Trouble,' the governor remarked.

'I'm no trouble,' Joanna protested.

Mrs Anstey leaned forward again. 'You will address me as ma'am, Orton. And you will speak when you are spoken to. Do you understand me?'

'Yes . . . ma'am.' Joanna had never addressed anyone as ma'am in her life before.

'And you can take it from me that you are

trouble,' Mrs Anstey told her. 'Looks, grooming . . . oh, trouble.' She looked down at a large chart on her desk.

'If possible, I would like a cell to myself,' Joanna said. 'Ma'am.' And then realised she had not actually been addressed.

Mrs Anstey looked up. 'You would like? If possible? You have a lot to learn, Orton. Number twenty-seven.'

'Twenty-seven, ma'am,' said the wardress.

'I will see you again when you've settled in, Orton,' Mrs Anstey said. 'I'm sure we will have things to discuss.'

'She likes you,' remarked the wardress, as Joanna was led away. 'You could do all right.'

'If she likes me,' Joanna said, 'I'd hate to be someone she dislikes.'

'What you want to remember,' the wardress told her, 'is that in here you're someone everyone will dislike. Just because you're different. Twenty years ago they'd have hanged you. Times change, they do.'

'Were you a wardress, twenty years ago?' Joanna asked, innocently.

The wardress stopped, and turned to face her. She made to step back, but found herself against the second woman, who held her arms. 'My name is Angie,' said the wardress. 'You want to remember that. I'm the difference between hell and purgatory in this place. You want to remember that too.' She dug her fingers into the bodice of Joanna's dress and pulled down, very hard. She was a strong woman, and the material split as if made of paper. She kept on tugging until she had reached Joann's groin, exposing petticoat and underclothes. 'Oh, dear,' Angie said. 'Now you've torn your dress. But you won't be needing it again, not for twenty-five years, darling.'

Joanna knew nothing but the killing fury she had experienced when Connor had assaulted her. She could not free her arms from the woman holding her, so she kicked with all her strength, slamming her high-heeled shoe into Angie's ankle. Angie yelped with pain and doubled over. With a supreme effort Joanna tore her arms free, and was hit a mind-shattering blow in the kidneys. She gasped and retched, and fell to her own knees, feeling that she was choking with pain. Dimly she heard a whistle, and then she was surrounded by uniformed women, who dragged her to her feet, and half carried her along the corridor, before bundling her through a doorway into a large storeroom, where several more women waited. 'What the shit is going on?' one of these asked.

'She's gone berserk,' Angie panted.

Joanna straightened as the pain began to

wear off, tried to brush hair from her forehead, and only then realised that her wrists had been handcuffed behind her back. 'You wouldn't think she was the type,' said the woman behind the counter. 'Not looking at her.'

She came round the counter and fingered the material of Joanna's torn dress. 'Nice.' She pulled Joanna's head forward, looked at the label inside the collar of the dress. 'Harrods, no less. What about the undies?'

'Listen,' Angie said, putting her face close to Joanna's. 'We're going to release your wrists. You start any more trouble and we'll put you in a straitjacket. You hear me?' Joanna hated herself as tears rolled out from her eyes. She nodded, biting her lip. But she was still aching too much to consider the possibility of being hit again. She could only think, when John Giffard comes to see me . . . 'So take them all off,' Angie said. 'Don't worry, darling; you'll get a receipt.'

Joanna stepped out of her dress and her shoes, took off her petticoat and underclothes. 'And the watch,' said the storekeeper. 'And the wedding ring.'

Joanna laid them on the counter, terribly aware of the eyes, watching her, seeming to investigate her every nook and cranny without actually touching her. But they were going to touch, sometime during the next twenty-five years, she knew. Some time soon. 'Rolex,' remarked the storekeeper. 'You're a right toff, darling. Height?'

'Five foot six,' Joanna whispered.

'Weight?'

'One hundred and twenty pounds.'

'That seems about right.' She began taking clothes out of the shelves behind her, while Joanna shivered. The room was suddenly chill, and the eyes were still there.

The woman laid two pairs of drawers, two brassieres, and two very plain blue dresses on the counter, together with a pair of trainers. To these she added a toothbrush, a tube of toothpaste, and a pack of sanitary pads. These are all I now own, Joanna thought. 'Get dressed,' Angie said.

Joanna pulled on the somewhat coarse drawers, added the brassiere, dropped the blue denim dress over her shoulders, thrust her feet into the trainers, stooped to tie the laces. 'Now pick up the changes,' Angie commanded. There were also two flannel nightgowns — how long was it since she had worn anything in bed? — and two bandannas. 'Tie it up,' Angie said.

Joanna tied the large square round her hair, gathering it into a mass. 'All the wisps,' said the storekeeper, and held a mirror for her.

'You keep it out of sight at all times. That's the rule.'

Joanna didn't really want to look at herself, at the vestiges of make-up left, at her expression . . . She tucked the stray golden wisps beneath the cloth. 'Come along,' Angie said.

'Mind you keep them clean,' recommended the storekeeper.

From the storeroom the corridor led to one of the cell blocks. They entered this on a catwalk, some twenty feet above the floor of the block itself; Joanna was reminded of walking the catwalks above the engine room on board *Caribee Queen*, and again her eyes filled with tears. She heard shouts and whistles, and opened her eyes again, looking down now. There were some twenty women on the floor beneath her, looking up, waving table tennis bats or magazines, cheering and cat-calling. 'They like you too,' Angie said. She led the way along the catwalk, then on to a more solid corridor, away from the noise beneath them. 'Number twenty-seven.'

The door stood open, as did all of the cell doors during this recreation period. Joanna stepped inside. There were two bunks, an upper and a lower, again reminiscent of a ship's cabin; there was even a wash basin and an exposed toilet, together with a table and two chairs. That the cell was already occupied was indicated by the book on the table, together with a couple of magazines, the toothbrush and a few other toiletries on the basin surround, the folded flannel nightdress on the lower bunk, and above all, the faint smell of humanity that hung on the air, not offensively, but very noticeably. 'Enjoy it while you can,' Angie said, enigmatically. 'And remember, the watchword in this prison is cleanliness. Nothing upsets the boss so much as lack of personal hygiene. You shower every day, right?'

She left the cell, the other wardress followed. Joanna remained standing in the centre of the cell for several seconds. Her home, for twenty-five years? She went to the window, which was above the table. By climbing on to the table and kneeling there she could see out, but the window looked down on to the prison courtyard, and did nothing to cheer her up.

She heard movement behind her, and turned her head, sharply. Three women had come into the cell. Two of them were older than herself, she could see at a glance, one considerably so. Her face was hard, but not vicious; she was overweight and had straggly gray hair. The other was in her middle-thirties, thin and pinch-faced, her figure totally concealed by the blue dress. The third was hardly more than a girl, Joanna reckoned. She was tall and had a very full figure, with long legs, and a mass of curling brown hair — obvious even beneath the required bandanna. She was the first to speak. 'You're Joanna Orton,' she said. 'We saw you on the telly. I'm Cindy.'

She held out her hand, and Joanna squeezed it. Could she possibly have found a friend? 'I'm Betty,' said the thin-faced woman, and also shook hands.

'I'm Mary,' said the older woman. 'Get down.' Joanna climbed off the table, no longer quite so sure that she had found any friends. 'Let's have a look at you,' Mary said, and pulled the bandanna from Joanna's head to allow her golden hair to drop to her shoulders.

'I thought we had to wear these at all times,' Joanna protested.

'Not in the cell, you don't have to. Nice hair.' Mary thrust her fingers into Joanna's hair. 'Wait outside.'

She was speaking to her two companions. Betty immediately stepped outside to stand in the corridor. Cindy hesitated. 'Not so soon, Mary,' she begged. 'Give her a chance to settle in.'

Mary snorted. 'So you can have first go,

eh? They'll all be after this one.'

Joanna looked from one to the other. 'Would someone mind telling me what is going on?'

Mary smiled at her; Joanna thought of a large cat surveying a small mouse. 'Think of it as an initiation,' she said. 'I'm just going to find out if you're going to be one of us.'

'And suppose I'm not?' Joanna asked.

'Then you won't enjoy your stay here, darling. And if it's going to be for twenty-five years, that's a long time not to enjoy. Right?'

Joanna stared at her, feeling the killing anger beginning to well up inside her again.

'Please don't hurt her,' Cindy begged.

She didn't specify to whom she was speaking, and she left the cell to stand beside Betty and ensure Mary had privacy. 'You really are a looker,' Mary said, sliding her hand down from Joanna's hair to caress her neck. 'Strip off, and let me look at the rest of you.'

'Bugger off,' Joanna told her.

'Listen, you little stuck-up runt, I run this floor, see? People do what I tell them to, or suddenly they ain't good-looking any more. You got it?'

'Then get this,' Joanna said, clasping her hands together and swinging the combined fist into Mary's midriff. Mary gasped, and bent double, and still keeping her hands together, as she had been taught by Matilda, Joanna struck her on the nape of the neck. Mary crashed straight down to the floor, her head hitting the concrete with a terrible crack. Betty screamed.

Cindy ran inside to kneel beside the older woman. 'Oh, my God,' she said. 'You've done her.'

People crowded the doorway, and were then thrust to left and right by Angie, followed by several other wardresses.

* * *

'I am sure you will be pleased to know,' said Mrs Anstey, 'that Mary Eldridge is not going to die. But she certainly has concussion and a nasty cut. Have you anything to say?'

'She made an obscene advance,' Joanna muttered.

'And whenever anyone makes an obscene advance you attempt to kill them, is that it? You have not yet been in my prison for twenty-four hours, and in that time you have assaulted one of my guards, and another inmate. Are you going to claim that Angie also made an obscene advance?'

'Yes,' Joanna said stubbornly.

'As I said, Orton, the moment I saw you,

trouble. Well, we don't want that kind of trouble here. I was going to give you a spell in solitary in any event, for the attack on Angie. Now this second matter . . . two weeks. Two weeks to allow you to think, Orton, and come up straight. Otherwise you will find it very hard.'

Joanna thought she had never heard anything so reassuring in her life. Two weeks in which she didn't have to speak to a soul, or react to a soul, either. Angie grinned as she was marched down the corridor to the punishment block. 'Two weeks,' she said. 'You'll have rubbed yourself raw by the end of it.' Joanna looked at her, and Angie flushed, and looked away.

* * *

Joanna lay on her bunk and stared at the ceiling. If she played her cards right she could spend the entire next twenty-five years in here. All she had to do was assault someone the moment she got out. That was all she felt like doing, at the moment. Twenty-five years! Two weeks! What difference did it make, really?

* * *

'Well, Orton?' Mrs Anstey asked. 'How are you feeling?'

'I am feeling fine, ma'am,' Joanna said.

'Good. Then may we hope for some co-operation?'

'Yes, ma'am.' Because she didn't really want to be left alone for another two weeks. She had never been utterly alone in her life before, and the initial relief of not having to respond, not having to *feel*, had quickly worn off.

'Good,' Mrs Anstey said. 'Your lawyer was down to see you, last week, but as you were in punishment he could not. He is coming back today. Do try to keep out of trouble until you have spoken with him. Who knows, it might be good news.'

'Well, hi,' Cindy said. 'How's the celebrity?'

'Am I a celebrity?'

'Oh, yes. Everyone's scared about what you might do next.'

'You mean no one is going to try to rape me?'

'Chance would be a fine thing.'

'But you're all queer. You too?'

Cindy flushed. 'It's a matter of, well, you've been here a fortnight. I've been here a year. And I have four to go.'

'Lucky you. What did you do?'

'I knifed my boyfriend. I thought he was my boyfriend.'

'But he didn't die.'

'No, worse luck. But five years . . . my solicitor says I'll be out after three. That's still two years off. So what do you do? I was used to it pretty regular. If a man was dropped in here today I'd lead the rush. But there's no chance of that. So you form . . . relationships.' Again she flushed, attractively. 'You and I could have a pretty good relationship.' She fluttered her eyelashes.

'I'll look forward to that,' Joanna said. 'But I'm not in the mood for sex right now. With anyone.' She still had hopes.

* * *

Kept alive by thoughts of revenge. She received, within her first month, a considerable amount of mail.

Couldn't have happened to a nicer person, Alicia wrote.

London won't be the same without you, Andy Gosling wrote.

Strange how apparent winners can wind up losers, Dick wrote.

When I get out of here . . . Joanna thought.

John Giffard smiled, as brightly as he could. 'Our grounds are going to be prejudice on the part of the trial judge,' he explained. 'Leading to mishandling of the case in that much of the evidence he accepted should have been inadmissable, and also to misdirection of the jury. I think it's pretty strong grounds.'

'When?' Joanna asked.

'Fifteenth of November.'

'But that's four months away!'

'It's as quick as can be.'

Her shoulders hunched. 'Tell me what's happening outside?'

'Well, Labour is getting the country back to work, gradually. But it's tricky without a real majority. There's talk Wilson will go back to the country later this year to gain more support. The economic situation is still pretty poor, with the price of oil set to go higher still. They're talking about twenty per cent inflation this year.'

'And the company? I'm so out of touch.'

'I believe Peter Young and William are coping. At the moment.'

'I want to see William. And I want to see Mrs Partridge, and the children.'

'You'll have to give me an order of priorities. You're only allowed one visit a week. I suppose the children and Mrs Partridge could be counted as one, but do you really want Helen and Raisul coming here? Seeing you like this?'

'Am I supposed not to see my children for twenty-five years?'

'Of course not, Joanna. I'll arrange it.'

'I want Peter to write to me, on a regular basis, at least once a month, to keep me up to date with company business.'

Giffard was writing busily. 'Will do. Anything else? Matilda?'

'She can come and see me, after the children, and after William. What about Charlie and Cummings?'

'The trial comes up next month. Not for Cummings. The charges against him have been dropped. But I suspect Charlie is for it.'

'That's very unfair.'

'If you are acquitted on appeal, or even if your sentence is reduced, we'll be able to do something about him. In any event, I imagine his sentence will be no more than half yours, if that.'

Joanna reached across the table to grasp his hand. 'What did you say?'

He looked embarrassed. 'It may be just a reduction. You see, there can be no argument about the fact that you caused Sean Connor's death. The only argument is about what was in your mind when you did it, and whether or not Crowther influenced the jury into believing you had planned it.'

'So whatever happens, I'm still going to be stuck in here for years,' Joanna said thoughtfully.

'Not so many years, perhaps. But it's important that you behave yourself.' She raised her head, frowning. Giffard flushed. 'I've been told about the fights and the solitary. You really want to avoid those, if you want to get out of here at the earliest possible moment. Parole boards take things like fighting very seriously.'

'Parole boards,' she muttered. She was going to be judged by a bunch of stuffy twits who wouldn't know the meaning of life if it got up and bit them in the leg.

'But that's some time in the future,' Giffard said. 'You have time to make up for what has happened by exemplary behaviour from here on in.'

'Exemplary behaviour meaning I accept being raped, is that it?'

'You're not serious?'

'Listen, there are over two hundred women in this dump, with not a man in sight. What do you suppose they do for kicks?'

'Good lord. I'll have a word with the governor.'

'I wouldn't waste your time. I suspect she needs her kicks as much as anyone. Listen,

John — just get me out of here. I don't care how you do it, but get me out!'

* * *

'Letter for you,' Angie announced. Joanna had been lying on her bunk — the upper bunk as Cindy, for all her youth, was the senior inmate at the moment — sat up and swung her legs over. Cindy took the letter and passed it up. 'Overseas,' Angie remarked.

'This has been opened,' Joanna protested.

'All mail addressed to inmates is opened, darling,' Angie pointed out and closed the door.

Joanna frowned at the envelope; she had supposed it would be from Peter Young. But it was postmarked Vancouver, Canada. She took out the pages inside. The handwriting was neat and educated. '*We have never met, but I followed your trial with interest. As I should. Sean Connor was my son.*' 'Jesus,' she muttered.

Cindy was on her feet, leaning against the upper bunk. 'Bad news?'

She was genuinely solicitous. She was, in fact, a very nice girl, Joanna had discovered, even if she had nearly killed her lover in a fit of jealousy; her clever lawyer had got the sentence reduced on the grounds of provocation. It all seemed a matter of luck. Now she was enjoying having the famous businesswoman-cum-murderess Joanna Orton as her cellmate. She enjoyed it even more during recreation; although she had made no move to cement her position, Joanna had taken over from Mary as boss of the block, and everyone wanted to be seen speaking with her, but Cindy was the one who was closest. That she wanted to be more than just friends was fairly obvious, but like everyone else in the cell block she was afraid of Joanna's reaction, which could be so violent, and she was also very patient. She reckoned that by providing unfailing support while Joanna remained so much on edge, they would have to get together some time.

'A hate letter,' Joanna said, and gave it to her. 'You read it. I'm not in the mood for that kind of muck.'

Cindy perused the sheet of paper. 'You have it wrong.' She read:

> "*Sean was the product of a liaison which I bitterly regretted. I brought him up as my own, but he proved so difficult I was happy to see him go out on his own, even when he took his mother's name. I continued to finance him, but we did not see each other over the last few years of his life. I wish*

you to know that you have my deepest sympathy, as I have no doubt that every claim you made in court was true. My son was a vicious monster. I tried to be in touch with you before the trial to ask if I could be of any assistance to you, but you declined to take my call. I cannot blame you for that. Now, I cannot of course do anything to help you while you are in prison. I have been informed that as I am neither a relative nor a member of your legal team I am not even allowed to visit you. But I shall be watching over you with great interest, and if you need any assistance when you are released, I hope and believe you will contact me. With every good wish.
Michael Johannsson.'

'Sounds a really decent guy.'

'Sounds a right crank, you mean,' Joanna said. 'We don't even know if he really was Sean's father. In any event, some hick from a Canadian town . . . '

'Vancouver,' Cindy said. 'That's a big city.'

'I still don't see how he's supposed to help me,' Joanna said.

'What shall I do with the letter?'

'Flush it.'

* * *

As the summer wore on, her tension grew. William's visits were an embarrassment. He avoided meeting her gaze, and muttered about how things really were bad and getting worse. 'I'm not sure I can cope,' he admitted.

'Just hang in there,' Joanna told him. 'I'll be back in charge by Christmas.' If only she could believe that. But she had to, or she would go stark raving mad. Matilda's visits were even more of an embarrassment, as she was obviously mortified by having to come to the jail at all. Peter Young's letters did nothing to dispel the gloom, but he had always been a pessimist.

Only the children lifted her spirits, but it was very briefly. They were doing their best to grasp the fact that somehow their beloved mother had turned into a wicked woman, who had to be locked up for the good of everyone who wasn't locked up, but they still apparently assumed she would be coming home any day, as they were told by Mrs Partridge. Mrs Partridge herself burst into tears every time she saw her mistress. But the days ticked by, the cruel combination of boredom and tension only slightly relieved by the October election, which again returned Labour with a sufficient majority to govern.

But only November mattered.

As the appeal revolved around legal arguments, Joanna was not required to go to court on the first day. When the time came for the justices to hand down their decision, however, she was taken up to London. Giffard and Norma had brought her some of her own clothes to wear, and Norma herself did her hair was well as she was able. Wearing a good frock and some jewellery, stockings and high-heeled shoes, and wrapped in her mink, Joanna suddenly felt like a million dollars again. The only discordant note were the two wardresses seated to either side of her. But to be driving through London, seeing the shops and the people, being again part of the real world, was a delight; the past six months need never have been. She felt so good she even smiled at the justices, three of them, seated in a row facing her as she sat in a chair in the centre of the room. They did not smile back.

The judgement was very long, detailed and involved. Joanna kept drifting off and not properly listening to what was said by the Lord Chief Justice. She did gather, however, that the court of appeal felt that Lord Crowther might have allowed his prejudice against the accused to influence his directions to the jury. On the down side, they felt he had not been wrong to allow aspects of her earlier life to be given in evidence. 'The case rested almost entirely upon the accused's motives for killing Sean Connor,' concluded the Lord Chief Justice, 'and her motives could only be understood by an understanding both of her character, and of the events that led up to that fateful night. It is however, the opinion of this court that the sentence imposed by Lord Crowther was unreasonably severe, and it is our intention to reduce the term.'

Joanna sighed, audibly; she had been holding her breath. The entire courtroom was shrouded in a mist of tears. 'The term of imprisonment will, accordingly, be reduced from twenty-five years, to twenty,' said the Lord Chief Justice.

Joanna could hardly see the man, or his colleagues, because of the tears, which were now flowing very fast. But these were tears of anger. She wanted to shout abuse at them. She wanted to pick up the chair and hurl it at them. She felt the killing rage she had known when assaulted by Mary, or by Connor himself. How dare you three old fuddy-duddies lock me up for twenty years? she wanted to scream. I have worked so hard, sometimes in great danger, to get where I am, and you can take it all away from me with a word and a stroke of the pen. Twenty years!

'That is very disappointing,' John Giffard said.

Joanna stared at him. '*Disappointing?*'

'We can go to the Lords, of course. But I'm afraid it would get us nowhere. I suppose you are paying the price of notoriety. Because you're so good-looking, so confident, so successful, and because you've lived such a . . .' he hesitated, 'a full life, people just feel you *have* to be guilty.'

'I thought judges weren't supposed to feel,' Joanna said, 'just interpret the law.'

'They're human.' He held her hand. 'I'm terribly sorry it had to turn out like this, Joanna. But, twenty years . . . you'll be out in eight, if you do nothing stupid.'

She withdrew her hand.

* * *

Cindy could tell at a glance that the appeal had not been successful. She sat on her bunk, hands dangling between her knees, and watched Joanna use the loo. Gone were the high heels and the fur coat, the stockings and the expensive lingerie. Gone forever, perhaps. Would she ever want to wear them again?

'They're a set of bastards,' Cindy said. Joanna sat at the table. 'Coffee?' Cindy asked, brightly, getting up. Joanna looked at her, and she sat down again. 'You have to — '

'Just don't say it,' Joanna said. 'Say it, and I'll break your neck.'

It really was quite unreasonable to take against Cindy, Joanna knew. The girl was only trying to be helpful. But she was part of the world, and Joanna hated the entire world at that moment. For the next week she hardly spoke to a soul, and ate sparingly. Cindy was clearly worried, but she kept her thoughts to herself.

Then she was summoned to the interview room, ten days after the appeal, to find both Giffard and William waiting for her. For just a moment her spirits soared. Something good must have happened. But a look at their faces convinced her that it hadn't. 'How're things today?' Giffard asked.

Joanna had never seen William looking so miserable. 'Tell me,' she said.

'We had a shareholders' meeting, three days ago,' William said.

'The week after the appeal.' They had been waiting for that. 'And?'

'The fact is, Jo, it simply isn't going to work. I mean . . . well . . . ' he looked hopefully at Giffard.

'Things are in such a state of flux it needs a great deal of positive thinking, and positive action,' Giffard said.

'William has full power of attorney,' Joanna said. 'Can't he be positive?'

'I'm afraid it isn't as simple as that,' Giffard said. 'Gosling is making a formal application to the high court to have you removed from the position of Chairman and Managing Director.'

'We have an agreement.'

'Which he claims is invalid in the case of a convicted criminal.'

'You'll fight it.'

'I shall oppose it, certainly. But my information is that the application will be granted.'

William looked about to burst into tears. Perhaps she was near to tears herself. But she was far more angry than tearful. 'What will happen if he wins?'

Giffard sighed. 'He will take over the company to do with as he sees best.'

'You mean he will sell out to Petherick.'

'I'm afraid that is a possibility.'

'The bastard.'

'I'm afraid there is more,' Giffard said. 'Once you cease to be Chairman and Managing Director, you lose control of everything. That is, Caribee House, the London flat, the car . . . '

'My children!'

'Oh, there's nothing to worry about there. No one can take them away from you.'

'I meant, where are they going to live?'

'We'll find somewhere,' William said. 'I mean to say, you'll still be a wealthy woman, Jo, owning twenty-eight per cent of the company shares . . . '

Joanna looked at Giffard. His face was red. 'One needs to be as optimistic as one can. The shares really have gone on a slide since your conviction. They're just on two at the moment, but they may go lower. This is what is going to influence the High Court judgement.'

'Apply to have trading stopped until after the judgement.'

'We shall try, of course.'

Two pounds a share, she thought. Once she had been worth six million pounds. Now it was just on half a million, and dropping. I am ruined, she thought. My family is ruined. And my company is ruined. All gone. As a result of a moment's madness.

'We'll sort something out, sis,' William said. 'Really we will.'

Joanna looked at him, and he flushed.

Giffard gathered up his papers and put them into his briefcase. 'We must be going. I really am sorry about this, Joanna.'

'You knew all along it was going to

happen,' Joanna said. 'Oh, get out. Both of you.' She pointed at William. 'And take care of my children.' The room was empty, save for the wardress. And at last she could allow herself to weep.

Part Three

Out of the Pit

'Life may change, but it may fly not;
Hope may vanish, but can die not;
Truth be veiled, but still it burneth;
Love repulsed, — but it returneth!

Percy Bysshe Shelley

9

The Proposal

'Recreation,' Cindy said. 'Let's play table tennis.' Joanna did not reply. Cindy scratched her head. Joanna not speaking was nothing new. She very seldom spoke. She very seldom did anything, except lie on her bunk and stare at the ceiling. Cindy thought she might be going quietly mad.

Outwardly, she was a model prisoner after her uneasy start. She did exactly what she was told to do by the guards. She went to the showers, she took her exercise, but in a zombie-like state, as if she had no idea who was around her or even where she was. And once in the cell she became totally withdrawn. It was eerie, and a little frightening. Even the other inmates were aware of it. None of them would dare interfere with her after the beating she had inflicted on Mary, but they were well aware that she was not one of them.

'Gives me the creeps, she does,' Betty said.

'I reckon she'll top herself one of these days,' Carrie suggested.

'In my cell?' Cindy cried in alarm.

'You don't want to leave her alone.'

Cindy had been so terrified she had run up the stairs; Joanna had, as usual, refused to join them in the recreation area. But Joanna continued to lie on her bunk and stare into space.

Cindy sighed, and sat at the table. She was just as afraid of her cellmate as was everyone else in the block. But she had also grown to like her, and sympathise with her. To have had so much — in the terms of Cindy's life and background to have had *everything* — and then have it all ripped away, and be left with four walls and a single change of clothing . . . she felt something had to be done to bring her back to the real world. But to risk arousing that searing temper . . .

Cindy was not the only one who was concerned. A few days later she was called into the office, where the guard was dismissed. This was not unusual. Mrs Anstey was fond of tête-à-têtes; the other girls called them tits-à-tit. Mrs Anstey was a closet lesbian, but she was also the Boss and there were always a dozen reasons she could provide for looking, touching, enjoying, providing the inmate was attractive enough. Cindy had herself had to endure an hour's 'physical examination' when she had first come to Liddleton. But she instinctively knew that she had not today been summoned to satisfy any of Mrs Anstey's suppressed desires. 'How is Orton?' Mrs Anstey demanded.

'She just lies there. She doesn't speak.'

'But she eats?'

'Oh, yes, ma'am. She has a good appetite.'

'Therefore her problem is entirely mental. She's applied for none of the jobs.'

'No, ma'am.'

'She has to have one. What do you suppose would suit her best? Garden or library?'

'She's very well-educated. She'd enjoy the library. I shouldn't think she's ever worked in a garden in her life, going by her hands. But the fresh air might be better for her.'

'Hm. What's she like as a cellmate?'

'Most of the time I don't know she's there.'

'But you like her,' Mrs Anstey suggested.

'Oh, yes,' Cindy said enthusiastically. 'She's so . . . so elegant. Even without make-up or proper clothes. Just elegant.'

'Yes,' Mrs Anstey said thoughtfully. 'Have you, ah . . . '

'Good lord, no,' Cindy said. 'You saw what happened to Mary, ma'am.'

'I did indeed. But that was a symptom at her despair at being in here at all. I think she has now surrounded herself by a cocoon, meant to resist the world in which she finds herself, until she can escape.'

'Escape, ma'am?' Cindy positively squeaked.

'I do not mean physically escape from Liddleton, silly girl. I hope she has more sense than ever to attempt that. I should punish something like that most severely, and anyone who attempted to assist her.' She glared at Cindy. 'I meant ultimate release. But she cannot remain inside that cocoon for what may well be ten years or more. She would never re-emerge. I wish you to break into her mind, Cindy. Release her mind. And her body, of course.'

'She'd scrag me if I laid a finger on her,' Cindy muttered.

Mrs Anstey was flicking through some papers on her desk. 'Let me see. You are due to come before the parole board in twenty-two month's time, Cindy. Should I feel that I could ask for, and obtain, your full co-operation in certain matters of internal discipline, I have an idea I could have that date brought forward by six months. Think of that. Just over a year. Wouldn't you like to be out of here in just over a year?'

Cindy licked her lips. 'I'll never be paroled if I'm put in solitary for fighting.'

Mrs Anstey raised her head and gazed at her. 'I give you my word, Cindy, that should there be a fight in your cell, no blame whatsoever will be attached to you. Nor will you be punished in any way, and no entry will be made upon your record, the record that will be submitted to the parole board.'

Cindy swallowed, and Mrs Anstey smiled.

'However, obviously it would be best if there was no fight. Handle the matter any way you like. Take your time. But not too much time. I want that cocoon removed.'

'Do *you* like Orton, ma'am?' Cindy asked, as innocently as she could.

'Come here,' Mrs Anstey said.

Cindy bit her lip, but stepped round the desk to stand next to the governor's chair. Mrs Anstey rested her hand on Cindy's leg, then moved it up, under the skirt, up the back of her thigh, to reach her knickers. Cindy found she was holding her breath; the trouble with Mrs Anstey was that one never knew what she was going to do next. Then she suddenly squeezed. However little in actual size, she was a very strong woman. Cindy gasped with the pain of it, and her mouth sagged open, remaining open as Mrs Anstey released her.

'I look forward to liking Orton, Cindy,' Mrs Anstey said. 'When her cocoon has been removed. But do not tell her I said so.'

'Look at that,' Cindy said. 'That woman is

an absolute thug.' The cell door had clanged behind her, and now she bent over, hoisting her dress so that Joanna could see the mark.

For a moment it did not appear as though Joanna was going to react at all. Then the bunk creaked as she rolled over. 'Shit,' she commented. 'Who did that?'

'Old Anstey.'

'Can she do that? Can't you complain?'

'Who'm I to complain to?' Cindy asked. 'Mrs Anstey?'

'Aren't there visitors? Inpectors?'

'Sure there are. And she knows when they're coming. Not for another month. What am I going to have to show them by then?' She sat down, and got up again immediately, to lie on her bunk, on her face. 'All we can do is grin and bear it.' She sighed. 'It's better when we're buddies. When you have a buddy. Everyone needs a buddy.'

Joanna hung her head over the bunk to look at her. 'You'd like us to be lovers, right?'

'Well . . . ' Cindy flushed. 'Buddies. And if we got physical, well, why not? We both have feelings.'

'You'd have to show me,' Joanna said.

Cindy couldn't believe her ears. Was it actually going to be this easy? But . . . she frowned. 'You never been with a woman? Not even when you were a girl?'

Joanna gave a savage smile. 'I was always kind of busy, when I was a girl. Going with men.'

To have sex with Cindy was actually to defy the world. Or so Joanna told herself. The world had gathered itself into one immense fist, and smashed that first into her face, sent her reeling out of its orbit into this specially man-made hell. Of course the world, all of those people who had spent the last, thirteen years reading about Joanna Edge, the city whizz-kid, or Joanna the Princess Hasim, the society beauty, or Joanna Orton, the city's most glamorous and successful widow, had also spent their time building up a mountain of envy, perhaps lust, certainly in many cases hatred. More importantly, they had taken refuge in the old Anglo-Saxon streak of puritanism, which still persisted whatever the breakdown in moral values during the swinging sixties. Joanna Orton had stuck out her chin time and again, and anyone who had tried to hit it either missed or fell flat on their faces. Ergo, Joanna Orton must one day fall flat on her own face, and then everyone could have a good laugh. She could almost hear them.

But there was no doubt that Cindy was right, and one simply had to share. Where one shared so little physical space, and so much of everything else, sex had to come into it. And she wanted, and needed, sex as much as anyone. At one level, therefore, life became almost tolerable. The level was when one was actually *doing*. Joanna was given a job in the prison garden, where Cindy also worked. Here was another exercise in full circles, she thought, remembering how, when her mother had come to live with her at Caribee House following Howard's death, she had allowed her to take over the huge garden — with the aid of several gardeners, of course — because Mums had liked gardening and Joanna had not known one plant from another.

Mums had been happy in that garden, perhaps for the first time since her husband's murder. And actually Joanna discovered that she too could be happy in the garden, even as she watched her beautifully manicured nails and her soft white hands become discoloured, and in the case of the nails, cracked and broken.

'Well, at least you'll be able to get a job when you leave,' Cindy joked, and then gulped, as she saw the expression in Joanna's eyes. Because the hate, the desire for revenge on all those who had done her down, was still there.

She would have liked to shut out the outside world altogether. But that was not possible. The children's visits were the most traumatic moments of the week. Joanna desperately wanted to see her children, but at the same time she didn't want them to see her, to see her broken fingernails, to pick out the gray strands in her hair, because these were gathering, to see her without her make-up and her mink, her aura of total authority. To see the real Joanna Orton, perhaps.

But seeing them was traumatic enough. William had managed to rescue something from the crash, and they weren't destitute, but they certainly weren't as well off as they had been, and she quickly spotted when Raisul's blazer was beginning to look brassy and Helen's dress had obviously been darned. As for where they were living . . . 'It's very small,' Helen confessed.

Joanna looked at Mrs Partridge. 'Well, madam, it's smaller than Caribee House, to be sure,' Mrs Partridge said. 'But Mr William said it was all we could afford.'

At least the children looked healthy and well-nourished. 'I do wish you'd come home, Mother,' Raisul said. 'I miss you quite a lot.'

Out of the mouths of babes and sucklings, Joanna thought. 'I'll be home as soon as I can,' she promised. 'But I'm rather tied up here at the moment.'

She still possessed a macabre sense of humour.

Businesswise, things were even more traumatic, seen from a personal point of view. The Labour administration seemed totally unable to control inflation, which had soared past twenty per cent during the great oil crisis and had not dropped far below it since. Shipping costs had soared too, but that was no concern of hers, save that it made thoughts of ever getting back into business, the only business she knew, more difficult than ever. The general air of depression was accentuated by the share plunge following the collapse of Burma Oil early in the new year, and in the spring unemployment shot past the million mark for the first time since the end of the War. Inflation was now twenty-two per cent. She received one letter from Peter Young, and one from Harriet. Both had been made redundant by the Petherick takeover, and while Harriet had quickly found another secretarial job, Peter was very gloomy about his prospects. He was fifty-five and had spent almost all his working life at Caribee Shipping. Matilda did not visit her at all, or write, but she gathered from William that Billy had found himself a job, albeit at nowhere near the level he had known at Caribee. William himself had also managed to find a job, but he too had had to accept a lower status, both in position and pay.

Dick Orton had disappeared following the decree nisi. Charlie was in gaol, like her, although his was a comparatively brief, three-year sentence. And poor old Cummings had died, some said of a broken heart. Something else to be avenged.

John Giffard wrote to her from time to time, always encouraging, but as nothing ever evolved in the direction of any other appeals she soon ceased to feel the least excitement when she saw one of his envelopes. Her past life was dwindling to nothing. As that policewoman had said on her very first day, only today mattered. And the day she got out, and could begin her revenge.

Today was cleaning the cell, showering, gardening, recreation, exercise, meal, lock-up, gardening, showering, recreation, meal time, lock-up. It was an unfailing, unceasing routine, varied only on visiting day, when the second gardening period was replaced by a chat with the outside world, and on Sundays, when the first gardening period was replaced by church parade. It was so unchanging an existence that keeping track of the days, much less the weeks and the months, and then the years, became very difficult. But for the use of the library she thought she would have gone mad. Joanna had always considered herself a very well-read person; now she discovered there were lots of authors, and lots of subjects, she had never touched, simply because she had been too busy. Now she found them a boon. Was she ever going to be able to use her mind, or her mental attitudes, again?

She depended very heavily on Cindy, who kept a very careful tally of the days and weeks and months. In many ways the younger woman, and Cindy was seven years her junior, was like a mother to her. Cindy had grown up in poverty, conditioned by the sixties, during which she had been a young teenager, enjoying the current philosophy of it you can get it, grab it, then spend it. She had been remanded twice, given two suspended sentences, and had actually spent six months in prison before the near fatal argument with her boyfriend. He had apparently been a petty thief and occasional pimp, and Joanna felt that if Cindy hadn't stabbed him, someone else would probably have done so eventually.

But that background meant that Cindy was well able to take care of herself, with the necessary caveat that she also understood when the odds were too heavy and she simply had to submit and hope to get away as lightly as possible. As she was an extremely pretty girl, with an impish sense of humour, she had been drawn into Mary Eldridge's orbit immediately on entering the cell block. This she had accepted as being a force too powerful to resist, just as she had accepted without protest the occasional summons to the Office, and the occasional hazing by the guards.

But she had not enjoyed any of it, and to have unearthed a real-life heroine of her own was, to her, paradise. She knew that the secret of Joanna's success was not physical; Joanna was only five-foot-six inches tall and she was a slender woman. It lay in the mind. Joanna dominated those about her simply because of the intensity of her personality. Any of the other inmates, and certainly more than one of them acting together, could have taken her apart. But they were all afraid of what she might do while being taken apart, or even more, after they had finished. Joanna was consumed with passion — and more than half of the time that passion was hatred, anger, an overwhelming desire to hurt. She had nothing to lose. Because she had already lost everything, and now she had only twenty years within these walls to look at.

* * *

'Don't you ever look back, and think, Christ, if it could have been different?' Cindy asked, as they lay together in her bunk after lights out.

'Sometimes,' Joanna said. 'And then I think, could it ever have been different?'

'If you hadn't jumped on that Connor's guts . . . '

'It had to happen,' Joanna said. 'That's how I figure it. The way I was, the way I thought I could do anything, it had to happen. Connor was just in the wrong place at the wrong time. His name could have been Smith.'

'Don't tell me you're feeling sorry for him?'

'Not in the least. Because he wasn't *there*. You follow me?'

'You mean, it was some kind of karma.'

'I mean, we are what we are. Everything else is what we see. *We* see. Not what they see.'

'You mean I don't exist. I'm just a figment of your imagination.'

'And I'm just a figment of yours.'

Cindy gave a little shiver, and held her close. 'That's philosophy. I'm not into that. What about his old man? In Canada.' Another letter had arrived that day.

'He gives me the creeps,' Joanna said.

* * *

Gradually the cell became filled with a growing sense of excitement, of anticipation, and of fear. Joanna didn't want to think about it. Apparently she had been here for two years. Two years! It seemed like two minutes, sometimes. Save when she looked at the children.

'She's menstruating,' Mrs Partridge said in a stage whisper that might have been heard outside the walls. Joanna reached across the table to squeeze her daughter's hands.

'It's no big thing, really,' Helen said.

* * *

Then, on the day of Cindy's parole hearing, it was a case of being alone, waiting. And then exploding. 'Yes!' Cindy shouted, returning after the interview. 'They're going for it.' She hadn't been inside three years!

'Listen,' she said, holding Joanna's hands. 'I'm here because I kept cool. That's what you have to do. Keep cool, and do what the Boss tells you, and it'll happen.'

Three out of five equals twelve out of twenty, Joanna thought. And Cindy didn't have a single black mark against her. Not a day in solitary. 'Listen,' Cindy said. 'When I'm out, anything I can do, you name it. You want me to go see your kids, just say so.'

Joanna bit her lip. Cindy sighed. 'Still a cut above the rest of us, eh? You don't want me showing up and upsetting what's left of their lives. I can't blame you. Well, the best of luck.'

Joanna found herself in the Office. 'I hope,' Mrs Anstey said, 'that you have learned something, Joanna, from Cindy. There was a young woman, from entirely the wrong side of the tracks, who got herself into a very similar situation.'

'Except that she got five years, and I got twenty,' Joanna pointed out.

Mrs Anstey regarded her for some moments. 'She didn't actually kill anyone, and she pleaded guilty,' she said at last. 'That always helps. She also behaved herself when she was in here. That was greatly to her advantage.'

'You mean she submitted to rape and mistreatment,' Joanna said.

Mrs Anstey sighed. 'You simply have to get over these antagonisms if you are going to prosper here, Joanna.'

'Is it possible, to prosper here?' Joanna asked.

'If you wish to do so, certainly. I have left you very much to yourself over the past couple of years, Joanna. This was because I felt you would need a longer period than was usual to settle in here. And I think I was correct in that judgement. I told Cindy to look after you, and I think she has done a very good job. But that has been a probationary period, so to speak. Now Cindy is gone, you have to consider the next few years. First, we have to consider your new cellmate.'

'I'd rather be left alone,' Joanna said.

'I'm sure. But that is simply not possible. Then we need to consider your job. Do you enjoy working in the garden?'

Joanna shrugged. 'Not really.'

'What would you prefer to do?'

Joanna frowned at her, while nervous bells began to ring in her ears; this woman was actually being kind to her? 'I'd like to work in the library.'

'Of course. An ideal job for someone of your intellectual abilities.' Mrs Anstey flicked some papers on her desk. 'Unfortunately, all the library jobs are held. For the next couple of years, at least. We shall have to find you something else to do, that you might find amenable, until one of those jobs becomes vacant.' Another flick of the papers. 'I think I have it. My personal secretary leaves next month. Would you like her job?'

Joanna raised her head. 'Doing what?'

'Principally filing and attending to my diary. It is a job that requires a good deal of initiative, and some intellectual capability. It also carries a great number of privileges. One which I am sure you would appreciate is a cell of your own.'

'I don't think you have finished,' Joanna said.

'We would have to work fairly closely together,' Mrs Anstey said.

'I thought that might be the case,' Joanna agreed.

'Would you enjoy that?' Mrs Anstey's cheeks were pink.

'No,' Joanna said.

'Oh, come now, Joanna, don't you think I know everything that goes on in my jail? You and Cindy were lovers. Don't you think I know that?'

'Yes,' Joanna said. 'I think we did become lovers. I was, am, still very fond of her.'

'And who do you think told her to become your lover? How do you think she got out of here so quickly?'

Joanna stared at her. 'I didn't know that. I'm very sorry.'

'Why should you be sorry?'

'Because I thought I had at last found a genuine human being.'

'They don't exist, not in prison,' Mrs Anstey told her. 'In here you do what you are told, or you are punished. Cindy did what she was told, and she made you happy, for a while. Did she not?'

'Yes,' Joanna said. 'She made me happy, for a while.'

'That's all that matters, in prison. Now, I am proposing to make you happy for as long as I can. Which will be as short a time as I can, if you follow me. There is no prospect of your appearing before a parole board for eight years after your sentence was confirmed, that is another five years from now. However, my recommendations carry a great deal of weight. I can save you perhaps a year, by having your hearing brought forward in front of others. And I can make those five or, hopefully, four years, very easy for you. Would you not like that?'

'Yes,' Joanna said. 'I would like that.'

'Good. Well, then, as soon as Marian gets her parole, which should be in about a month, I will have you regraded as my secretary, and you will move into Marian's cell.'

'And you will come and sleep with me every night,' Joanna said.

Mrs Anstey raised her eyebrows. 'Why, no, my dear. You will come and sleep with me, whenever I wish you to.' She smiled. 'My bed is far more comfortable than any prison bunk.'

'I will see you damned first,' Joanna said.

Mrs Anstey leaned back in her chair. 'I'm not sure I understand you. You and Cindy . . . '

'Cindy and I had something going,' Joanna said. 'We liked each other, and maybe we did get to love each other. We *loved*. I don't suppose you can understand that. We loved. I'm not a whore, about to jump from one bed into another for the sake of a kiss and a cuddle and a hand between the legs. Not even to get a year off my sentence.'

Mrs Anstey glared at her. 'You are a stupid woman, Joanna Orton. And an arrogant bitch. I would have thought you'd have learned to come to terms with life by now.'

'Not your terms, ma'am.'

They held each other's gaze for several seconds, then Mrs Anstey suddenly swept her hand across her desk, scattering papers, pens, paperclips, files, in every direction. At the same time she leapt to her feet, leaned across the desk, seized Joanna by the bodice and the headscarf, and jerked her forward. Taken by surprise, Joanna thudded into the desk with a force that winded her. Her knees gave way and she fell down the outside of the desk, jarring her chin.

Mrs Anstey had released her, and now fell backwards, with a deliberate force that sent her chair also tumbling over. Then she regained her feet, pressing her bell. Joanna held on to the desk and pulled herself up, gasping, stroking her chin where it was sore from the blow. And behind her the door burst open and several guards ran in, headed by Angie. 'She attacked me,' Mrs Anstey shouted. 'The bitch attacked me.'

Joanna gasped, and turned to face them, to have her arms seized and pulled behind her back, and handcuffs affixed to her wrists. She panted with desperate anger, and kicked at her, had her legs swept from beneath her so that she struck the floor with a thump, and was again winded. 'Don't break anything,' Mrs Anstey warned, getting up and pushing hair from her eyes. 'I don't want anything to show.'

Angie grinned. 'Bruises won't show more than a week. Eh, Joanna?'

Joanna managed to sit up painfully, and Angie put her foot between her breasts and pushed her flat again. 'Not in here,' Mrs Anstey said. 'Is there anyone in solitary?'

'Not at the moment, ma'am.'

'Well, that's where she's going anyway. Take her along there.'

Joanna got her breath back, and now she screamed, as loudly as she could. 'Can't have that,' Angie said, kneeling beside her head, rolling up a handkerchief and stuffing it into her mouth. My God, Joanna thought. This can't be happening. Not to me! 'Up,' Angie said, holding her shoulders and dragging her to her feet, now assisted by two of the other women. 'You know what I think, ma'am,' Angie said. 'A good old-fashioned thrashing. That's what she needs.'

'No,' Mrs Anstey said. 'She'll have to be examined by Dr Prinney, soon enough. There can't be any marks. Put her in a straitjacket. She's hysterical. We have to let the fit pass. Right?'

'Right, ma'am.' Angie grinned, and jerked her head. Joanna was dragged out of the office by the four women. She tried to kick again and again had her legs swept from under her, so that she was frog-marched the next few feet. 'You going to walk?' Angie asked. 'Because we might just drop you.'

She was holding Joanna's right thigh, under her dress, fingers tightening and relaxing, moving to and fro. That was almost worse than the prospect of being dropped, face down, on to the stone floor; but her hands were still handcuffed behind her back, and she knew she would bruise her face terribly. 'Scream, and I'll shove this stick right up your ass,' Angie told her. 'Now, you walking?'

She pulled the handkerchief from Joanna's mouth.

'I'll walk,' Joanna panted.

'Now you're showing a little sense,' Angie said.

* * *

'Hm,' Dr Prinney commented. 'Hm.'

He was a small, precise man in his forties, who, if he enjoyed having charge of the bodies of more than a hundred women, some of whom were quite attractive, and one, at least, now stretched out before him, was quite beautiful, never revealed the slightest emotion.

'You really are quite fit, Orton.'

'Do you know what they did to me?'

'I have received a report. You were in a straitjacket for two days. I'm afraid that was inevitable, after you went berserk and attacked the Governor.'

'I did not attack the Governor,' Joanna insisted. 'She attacked me.'

'I would keep your voice down, if I were you,' Prinney said. 'I'm afraid I find such wild accusations quite impossible to believe. You say you were beaten? That is absurd, in an English prison. There is not a mark on your body.'

'They were careful not to leave marks.'

'Orton,' Prinney said severely, 'I am not going to keep you in this hospital, because there is nothing at all wrong with you, physically. You could do with a little more weight, but that is up to you; the food is available, all you have to do is eat it. Now, you are leaving here within the hour. If you keep your mouth shut and behave yourself, you will go back to your cell and the company of your, ah, fellow convicts. If you persist in throwing out wild and unsubstantiated accusations, I am going to have to send you to the psychiatric ward, and you may not find that as pleasant. It's entirely up to you.'

'And I suppose all of this is going to go on my record? Even if it is a pack of lies.'

'I'm afraid it is already on your record, Orton.'

So, once again she had to surrender, to suppress the boiling anger that kept threatening to overwhelm her, to drive her into some fresh act of violent defiance, which would put back her release. Survival was the name of the game. No matter what was done to her, or what she had to accept. Actually, this second explosion made her life far more acceptable than before. Mrs Anstey had apparently got the message, and Joanna had a sneaking feeling that Dr Prinney might also have had a word with her. After all, Joanna Orton had once been an important and respected figure; while she was in prison it might be possible to suggest to her that no one was going to believe anything she said anyway, and that she would be making life much worse for herself. But once she got out . . .

The plot, on the part of the guards and the Governor, became to ignore her and let her get on with it. Because, hopefully, once she got out she would be a forgotten, irrelevant figure. While in the eyes of the inmates, she was even more the heroine, to be revered rather than ignored. She might deny that it ever happened, but it was accepted that she had attacked the Boss. After having attacked Mary Eldridge! She had become a legend in her own lifetime, in prison no less than she had once been in the business world.

Her new cellmate, Belinda, was a handsome if raw-boned young woman in for manslaughter. She found the prospect of several years behind bars just as unacceptable as had Joanna, and needed a good deal of comforting and reassurance. Within a few months she was Joanna's abject slave, and as she was large, and had been convicted for kicking a rival in love to death after having knocked her down, she equally was someone the other inmates preferred to please than to pester. While she wanted only to please Joanna, not only because of her reputation, but because she recognised the intellectual superiority of her cellmate.

But for Joanna the hell into which she had stumbled grew ever more inescapable as the seventies reached their end. According to William, Petherick was keeping his head above water, although with inflation well into double figures, and the country beleaguered by strikes as the steadily weakening Labour administration failed to get to grips with any of the real problems, survival in business was just as grim a task as survival in prison. When in 1979 the Conservatives won back power after six years, everyone was looking for an upturn in business affairs, but for the moment things only seemed to get worse. Not, Joanna thought bitterly, than any of it mattered to her!

William himself was apparently doing quite well at his new job, and he seemed content enough in his marriage, although as Norma had never become a mother Joanna had to suppose that his problem was a residue of that bullet that had so nearly killed him all those years ago. But Billy had lost his job again, and William said that he and Tilly were having a difficult time.

He had no news of Peter Young, but when she asked if John Giffard would visit her, he pulled a face. 'Giffard is dead.'

'Eh?' Joanna could not believe her ears.

'He had a heart attack.'

'Oh, poor John!' She had never been quite sure how old he was, but as he had been Howard's lawyer before she had even come on the scene he had to be at least twenty years older than herself. Still, a heart attack . . . 'Would you like me to get one of his partners?'

Joanna considered. She had been so sure that Giffard would believe what she had to tell him, that he might be able to get back at Mrs Anstey in some way, but she knew none of his partners, except for one. 'There was a woman,' she said. 'Jeanette Corder. Perhaps I could see her.'

'I'll arrange it,' William promised.

* * *

Her own investments were a source of concern. What little capital William had been able to rescue for her from the wreck of Caribee Shipping barely provided the income for the upkeep of Mrs Partridge and the children. The following week they should have visited her. But Mrs Partridge came alone. 'What's happened?' Joanna's voice was sharp.

'Well, madam, I thought I should come alone this week, because you'll have to instruct me.'

'Go on.'

'It's Helen. She's been seeing a man.'

'Just what do you mean?'

Mrs Partridge sighed. 'I think she's having an affair.'

'She's only sixteen!' Joanna bit her lip. She had been only sixteen when she had first attracted the attention of Howard Edge. Of course, she had waited another two years before surrendering, but morals at the beginning of the sixties were a little different to morals at the end of the seventies. And without a mother . . .

Mrs Partridge was sighing again. No doubt she was remembering that teenage girl Howard had brought home on that never-to-be-forgotten night. 'How do you know this?' Joanna asked, trying to keep her voice down as she knew that the women at the other tables were trying to listen.

'Staying out late, telephone calls, things about her clothes . . . I don't know if I can cope, Madam.'

'You have to cope,' Joanna said fiercely.

‘Please, Mrs Partridge. If you gave up . . . I’d give up too.’

‘You are coming home, soon, Mrs Orton?’

‘Soon,’ Joanna said. It had to be soon. ‘But please send her to see me, next week. It would be best if she came alone.’

She had, in fact, noticed a certain furtiveness creeping into Helen’s personality over the past year. She had reckoned this was to be expected, as the girl had grown into a teenager having to live with the concept that her mother was a condemned murderess; it had not occurred to her that there might have been an outside cause. Although possibly the two were connected.

Now, as she sat across the table from her daughter, she wondered why it hadn’t happened sooner. Helen was almost a carbon copy of herself, her beauty perhaps enhanced by the slight sharpness of feature she had inherited from Howard. While at sixteen her figure was perfection. ‘Why do they all look at me like that?’ she asked. ‘One would think they were men.’

‘Half of them wish they were,’ Joanna pointed out. ‘There’s not much else to do in a place like this. Don’t tell me you’ve never had a girlfriend.’

Helen flushed. ‘I prefer men.’

‘Doesn’t everyone, when they’re available?

When you say men, I assume you mean boys.'

'Well . . . ' Helen's flush deepened. 'Boys are such creeps.'

'True. Would you like to tell me about him?'

'Mrs Partridge has been at you.'

'She's concerned, yes. I don't find that unreasonable. She feels responsible for you. She *is* responsible for you.'

'Just so long as she doesn't interfere.'

'Whether she interferes or not depends on what I tell her to do. So why don't you tell me, first?'

Helen leaned across the table, grasping her mother's hands. 'His name is Harry and he's an absolutely dreamboat.'

'I'm sure he is. What does he do?'

'Well . . . ' the flush was back. 'Actually, he's not doing anything right now. But he's all right. He's old enough to be unemployed, and collect the dole.'

'That being?'

'Twenty-four.'

Joanna actually felt a sense of relief. She had immediately supposed he would be an ageing lecher — rather like Howard, in fact. But Howard had not been on the dole. 'And you're madly in love,' she suggested.

Helen pulled her hands away. 'We're very fond of each other.'

'How fond?'

'Oh, Mummy! We use a condom, if that's what's bothering you.'

To Joanna's distress, she had clearly upset the girl, because Helen did not visit the following week. Or the week after. But then, neither did Raisul. Mrs Partridge came as usual.

'It's very difficult for him,' she explained. 'There's been some trouble at school.'

'What kind of trouble?'

'Well, madam, boys will be boys. And Raisul is obviously not English, even if he speaks like an Englishman. He has a temper.'

'Will you please tell me what has happened?'

Mrs Partridge sighed. 'They started taunting him about coming here, visiting his murdering mother, and he attacked them.'

'He attacked them?'

'He seems to have gone berserk. I had to go and talk with the headmaster. He was suspended, you see. But I managed to sort that out. Only . . . he told me . . . ' she gazed at Joanna with enormous eyes.

'Go on.'

'Raisul told me that he didn't want to come here any more. Not right now. I didn't feel I could force him.'

'Of course you must not force him,' Joanna said. She had shed all her tears.

'Kids,' Belinda commented. 'They're more trouble than they're worth.'

'Do you have any?' Joanna couldn't believe she did; she was only twenty-two.

'Sure, I had one,' Belinda said. 'I gave it away.'

'You what?'

'I wrapped him up nice and snug and left him on a doorstep.'

'My God!'

'Oh, he was found, and looked after, and adopted. I think he's doing fine.'

'And you have no regrets?'

'In here? Wouldn't you be better off without any?'

Joanna wondered if she was right. But gradually it seemed she was being more and more isolated from the world. Her world.

But her world no longer existed.

* * *

Jeanette Corder came, as requested. 'I gather you're having a difficult time,' she remarked.

'Not any more. I'm a senior citizen. But . . . ' she told the solicitor about the straitjacket, the assaults.

'Sounds beastly,' Jeanette commented.

'Can't we do something about it?'

'Can you prove your allegations?'

'We've all experienced it, in some degree or other.'

'You mean your fellow prisoners would give supporting evidence?'

Joanna considered. While they were mostly afraid of her, very few of them had ever shown any sign of liking her. Even Cindy had found her a convenience. Jeanette was studying her expression. 'If you were to bring accusations like that into the open, and you failed to have them confirmed or accepted, it would set back your chance of a parole by a good distance.'

'Have I any chance of a parole?'

'Of course. As you say, that rumpus was a long time ago. You've been here four years. You're halfway there.'

'Have you any idea what it is like to contemplate spending another four years in this place, losing touch with my family, my own children, for God's sake, watching my business collapse . . . '

'Your business collapsed four years ago, Mrs Orton. I know the situation with the children is difficult, but your aim in life should be to get out of here just as quickly as you can, so you can get back to them.'

'And, of course,' Joanna said. 'I am a convicted murderess, so I shouldn't really complain.'

'I'm afraid that sums it up,' Jeanette said.

* * *

Once again, the idea of suicide became attractive. And this time it would not, apparently, have a great impact upon Helen and Raisul — they wanted nothing more to do with her. She did not suppose there was a single solitary soul in all the world who would give a damn. She would be buried in the prison cemetery, and forgotten. All those great days in the past, the adventures and the romances, the thrill of being written about in the newspapers and interviewed by the media, the crises that she had always successfully negotiated, would all be history. But they were already history.

'Mail,' Belinda said.

'Throw it in the can,' Joanna recommended.

'It's from Canada. You know anyone in Canada?'

'It's from the creep who was Sean Connor's father. Or so he says. He's been writing me for years.'

'Shit! What does he say? That you

should've been torn apart with red hot pincers?'

Joanna actually smiled. 'No, funnily enough. He says that he forgives me, understand me, sympathises with me. Seems Sean always was a bad egg. So his dad sent him off. Oh, he always supported him, bought him expensive cars, but they were effectively estranged. And he knew just how much of a satyr Sean was. I didn't.'

'Sounds like he's pretty well-heeled,' Belinda remarked.

'I suppose he must be. I've never really thought about it.'

'But you don't want to read his letter.'

'I'm not in the mood. Bin it.'

'Ah . . . would you mind if I read it?' Belinda asked. 'Nobody ever writes me.'

Joanna rolled on her stomach. 'Go ahead, if it turns you on.'

Belinda climbed into the upper bunk, and slit the envelope. Then she lay down to read it, slowly, Joanna knew, because she was no great reader. 'Sounds a real nice guy,' she remarked. 'Complains a bit that you've never replied to any of his letters.'

'Chance would be a fine thing.'

'Yeah. And . . . holy Jesus Christ!'

'Eh?' Joanna rolled on to her back again, stared at the heaving mattress above her.

'You won't believe this.'

'I don't see how I can, if you won't tell me what it is. He's being abusive, I suppose.'

'No,' Belinda said, and started to laugh.

'I am going to break your neck,' Joanna threatened. 'Give me that letter.'

Belinda hung it over the edge of the bunk. 'You'd better read it. He wants you to marry him.'

10

The Bride

Joanna found it difficult to believe what she was reading.

'*Although you have never replied to any of my letters,*' wrote Michael Johannsson, '*I feel a definite affinity between us that has nothing to do with my son. I have not been able to say exactly what my feelings are, previous to now, because my wife was still living. Although we have been estranged for many years, we were never actually divorced, nor did I consider this to be appropriate over the last three years, aware as I was that she was dying of cancer. That is behind me now, and I am only aware that I owe you more than I can possibly convey, perhaps an entire lifetime. I have, as you know, followed both your case and your situation with great interest, and I am aware that there remains four years before you can be released from prison, but that is no reason why we should not marry now.*

I understand that it would be an

enormous step for you, to agree to marry a man you have never seen, and who is the father of a man who so outraged you. However, I believe there are certain mitigating factors which may make me acceptable to you. You will forgive me, I am sure, for raising matters that must still be painful for you, but I know how much you have suffered, both financially and socially, by your imprisonment. May I take the liberty of saying that I am an extremely wealthy man, and that I intend to do everything in my power to restore you to that position you once enjoyed and so richly deserve. In token of the above, should you agree to my proposal, I would be prepared immediately to take all the financial burden of your children off your hands, relocate them to more salubrious surroundings, if that is what you wish, and generally in every way alleviate their position. Again, if that is your wish. As for the future . . .'

Joanna laid down the letter. She had thought she had shed all her tears. This poor, lonely old man!

'You are going to say yes?' Belinda begged.

'Of course I can't accept.'

'Why not? If he's as rich as he claims, you

have it made. So do your kids.'

'The idea is obscene.'

'Because you had his son? So what's a bit of incest between friends? It wasn't as if you married the guy.'

'I'd be selling myself,' Joanna said.

'Shit, darling, don't we all? Would you have married your first husband, that shipowner, if he'd been a busker playing outside the Odeon? Would you have married that Arab guy if he hadn't been a prince?'

The temptation was enormous. *I will restore you to the wealth and position you once enjoyed, and deserve*. How she wanted that. How she wanted to revenge herself on all those people who had abandoned her to a lifetime in this cell. How she wanted to emerge from ashes of her life, like a phoenix, and cock her finger at them all. Did he understand that? Could he possibly guess it? And would he accept it?

What did she have to do to achieve her objective? Say yes, to a man she had never seen. He had not even sent her a photograph. Perhaps he was too grotesque to risk it! And then, eventually, go to bed with him. He would be getting the best of the bargain. Even in four years time she would only just be forty, and if there were silver threads amongst the gold, a bottle would very quickly take care of those. As for the rest . . . her body was as strong and as desirable as it had ever been. There was the problem. Her body. It had become an intensely private matter to her, to be yielded on very rare occasions, when the sexuality in her nature took control. But those moments were becoming more and more rare. Now she would be required to uncover herself, in every possible way, all over again. Perhaps he was too old for sex!

She showed the letter to the Reverend Ingle the following Sunday. 'Remarkable,' he commented. 'You say this man has been writing to you for years?'

'Since I was convicted,' she said. 'And I think he was trying to get in touch with me before that.'

'And you have never replied?'

'He's the father of the man I am supposed to have killed, Reverend.'

Ingle stroked his chin. 'And now you want to marry him.'

'No. He wants to marry me.'

'Hm. I think you want to think very carefully about this, Orton. You described his son in court as a satyr, if I remember correctly.'

'He behaved like one, certainly.'

'And this man is his father.' Joanna bit her lip. 'He may have some thoughts of revenge,'

Ingle suggested. 'This business of taking over the care and upbringing of your children. I don't like the sound of that. Suppose he's a paedophile?' Joanna's head began to spin. 'And then, he claims to be a wealthy man. What proof has he given you of this?'

'Shit,' she muttered.

'Of course I understand how important it is for you to have something to look forward to, and there can be no doubt that *were* you to marry the father of the man you killed, it would weigh very heavily with the parole board. But you need to be very sure that you are not exchanging one hell for another.'

'And you won't advise me.'

'I have advised you, Orton. But the decision must be yours.'

Once upon a time, Joanna reflected, she would not have needed, or heeded, advice. She would have sized up a situation and made her decision. Had being sent to prison, being in prison, so reduced her personality? She asked William to come and see her, showed him the letter. 'Wow!' he commented.

'Can you find out something about him for me?'

'I'll try. If he's a really wealthy man something should be available.'

* * *

Meanwhile she replied to Johannsson's last letter.

> '*Forgive me for never having written to you before,*' she wrote, '*but I found it difficult to accept that you actually wished to be friends with the woman who was responsible for your son's death. And now, to wish to marry me . . . I am enormously flattered, of course, but again, if you'll forgive me, while you appear to know everything about me, I know nothing about you, except what you have chosen to tell me. I do not even know what you look like!*
>
> *Nor do I know any of your plans, supposing we did marry. Would we live in Canada, or in England? Would you wish to have children? There are so many questions to be considered.*'

She waited with some anxiety for a reply, because she knew that her mind was slowly making itself up. Worse than the thought of the four years left to her had always been the thought that she would emerge to nothing, no money, no career, and now, it seemed more and more with every week that her children did not come to see her, no family either. Michael Johannsson promised a new life — if anything he claimed was true.

* * *

'Here we go,' Belinda said. 'It's another biggee.'

Joanna's hands were trembling as she slit the envelope, which contained several separate pieces of paper and a photograph. Michael Johannsson was standing beside an expensive car; she thought it might be a Cadillac. He looked as if he was several inches over six feet tall, with a build to match. His face was large, and strong, his hair white and receding. He was casually dressed, but the clothes were clearly expensive. 'Let's see,' Belinda asked.

Joanna handed her the photograph without a word, picked up the balance sheet, which covered the last year of the Johannsson Mining Corporation, revealing assets of twelve-point-four million dollars, a turnover of eight million, and a profit of three-point-two million. This, too, she handed to Belinda. 'Jesus,' Belinda muttered. 'Can I be your maid?'

* * *

This time the letter itself was short.

'We shall live wherever you wish, and we shall start a family whenever, or if ever, you

wish. Unless I hear from you in the negative within the next month, I shall start things moving. I have a nodding acquaintance with the Home Secretary, so we shouldn't have too many problems.'

She had to do nothing but sit back and wait. 'Oh, please let me be your maid,' Belinda begged.

* * *

William came to see her the following week. 'He seems to be genuine,' he said.

'I know.' Joanna gave him the balance sheet.

'Wow,' he commented.

'What position does he hold?'

'President.'

'And his equity?'

'Eighty-five per cent.'

It was her turn to mutter, 'Wow. What's the current rate of exchange?'

'Low. Roaming around one-fifty.'

That meant Michael Johannsson's company was worth about eight million pounds, of which six-point-eight belonged to him. She had once been just about as wealthy as that. Once! 'So you're going to go ahead?'

Suppose he's a satyr, like his son, or a

paedophile, Reverend Ingle had suggested. But she could insist that Mrs Partridge remained in charge. As for his bed manners . . . she thought she could suffer anything to get her hands on six million pounds. There was that old mercenary streak, what the tabloids had called her ruthless determination, surfacing again. And how good it was to feel it, when she thought it had been crushed out of her for ever! 'Tell me about Petherick.'

'As I have told you before, times are hard. But getting better. Or at least, people are coming to terms with a high rate of inflation. Every government says it means to tackle it, but as long as the governments all have commitments to the welfare state which far outrun their income, it doesn't look likely to go away.'

'About Petherick. Is he MD?'

'Actually, no. Your old friend Andy Gosling is now MD.'

Joanna frowned. 'I thought he sold out to Petherick?'

'That was the original deal. But when things were very bad, Andy bought back a controlling interest. Petherick has sold his entire stock. Rumour has it that Andy really stretched himself to make it. But now he and his friends own the company.'

'You never told me.'

'I didn't want to upset you. You were having a pretty hard time, remember.'

'Andy Gosling,' she said, thoughtfully.

'With that fellow, Holroyd. You know, the chap who bought Dick's shares.'

'Let me get this straight,' Joanna said. 'Holroyd works for Andy?'

'He does now. There's a suspicion he always did. It's not something one can say openly, of course, because of the risk of slander or libel. But it was all fairly pat. As you may remember, Townsend's involved as well. He's the second biggest shareholder, but that fellow Amalia has a sizeable holding as well.'

'I remember them all,' Joanna said.

It was William's turn to frown. 'You're not going after them?'

'I am going to turn them inside out,' Joanna said. 'But that's between you and me.'

He was looking very uneasy. 'It'll cost you.'

'I'm going to have it.'

'You mean this chap Johannsson has it. Will he go along with a hostile takeover which could cost a million or two?'

'He's said he will. I'll just straighten that out.'

* * *

Joanna was summoned to the Office. 'Is this some kind of a joke, Orton?'

Joanna raised her eyebrows. 'What, ma'am?'

'I have a communication here from the Home Office, informing me that you are to be married, here in Liddleton, on Saturday next.'

'Oh, that,' Joanna said, as casually as she could.

'Why was I not informed of this development, before?'

'I did not think you would be interested, ma'am.' Mrs Anstey glared at her. 'My fiancé told me he would make all the arrangements. As he seems to have done.'

'This man . . . this Johannsson — what do you know of him?'

Joanna smiled at her. 'I know that he is very rich, and that he is a personal friend of the Home Secretary.'

Mrs Anstey's jaw dropped. But she quickly recovered. 'And does *he* know that you have at least another four years to spend in here?'

'Yes, ma'am, he does. He knows all about me. You see, he's the father of the man I killed.'

Coup de grace! Mrs Anstey was left speechless. While Joanna and Belinda hugged each other. 'I'm to have a night with him,'

Joanna said. 'Would you believe that I'm scared stiff?'

'I wouldn't believe it,' Belinda said. 'Not you, Joanna. Please can I be your maid?'

'Come and see me when you get out,' Joanna promised.

Because she *was* nervous. Indeed she was terrified, more afraid than at any previous time in her life. Her relationships with Howard Edge and Prince Hasim had just happened, overtaking her before she had been properly aware of them. Taking over the management of Caribee Shipping had been a similarly instant event, a matter for quick decisions, supported by the devil-may-care attitude of knowing that she had nothing to lose. Well, she told herself, did she have anything to lose this time? The difference was that she was thirty-seven instead of twenty, and that she had suffered every indignity a woman could. But that had to have made her tougher, stronger, more than ever ruthlessly determined to regain the top. Surely.

But to share . . . had she ever shared, with anyone? She had never shared with Howard, because she had been his mistress for most of their relationship, and he had been a secretive man, tending to keep his plans as well as his fears and fancies to himself. She had felt they were going to share, after their marriage, but that had lasted less than a fortnight. She had never shared with Prince Hasim, because to him she had always been a magnificent toy, a thing of enormous value, to be handled with the utmost gentle care, but nonetheless never to be considered as an equal.

She had never shared with Dick, because the reverse had been the care with him, only he had never even been a magnificent toy. Sometimes she felt she had come close to sharing with Cindy, or even Belinda. But she knew these were temporary situations, born of a mutual misery, a mutual need to have another's arms to hold one tight, when the misery threatened to overwhelm. Such relations would not stand the cold light of day. And now . . . Michael Johannsson. A big man, in every way. She had never had relations with a *big* man.

* * *

'You may use the interview room,' Angie told Joanna, escorting her along the catwalk. The entire block was singing and cheering, while Joanna's knees seemed to have turned to jelly.

Then they were in a more solid corridor, and she was being shown into the room where last she had met John Giffard. 'I'll be right outside,' Angie told her.

Joanna took a deep breath, and the door clanged behind her. 'Would you believe,' Michael Johannsson said, 'that this is the first time I have ever been inside a prison?' He was exactly as he had appeared in the photograph, a huge bear of a man.

Joanna licked her lips. 'It's not all it's cracked up to be.'

She waited, unable to move, uncertain what was required of her. 'Pretty grim, huh?' His accent was only slightly nasal.

'Pretty.'

There were two chairs at the table. He pulled one out for her. She moved towards him, and sat down. Still he had not touched her. He sat in the other chair, facing her. 'I've never been in a situation like this before, either,' he confessed.

'Me neither. I was sorry to hear about your wife.'

He shrugged. 'As I said, we lived apart for the past ten years.'

'Yes.'

They gazed at each other. 'About your son . . . '

'No,' he said. 'Never again. Promise me.'

'Oh! Right.' She felt an enormous sense of relief. But that didn't mean Sean wouldn't lie in bed between them.

'I bought you this.' He felt in his pocket and produced the ring box. 'I've been told it's not a good idea for you to wear it in prison, but I'd like you to look at it.'

Her hands trembled as she opened the box and gazed at the sapphire set in diamonds. It must be just about as valuable as my ruby, she thought. That was locked away in her safe deposit box. 'It's magnificent.'

'It's yours. Waiting for you, I guess. As am I.' Once again they stared at each other. 'There's so much that needs saying,' Michael Johannsson said. 'And I'm not sure now is the time or place. I want you to know that I meant every word I have ever said, and that once you get out of here I am going to make you the happiest woman in the world.'

'As I shall try to be everything you expect of me.'

He grinned. 'Kind of formal. But I guess we both know what we mean. Would we be breaking any rules if I were to kiss you?'

'I suppose we would. But I don't think it would matter.'

'What about you?'

'I would like that,' Joanna said.

* * *

'You will be married in the prison chapel,' Mrs Anstey told her. 'You may have one attendant.' She paused.

'Belinda, please, ma'am.' Mrs Anstey nodded; she had expected that. 'And my children,' Joanna said.

Mrs Anstey raised her eyebrows. 'I will see if permission can be obtained.'

'And my brother and his wife.'

'My dear Orton, this is a prison.'

'I have made the request, ma'am.'

'And I will forward it. After the ceremony, you will be allowed one night with your husband. The Home Secretary has very generously allowed this to be spent outside the prison, at an hotel. You are being granted parole for that one night, and your husband has guaranteed that you will be returned here the next morning. I assume you have enough sense to go along with this.'

'Yes,' Joanna said.

'Well . . . ' Mrs Anstey's smile was cold. 'I will wish you joy of it.'

'Will you be attending the ceremony, ma'am?'

'Why, do you know, I think I might.'

Someone else to get even with, Joanna thought, when I am finally out of here.

* * *

Mrs Partridge was allowed to bring down a choice of Joanna's clothes — she had rescued them from Caribee House before the company had reclaimed it — and Joanna chose a simple white suit. As she had lost weight it required altering, but was promised for the day. 'How are the children taking the idea?' she asked.

Mrs Partridge flushed. 'Helen doesn't approve.'

'Has she met Mr Johannsson?'

'He came to call. And he's taking a new apartment for us.'

'But you're staying on?' Joanna was anxious.

'I'll be there just as long as you want me, madam.'

'Dear Mrs Partridge.' Joanna squeezed her hand. 'Why doesn't Helen approve? Was it something about him she didn't like?'

'Well, madam . . . ' Mrs Partridge went into one of her flushing routines. 'I don't think there is anything about the gentleman himself she didn't like. It's the idea. She's at that age, you see. Romance, love, belief in love, is everything. She doesn't believe you love Mr Johannsson, or can possibly love him. Ever.'

I am selling myself, for freedom and power, Joanna thought. Something out of Faust. But she did not think Michael Johannsson was Mephistopheles. 'I think he'll have to grow on her, as he'll have to grow on me. What about Raisul?'

'He doesn't say much. He's a deep one.'

'And you? What do you think about Mr Johannsson?'

'It's not for me to say, madam.'

'I'm asking you to.'

'He's seems a very nice gentleman, madam.'

Joanna knew that was all she was going to get out of her.

* * *

The wedding suit duly arrived on the day before the ceremony, and the entire block attended the fitting, which was made in the recreation area. Mary collapsed into tears.

'You're going to be so happy,' she sobbed. 'I know it.'

The following day the whole prison seemed to be humming. This was an event that transcended the grim reality of their lives, a sort of fairytale taking place in their very midst. Belinda had also been allowed to wear her own clothes for the occasion, and Angie dressed Joanna's hair. It was the first time in five years she had had a shampoo and set, and it felt so good. 'Used to be a hairdresser, a long time ago,' Angie said.

She had even managed to find a bouquet of flowers. Once again they were clapped and cheered all the way out of the block, and straight into the chapel, where Reverend Ingle was waiting for them, together with William and Norma, looking apprehensive, Mrs Partridge, looking even more apprehensive . . . and Raisul. 'Oh, madam,' Mrs Partridge said, hugging her. 'She wouldn't come. She just wouldn't come. And I couldn't force her.'

'Of course you couldn't,' Joanna said.

'I'll sort it out,' Michael said. Joanna looked up at him, the solid bulk of him, so massive, so reassuring. He could sort anything out, she was sure. And he had a lot to do.

She hardly heard the ceremony, hardly felt the kisses and the congratulations, even from Mrs Anstey. She stared at the two rings, because Michael had insisted upon slipping on the engagement ring first. 'Just for tonight,' he said.

Then she was sitting in the back of a car and the gates were swinging open. The last time those gates had opened for her had been the day she had gone to her appeal hearing. When they had closed on her return she had supposed that was the end of her life. When they closed on her return this time, it would be merely another chapter, opening, towards the future. But before then . . . she glanced at Michael, found him staring at her. 'It would be banal to ask if you are happy,' he said. 'But are you content? Be truthful.'

'I think I am as content as a woman in my position has any right to expect,' Joanna said. 'I'm sorry about Helen. You understand that it's been fairly traumatic for her.'

'I understand. Have you any objection if I see what I can do?'

She continued to gaze at him for several seconds. He could be a paedophile, Ingle had said. But she couldn't believe it of this man, save that she was conditioned to be suspicious of all men. 'I'd be grateful,' she said.

'Kid gloves, I promise,' he said.

'Yes, please.' She forced a smile. 'I'm afraid she has a lot of her mother in her.'

'I figured that the first time I met her,' he said.

They drove in silence, while Joanna looked out of the window at the countryside. It was all but dark, but she savoured every tree, every winking light in a house window. Yet was totally aware of the man sitting beside her, who had not yet touched her, who had only, in fact, touched her twice in his life. Am

I going to scream? she wondered. The last man who had touched her, sexually, had been this man's son, and that had been five years ago. They turned through wrought-iron gates and down a tree-lined drive. 'It's not the Savoy,' Michael said. 'But it's quiet. And they don't have a clue who we are. So, no honeymoon special. We're just passing through. Right?'

'Yes,' she said. Yet it was all she could do to stop herself shaking when they reached reception. Michael, who seemed to have thought of everything, had provided two heavy suitcases, although she didn't even have a change of clothes, to her knowledge. She stood to one side, trying to ignore the glances of the other guests in the lobby — their interest had only to be because she was a good-looking woman, she kept telling herself — and then they were in the lift and mounting upwards. The bellhop took them along to their room, drew the curtains back from the picture window to show the floodlighting in the hotel park, placed their suitcases on the stand, accepted Michael's tip, and withdrew.

Joanna stood at the window, looking out, listening to what was happening behind her. The door closed. 'I thought we'd eat in the room,' Michael said. 'We have so little time.'

She turned. 'Of course.'

'Would you like to look at the menu?'

'You order.'

He did so, then opened the minibar and uncorked a bottle of champagne, filled two glasses. 'Here's to us.'

She drank, gazing at him. He kissed her, very lightly. 'What would you like more than anything else in the world, at this moment?'

'A hot bath.'

'Voila!' He gestured at the bathroom, then went into it and turned on the taps.

'Should I have said something different?' she asked.

'Not in the least.'

She took off her coat and hung it up, then unzipped her dress. He sat on the bed. 'Do you mind if I watch?'

'You're my husband.' She hung the dress up next to the coat, stepped out of her shoes, sat down to roll down her stockings.

'I suppose you know that you are an incredibly attractive woman,' he remarked.

'It's got me into a fair amount of trouble.' She realised her hands were trembling as she dropped the second stocking on the floor, and reached behind herself to unfasten her bra. It was a very long time since she had done that in the presence of a man. Indeed, as in her heyday she had never worn such things, she could not remember the last time she had done so. And this man was still a stranger. She dropped that too on the floor.

'That bath must be just about ready,' he said, and went into the bathroom to turn off the taps. He was such a gentleman!

She stepped out of her knickers, went to the bathroom door, encountered him coming out. They stared at each other. 'I'm flesh and blood,' she said.

'So am I,' he said, and took her in his arms.

She soaked, slowly and luxuriously, while she listened to their dinner being served. When she got out of the bath, Michael was there with a white robe to wrap her in. She had washed her hair, and it lay damply on her shoulders. He had also undressed and wore a dressing gown. They sat opposite each other to eat, and drink champagne. 'Can you stand the thought of sex?' he asked.

'I'm your wife.'

He grinned. 'Doesn't mean all that much nowadays. I want you to want it.'

'I do,' she said. 'But . . . you'll have to be gentle. It's been a long time.'

'I'll be gentle.'

He lifted her in his arms to carry her to the bed, carefully removed the bathrobe, kissed her mouth, her lips, her eyes, her cheeks, her chin. When his mouth moved lower she closed her eyes. He was taking possession of her, in his own way, and she wanted to be possessed. Even when he rolled her on her stomach to her back and her buttocks, while she instinctively tensed as memory flooded back, she slowly relaxed as she realised that this man was a gentle man.

When he entered her, she felt like a virgin again. Now his movements grew more violent, but they were always controlled, always careful to avoid pain. She did not climax, but she had not expected to, after so long. It was sufficient to have him covering her, his passion spent, his sweat mingling with hers.

He raised his head to look at her, and she kissed him. 'We have all the time in the world, my darling,' she said. 'All the rest of our lives.'

'To hear you say that . . . hey, I never gave you your wedding present.'

'Do I get one?'

He rolled off the bed, went to his suitcase. 'You get fifty thousand,' he said.

11

Family Matters

Joanna sat up, heart pounding, as he brought the share certificates back to her. 'Oh, my,' she said. 'Oh, my. But how?'

'I, or rather, my brokers, made the lady an offer she couldn't resist.'

'Alicia? But . . . she said she always wanted to maintain a stake in the company.'

'In Caribee Shipping. That no longer exists. Nor will it ever again, unless someone takes control of Petherick Shipping and restores the name.' Joanna clasped both hands to her neck. 'Her shares in Caribee were exchanged for shares in Petherick,' Michael explained. 'But of course whereas Caribee had a million, Petherick has four, so fifty thousand shares does not represent a very big part of the company. And the price has remained low, because of all the inflationary pressures we've been suffering. So, as I said, the lady couldn't refuse an offer of virtually twice their current value.'

'I never thought Alicia would sell out to me, under any circumstances,' Joanna said.

'I doubt she would, and she didn't. In any event, I don't think it would be a good idea were anyone in the City to discover that you are back in business. Nor did I think it a good idea for me to be involved, as the story of this marriage is going to be public all over Britain tomorrow. The shares have been bought by a holding company, J & J Ltd., which I have set up on your behalf.'

'J & J?' she said.

'Joanna and Johannsson.'

'Oh, Michael,' she said. 'I think I'm going to cry.'

'My agents will keep their eyes and ears open, and buy whatever snippets they can, until you're ready to go to work,' Michael said.

She lay with her head on his shoulder, while outside the darkness began to fade. Neither had slept; there had been no time for sleep. And they had had sex twice more. She had not expected that in a man of fifty-six. He had been insatiable. But then, so had she. She felt she was in a dream. 'Will you really back me to regain control of the company?' she asked.

'That was the deal.'

She raised her head. 'Do you think that matters, now?'

'Yes, I do. I intend to make you the

happiest woman in the world.'

'Suppose I told you that I already am the happiest woman in the world?'

He kissed her. 'You'd be lying. And even if you were, I'm going to make you happier yet.' They had not once mentioned Sean's name.

* * *

The cheering and the hand-clapping, the stamping of feet and the banging of utensils, echoed through the prison for a good hour after the gates had again closed behind Joanna. Mrs Anstey's mouth was twisted. 'I can see you've had a good night, Orton,' she said. 'Or, I suppose, I have to start calling you Johannsson. Joanna Johannsson. What a mouthful. I hope you are not expecting any special treatment.'

'No, ma'am,' Joanna said as primly as possible. She was back in her prison uniform, and yesterday and last night might never have been. But it had been, and her new engagement ring was on its way to her safety deposit box to join her old engagement ring — together with fifty thousand shares in Petherick Shipping. She was on her way, with less than four years to go.

Considerably on her way, although she didn't then know it. 'You must tell us all about it,' the women said during recreation.

Joanna was happy to do that, omitting all the really important matters such as the shares and the promise of the future, concentrating on the food she had eaten, the room in which she had spent the night — which was what they really wanted to hear about in any event. 'You must be the happiest woman in the world,' Belinda said, when they were alone in their cell.

'That's what Michael said,' Joanna mused. 'And I believed it, then. Now . . . '

'So what's another four years? You have so much waiting for you.'

So much, Joanna thought. Helen! Four years might just complete an irreconcilable break, unless Michael could work something. Four years.

⋆ ⋆ ⋆

'This is incredible,' Mrs Anstey said, slapping the report on her desk. 'You are allowed out, for one night, and you're pregnant? At your age?'

'With respect, ma'am,' Joanna said. 'I am thirty-seven. That is not too old to have a child.'

Mrs Anstey snorted; presumably she had never had children. None of the inmates were even sure that she had ever actually been married. 'This will have to go to the parole board, and probably the Home Office as well,' she said disdainfully. 'I suppose you think it will help you get out of here sooner.'

'Yes, I do,' Joanna said.

Mrs Anstey glared at her.

⋆ ⋆ ⋆

'Must be some guy,' Belinda had said enviously. 'Nervous?'

'Scared stiff,' Joanna confessed. But she gave no sign of it as she sat in a straight chair before the board.

'This is about the most unusual case I have ever come across,' said the chairperson, a rather large woman, who was flanked by another woman and by a man who looked almost as scared as Joanna felt — but she suspected he was scared of the chairperson. 'I can't see any point in asking you any questions,' the chairperson said, 'as we know where you are going and what you will be doing when you leave here. Nor does there appear to be any point in considering your record of misbehaviour while in here; indeed, we have been specifically instructed not to do so. You have friends in high places, Mrs Johannsson. Just remember that even such friends will not be able to help you if you get into trouble again. Dismissed.'

Belinda was waiting to hug her and kiss her. 'Can I be your maid?'

'Just as soon as you get out,' Joanna assured her.

Michael himself came to collect her. 'Who says miracles never happen?'

Joanna hugged him and kissed him, then leaned back in the front seat of the Mercedes; he was driving himself.

I am free, she thought. Free, free, free. Minutes later they were on the M4. 'Where are we going?' she asked.

'I have a flat in London. I've arranged a little party there.'

She sat up again. 'Oh, lord!'

'Don't you like the idea?'

'Well . . . these clothes don't fit very well any more, and I haven't had my hair done, and — '

'Just relax,' he suggested. 'It's you that's important.'

'Who's going to be there?'

'Raisul and Mrs Partridge will be there, and your brother and his wife . . . '

'And Matilda?'

'Ah, no. She declined. Sorry about that.'

'And Helen?'

'She declined as well.'

'I've a lot to do,' Joanna said, half to herself. She was looking at houses. They were entering London's suburbs She didn't really want to meet anyone, until she had got her bearings.

'Did I do the right thing?' Michael asked, anxiously, glancing at her expression.

'Of course you did. They're my family.'

'My family too, now,' he reminded her.

She squeezed his hand.

They left the motorway and were in Chelsea. They turned off the main road and into a quiet square. 'Shit!' Michael commented.

Joanna had been leaning back again. Now she sat up, and saw the crowd of photographers and reporters outside one of the houses. 'Now who the fuck would have done that?' Michael asked. He was clearly very angry.

'Mrs Anstey, I would say. I'm not her favourite person. Michael . . . '

'I know.' He turned left and drove out of the square, rejoined the main road. 'We'll go to an hotel.'

'But the party?'

'We'll have it there.'

* * *

It was not a howling success. Quite apart from having the venue so suddenly shifted, there was so much between them all, to be said, alleviated, at some time in the future, but not all at once. At the wedding there had been no time for anything more than perfunctory greetings and congratulations, with William no doubt remembering how bitter she had been when last they had met. Now she smiled at them all, but the bitterness remained. 'What do you want to do now?' Michael asked when the guests had departed. 'I mean, tomorrow, or whatever. Bearing in mind that you don't *have* to do anything.'

'I know,' she said. 'Believe me, one half of me just wants to get into bed beneath scented sheets and lie there for ever and ever. But I've already lost five years out of my life. Then the other half of me wants to take off to some deserted island and just lie in the sun for a month.'

'That's entirely practical.'

'It isn't really. What about the baby?'

'A month in the sun will probably do him good. Or her.'

'And Helen?'

'As she's been behaving oddly for a long time now, I can't see that another month is going to do harm.'

'Did you see her?'

'No. I got her address from Mrs Partridge, and called and asked her to lunch, but she hung up on me. I didn't figure I had the right to go round and slap her bottom, so I left it there.'

There was so much to be done, but the baby came first. Although she desperately wanted to have Michael's child, for the first time Joanna regretted being pregnant at such a time. Even when Howard had died and left her carrying Helen, the pregnancy had worked to her advantage. Now it was only a handicap. But, she reminded herself, had she not been pregnant, she would still be in jail.

'What about Raisul?' Michael asked, when they were able to get into the flat, in the small hours of the next day, when the papparazzi had gone home to bed. Joanna had spent two hours at her hairdressers, and felt a new woman. 'Do you wish him to move in with us?' It was a two-bedroom apartment.

Another problem. Raisul had seemed to be delighted to see her again, but there had been no spontaneous warmth in his hug. She was virtually a stranger to him, and he, taller than she, broad-shouldered, every inch the young man rather than the little boy she remembered, was most certainly a stranger to her. If they were to live together again beneath the same roof, it was going to have to be a large roof.

There was also the matter of Michael himself. He was her saviour in every possible way, but they remained largely strangers, only slowly feeling their way towards that mutual understanding, and acceptance, that is essential where two people are to live together in harmony. He was going out of his way to be nice to her, to satisfy her every whim, but there were certain whims she could not convey to him without risking causing offence — and that she dared not risk. Her principal problem was coming to grips with the total lack of privacy in which she found herself. She had always been an intensely private person. During the year she had been Howard Edge's mistress, she had always had a room to herself. What might have happened after their marriage she did not know, because Howard had died on their honeymoon.

Prince Hasim had also maintained a separate bedroom, because that was how Arab princes lived. Nor had he encroached on her life at all. That she wanted to continue running her shipping line had amused him. That she had had a house in the country amused him even more. But all he had ever wanted from her was her body when he felt the urge, and her company in society. Dick had always been very much the junior partner, and she had continued to sleep alone, except when *she* had the urge. Even in prison, although she had had to share a cell, both Cindy and Belinda had quickly gathered that she wanted her privacy, and as they had both been afraid of her, they had accepted the situation.

Such a point of view was totally foreign to Michael's way of life, and she could tell that he had never even considered it a possibility for a married couple. Equally, his concept of the best way for them to form a couple was to share every moment, awake or asleep. This was something she had to go along with. But to have others in the house would surely complicate matters, especially where one of the others would be her son, and the other . . . 'And Mrs Partridge?'

'Hm. I can see we will have to buy a house.'

'Who's occupying Caribee House at the moment?'

He raised his eyebrows, then grinned. 'I can find out. Do you really think they'd sell?'

'Depends who it is,' Joanna said. 'And what state his finances are in.'

Michael still had Helen's phone number, but Joanna decided against telephoning, and got her address from Mrs Partridge. Mrs Partridge and Raisul had been removed to a more upmarket apartment, and the old lady was looking quite prosperous. But she was as worried and anxious as ever. 'You realise she's living with this man of hers, madam?' she said.

'I do. I'm not going to come over the heavy-handed mother, Mrs Partridge. But I do want her to do something with her life.'

'I don't think she'll go back to school.'

'I left school when I was sixteen,' Joanna pointed out. 'She can go to a secretarial college. That's what I did.' And who knows, she thought: she might meet another Howard Edge.

Michael wanted to accompany her, but she decided against it. 'This is mother and daughter talk,' she said.

'Remember, she's not yet an adult in the eyes of the law,' he said. 'If you don't like the set-up, you can make her come home.'

Joanna smiled. 'Invoke the law and drag her home with a couple of bobbies. I've had just about all the law I can stand, Michael. This has to be done with TLC.'

She took a taxi to the address, disturbingly, a street in Brixton. The moment she stepped down from her taxi she regretted having worn her mink. But she had faced tougher opposition than these jeering youths, so she merely looked at them before entering the house; there was no bell and the street door was open. Mrs Partridge said that as far as she knew Helen had a job, so Joanna had waited until half-past six. The apartment was a walk-up, three flights, and she was quite out of breath by the time she reached the landing. She didn't care much for the cleanliness of the stairs, or the rather sour smell with which she was surrounded.

She rang the bell, and again, before the door was opened by an unshaven young man wearing a vest and pants, who goggled at her mink in consternation. 'You must be Harry,' Joanna suggested. 'Is Helen in?'

'Shit!' he commented, as the penny dropped. 'No, she ain't.'

'But you are expecting her, I suppose?'

'Yeah.'

'Then do you mind if I come in and wait? I'm her mother.'

'Yeah,' he said again, hesitated, then stepped back. Joanna stepped inside, and was even more assailed by the sour smell. But the whole room was sour, with various discarded articles of clothing draped over the chairs and the overstuffed settee. Only the tape deck in the corner looked either new or cared for. There was a door leading to a bedroom at the rear of the room; as it was open, she could tell it was hardly more tidy in there. 'Helen ain't the neatest person in the world,' Harry explained, scooping some clothes off of a chair.

'And it's not part of your business to help her,' Joanna commented.

'I'm the man of the house,' he agreed. 'Why don't you sit down, Mrs Orton.'

'The name is now Johannsson,' Joanna pointed out, and took off her mink before sitting in the vacant chair; the mink she draped across the other chair, mainly occupied by clothes.

'Yeah. I forgot. Drink? There's beer.'

'I don't suppose you have a cup of tea?'

'I don't drink tea. Maybe Helen will make you one, when she gets in.'

'I'll look forward to that.' She was trying to determine whether this was his natural appearance and behaviour, or whether he was being deliberately antagonistic to a woman he had to feel had come to disrupt his living arrangements. She hoped it was the latter. 'What sort of work do you do?' she asked.

'Work? How'm I to get work?'

'You mean Helen supports you.'

'Only in a manner of speaking. I get the dole.'

'Of course. But I am sure you hope to do better.'

'I'm happy.' He opened a beer for himself, cleared some more clothes off the settee with a sweep of his arm, slumped on to the cushions, legs thrown wide. 'What's it feel like, to be out?'

'It feels very pleasant,' Joanna said.

'But you're on parole, right? You step out of line, and it's back inside. Right?'

'That depends what you mean by stepping out of line,' Joanna said carefully, wondering if he was going to assault her.

But at that moment a key turned in the lock, and Helen came in, puffing, her arms filled with bags of groceries. 'Sorry I'm late, love. There was this man . . .' she paused, her mouth open.

'She wants a word,' Harry said. He didn't get up, either to greet Helen or to relieve her of any of the bags.

Helen crossed the room and dumped the lot on the table, stayed there for a moment, facing the wall, obviously getting her emotions and her thoughts under control. Joanna observed that she looked quite well, had her figure under control, her hair neat and clean, but her clothes were shabby, her shoes down at the heel, and the cloth coat had had some loose threads. Now she turned. 'Well, it's good to see you, Mother. After so long.'

Joanna had got up, and was standing, waiting for her to come to her. Helen did move towards her, halfway across the room, then checked, glancing at Harry. 'I see you two have met.'

'Yes,' Joanna said.

'Well . . . I wish you'd called to say you were coming.'

'So you could have been out?'

'No, I would have tidied the place up.'

'Do you think we could have a little time together?' Joanna asked. 'Alone?'

Helen hesitated, then looked at Harry again. 'Would you mind?'

'I'm not being put out of my home by an ex-con,' Dave declared.

Helen bit her lip, while Joanna felt as if she had been slapped in the face. 'You can go down to the boozer for half an hour,' Helen said.

'What with?'

She opened her handbag and took out a five-pound note. 'Use this.'

'No,' Joanna said. 'I'll leave. Perhaps you'd telephone me, Helen, and we'll meet up.' She stumbled down the stairs and into the street; she felt physically sick.

* * *

Joanna did not dare tell Michael the truth about her meeting with Helen; she felt he would be so angry he might assault Harry. She had to stick to half truths, tell him that she and Helen were going to have a meal together, as they'd found talking difficult in the flat. Michael was, in any event, preoccupied, and pleased with himself. 'I've found out about Caribee House,' he announced. 'It belongs to Petherick, of course, but it's for sale. Seems large country houses aren't viable in the days of looming recession and rising interest rates.'

'Gosh,' she said, and looked at him.

He grinned. 'Would you really like it? Seems it's gone down a bit. It hasn't been occupied over the last few years. We'd have to spend some money renovating it. But I have an idea you'd enjoy that.'

'Oh, Michael,' she said. 'Would you really buy it?'

He winked. 'If it's in as bad condition as they say, we'll get it cheap. We've a viewing tomorrow.'

Joanna was so excited she hardly slept. And again she felt physically sick as the Mercedes turned into that so familiar drive. But maybe it was just the baby.

A young man was waiting for them with the keys. 'I feel I should tell you, Mr

Johannsson, Mrs Johannsson, that this house used to belong to that Mrs Orton, you may remember, the woman who murdered her boyfriend, way back.'

Joanna looked at Michael, and they both smiled; he didn't have a clue. 'We're not superstitious,' Michael assured him.

The salesman unlocked the door and they stepped into that so familiar hall. Everything was very much as she had left it, save for the dust and the cobwebs. 'When Mrs Orton was sent down,' the young man explained, 'her children lived here for a while, with their nanny, but then the company was wound up, and the new owners took it over.'

'What happened to the children?' Joanna asked.

'Haven't a clue,' the young man said. 'Then the new owners lived here for a while, not as a home, but as a weekend cottage, really.'

'When you say the new owners, who exactly do you mean?' Joanna asked.

The young man opened his file, hunted through the various documents there. 'Chap called Gosling. But he wasn't married, and I suppose he found it a bit large for him. He stopped using it at all about four years ago, and since then it's stood empty.'

'Let's go upstairs,' Joanna said.

She led them up, and from bedroom to

bedroom. 'My word,' remarked the young man. 'One would almost suppose you had been here before, Mrs Johannsson.'

'I'm clairvoyant,' Joanna told him.

'I am so excited,' she told Michael, as they drove home.

'No ghosts?'

'Oh . . . oh, my God! What about you?'

'Not for me. But we'll completely redecorate that drawing room. It's a big house. You will be able to have Raisul and Mrs Partridge move back in. Think they'll like that?'

'I should think they'll adore that. Are you going to tell Gosling who we are?'

He shook his head. 'Not until we're in a position to topple him off his perch. The house will be bought by J&J. What about Helen? There's room for her too.'

'That's up to her,' Joanna said. 'There isn't room for that slob she's living with.'

* * *

They met for lunch at a bistro in Soho. 'He's not bad, really,' Helen said. 'It's just that he regards himself as unfortunate.'

'Because he can't get, or hold, a job? Has he tried hard enough?'

'He gets angry with people, and answers back, and then gets fired.'

'Why do you stay with him?'

Helen flushed. 'We get on.'

'You mean he's good in bed. Men who are good in bed aren't altogether unique, you know.'

'You don't understand,' Helen said. 'I can't live lies. I like to talk, and I like to tell the truth.'

'Ah,' Joanna said. 'And the moment, in your spells of candour, you tell your date that your mother is in jail, for murder, they sort of sidle off.'

'Well . . . perhaps it's not quite as simple as that.'

'Whereas Harry didn't sidle off. He waited to insult me.'

Helen bit her lip. 'He always says what comes naturally.'

'But I am no longer in gaol. I am now again a wealthy woman, or at least I'm married to a very wealthy man who happens to be indulging me. Suppose I told you that we are buying back Caribee House? Would you move back in?' Joanna asked.

'Back there? How can you? It's where . . . ' guiltily she glanced at the nearest tables. 'You'll have nightmares!'

'I think I've learned to cope with nightmares,' Joanna said. 'Will you?'

Helen ate, slowly. 'I must do my own thing,

Mummy. I simply have to.'

'And your own thing is working as a shop assistant and living with a layabout.'

Helen flushed, but this was at least partly anger. 'That is my own thing, at the moment, yes.'

'What happens when you get pregnant?'

'I get pregnant. But it won't happen. I'm on the pill.'

'Clever you. Helen . . . ' Joanna leaned across the table and held her daughter's hand. 'If you won't come back home, will you work for me?'

Helen frowned. 'For you? What as?'

'As soon as I'm back in business, I'll give you a job.'

'You're going back into business? Who'd employ a — ' she bit her lip.

'Ex-con?' Joanna gave a grim smile. 'Probably no one. But I don't intended to be employed. I intend to do the employing.'

'You reckon?' Helen drank her coffee. 'Thanks for the meal, Mummy. I don't want us to quarrel, really. But . . . '

'You need to do your own thing. You haven't answered my question. Will you come and work for me? It's not going to take too long for me to set things up. As soon as my baby's born.'

Helen's jaw dropped. 'You're pregnant?'

Joanna grinned. 'Unlike you modern women, I have never taken the pill. Yes, I'm pregnant.'

'But you hardly know the man!'

'Well, now, I have actually known him, in a Biblical sense, for four months.'

'You mean you got pregnant on your wedding night? What a hoot!'

'Absolutely. But you are going to have a little baby brother, or sister, in five months' time. Now answer my question?'

'Tell you what,' Helen said, 'ask me again, when you're back in business.' Her tone said, if it ever happens.

Joanna reckoned she had made as much progress in that direction as she could, short of making Helen a ward of court, and she did not want that kind of publicity right now. She wanted time to stand still until she had her baby. It was amusing to remember that she had been in this position once before — when she had been carrying Helen! Then all her dreams, plans, fears and hopes had had to be put on hold, until her delivery. Then she had desperately wanted a boy, because a boy had been necessary, by the terms of Howard's will. Well, she had survived having a girl. Now it didn't matter.

For the time being she could occupy herself with redecorating Caribee House. She so wanted to have the baby in that house, where both Helen and Raisul had been born. But five months . . . It seemed an eternally long time, as the new Conservative Government set about putting the nation's finances in order, which inevitably brought on a recession, with unemployment threatening to go through the roof. This meant that it was easier to get the various contracts on the house fulfilled; Joanna went down almost every day, even when her belly was swollen. It was a dream to keep her going, until she was ready for . . . she wasn't quite sure for what. 'Do you think I am a mean and vicious woman?' she asked Michael.

'You mean because you wish to get even with those wretches who sold your company from under you? No, I don't think that is at all mean and vicious. Providing you don't let it take over your life.'

'Um,' she said. Because in many ways it had already taken over her life. Buying Caribee House was less gaining a victory over Andy Gosling than slapping Alicia in the face. The remarkable thing was that no one had yet worked out who J & J was. And she didn't want them to until she was ready.

She gave birth at the beginning of June, 1981. Caribee House was only just ready, and her doctor was astounded when she insisted upon having the baby at home, in such ill-prepared conditions. But he, like so many people in the past, was getting the message that when Joanna Johannsson made a decision, it would be implemented. He moved in a staff of nurses and they coped very well. The baby was a boy, who she named Howard. Michael did not object.

Then she could sit back and relax. Mrs Partridge and Raisul duly moved in, but the rest of the servants were new. However, Charlie was out of gaol and she contacted him to let him know that his old job was waiting for him; he was back behind the wheel of her Mercedes a week later.

William and Norma, and their children were, of course, totally supportive. She did not know what they made of her, or said of her, in the privacy of their own home, but they came down to Caribee House to watch the last redecorations set into place, and complimented her on her taste. William did mention, when they were alone together, 'Quite an achievement, Sis, getting the old place back together.'

'I'm pleased,' Joanna said.

'So . . . what next?'

'The company.'

He pulled his nose. 'Have you any idea what that is going to cost?'

'Some.'

'But you're going to do it anyway?'

'In time. But now, you see, I have all the time in the world.'

He went away a sorely worried man, although as with Helen, Joanna promised him a job once she had regained the company.

And it was happening. 'Here's an item of news that may interest you,' Michael said at dinner. 'There's talk in the city that entrepreneur James Holroyd is in financial difficulties.' Joanna put down her wine glass. He grinned at her. 'I've told your man Prim to make him an offer for his portfolio. In the name of J & J. And providing he still has any Petherick stock. We may have to accumulate some worthless paper, but as long as there's good stuff as well . . . '

'Oh, Michael,' she said. 'I don't deserve you, really I don't.'

'Well,' he said, 'there's more than one opinion about that.' A fortnight later the deal was completed. 'You now hold, anonymously, twelve percent of Petherick Shipping,' Michael said. 'Mind you, Gosling, or his accountants or stockbrokers or whatever, are going to start to think some time soon.'

'Start to worry, you mean,' she said happily.

But in fact she reckoned Andy, like all of London, was getting geared up for the royal wedding in a month's time. So was she. But she was jerked out of her contentment on the evening of fourth July when the phone rang. She picked it up and gave the number, as was usual.

'Mummy!' Helen screamed. 'Help me! Mummy! They're breaking down the door! Help me!'

12

The Phoenix

'Helen!' Joanna shouted. 'Call the police!'

'They're all around,' Helen screamed. 'But they can't stop the mob. Mummy!'

'I'll be there as soon as I can,' Joanna promised, and slammed down the phone. 'Charlie!' she bawled, as she ran down the stairs.

'What's happened, Mother?' Raisul stood in the door of his bedroom, where he had been doing his homework.

'There's some kind of riot in Brixton,' Joanna said. 'Helen's in trouble. Charlie! Get out the car.'

'I'll come with you,' Raisul said. Joanna looked at him in surprise; he had never offered to go anywhere with her since her return from prison. He flushed. 'Well,' he said, 'if Helen needs help . . . '

'Mrs Partridge!' Joanna shouted. 'I have to go out. Keep an eye on the baby, will you?' She grabbed her mink and pulled it over her shirt and jeans as she ran down to the front hall. Charlie was holding the door for her.

Just like old times, she thought; just like old times. Only now she had Raisul, helping her into the car. 'Find out what's happening,' she told Charlie, as the Mercedes roared down the road.

He switched on the radio. ' . . . huge gangs of black youths,' said the announcer. 'Police are trying to contain them, but the situation is completely out of hand. As I watch, a police van has been overturned and set on fire. Thank heavens there doesn't seem to have been anyone inside. Listen to the shattering of glass; there is wholesale looting going on. It will be a miracle if no one is killed tonight.'

'God, God, God,' Joanna said. 'Charlie . . . '

'We'll get there, Mrs Johannsson. You got any idea where Mr Johannsson is?'

'He was at his club. I should've called him.'

'I reckon he must know there's a riot,' Charlie said.

'But not that Helen may be involved,' Joanna said. Raisul squeezed her hand, and impulsively she threw her arm round his shoulder, hugging him close.

Now they were in the city, and forced to drive slower. Charlie knew all the best routes, yet it was still an hour after they had left the house before they got close to Brixton, and now progress was slowed even more by the traffic jams, as people either tried to get towards the riot or away from it. 'This isn't doing any good,' Joanna said. 'Let us out.'

'You going in there on foot?' Charlie demanded.

'Park the car and follow,' Joanna said. 'You know the address.'

She got out, Raisul at her side. They certainly made much quicker time on foot, jostled from time to time by the gathering crowd, some of whom were quick to notice and take offence at Joanna's mink, but with Raisul at her side, taller than most of them and heavily built, no one actually interfered with her. Now the noise from in front of them was immense, and at the end of the street they were stopped by several policemen, who wore riot gear. 'Where do you think you're going, lady?' one asked.

Joanna checked the street sign; Helen's flat was one block away. 'My daughter is down there,' she said.

'Well, she shouldn't be,' said another policeman.

'She lives there,' Joanna snapped. 'I have to get her out.'

'Listen,' said the first policeman, 'you go down there, wearing that coat, and you'll be lynched.'

'Then here.' Joanna took off the mink and

crammed it into his arms. 'You keep it.' He was too surprised to react, and she darted past him, Raisul behind her. Both policemen shouted after them, but they could hardly hear them because of the racket around them.

To their right, several cars were on fire, with people dancing round them. At the end of the next street there was a solid phalanx of policemen, advancing behind riot shields. To their left where there were several shops, a mass of people were looting the various smashed windows, and some of the buildings were on fire. But in front of them there were more fires. Where Helen lived! 'Hurry,' Joanna said, and they ran across the street to the far pavement. No one paid them any attention; there were people running to and fro all around them, screaming and shouting. Nor did Joanna's yellow hair seem to antagonise people; wearing jeans and a jumper she could have been a rioter herself.

Joanna turned down the next street, and checked. Two of the houses were on fire, and one of them was the apartment building. There was a fire engine, but it was temporarily inactive as it was being bombarded with stones and other missiles from further down the street. Panting, Joanna and Raisul got into its shelter, and found themselves beside a helmeted officer. 'Animals,' he said. 'Goddamned animals.'

'That house,' Joanna panted.

'If we could get some water on it . . . '

'I think my daughter may be in there.'

He gave her a devastated look. 'You know that?'

'She was there an hour ago. She telephoned me.'

'Well, if she has any sense she'll have got out.'

'Maybe she couldn't. I have to get inside.'

The man tilted his helmet to scratch his head. But as with so many men, and women, he was feeling the force of Joanna's personality. 'Hey,' he bawled at his men, who were all sheltering from the missiles. 'Let's get some water on that house.'

The engine was started up. The hose was already connected to the nearby hydrant, and now a jet burst upon the street door. It was the ground floor flat that was actually burning, set alight by a molotov cocktail hurled through the window. Joanna was more worried about the smoke that was billowing up the stairwell. 'The ladder,' she shouted. 'We have to use the ladder. The third floor.'

More orders, and the turntable swung round to place the ladder against one of the the third floor windows. The mob hooted their derision, and more missiles were thrown, but now a line of policemen arrived behind them, and they began to break up. One of the firemen clambered up. Joanna followed. 'Hey!' bawled the officer. 'You can't do that! Come back down here!!'

Joanna ignored him and kept on climbing. 'You'll fall!' the officer shouted in desperation. 'Dick, go get that crazy woman.'

'Take care, Mum!' Raisul shouted.

The fire officer glared at him. 'That your mother? She ought to be locked up!'

'Been there, done that,' Raisul told him.

The lead fireman, concentrating and unaware of the chaos behind him, reached the window and peered in. The sash was down but not locked, and he threw it up easily enough. 'Anyone in there?' he shouted.

'Help me, please!'

'Helen!' Joanna shouted.

The fireman looked down. 'What the fuck . . . ?'

'Listen,' Joanna snapped. 'Get in there and get my daughter.'

He gulped, and climbed through the window, Joanna climbed behind him, while the man sent to fetch her down paused in the opening, having made an ineffectual grab at her. 'Jesus, this floor is hot,' the first fireman said. 'It'll go any moment.' He pointed at wisps of smoke seeping under the door. 'I don't see anybody.'

'Help me, please!' Helen screamed.

Joanna pushed the fireman aside and ran across the floor, feeling the heat rising about her. She threw open the bedroom door, blinked in the gloom, saw a bare foot sticking out from beneath the bed. She dropped to her hands and knees, peered into the gloom; the fireman joined her and used his flashlight, and they both looked at the naked girl, huddled against the far wall. 'Come on,' Joanna said. 'You're safe now.' She grasped Helen's ankle and dragged the girl towards her.

Helen whimpered with pain and misery. The fireman hastily got up, shone his torch round the room, and located a bathrobe hanging from the hook on the door. He handed this to Joanna, and Joanna wrapped Helen in the robe as she drew her out. 'Oh, Mummy,' Helen moaned. 'Oh, Mummy.'

'We have to get out of here,' the fireman said.

Smoke was now definitely filtering into the room, making breathing difficult, and the heat was increasing. Joanna held Helen close as they stumbled across the bedroom and into the lounge. Dick was still sitting astride the windowsill. 'This building is about to go,' he said.

Joanna handed him Helen, and he retreated on to the ladder, now bathed in the glare of a searchlight. The crowd actually applauded.

* * *

'She's in a bad state,' said Dr Hobart. 'She really should stay in hospital for a few days, for observation.'

'I want her home,' Joanna said.

'I'm not sure she wants that.'

'She's not eighteen,' Joanna said. 'I'll decide what she wants.' He surrendered, and Helen was transferred to the Mercedes. Joanna sat beside her. 'There's no necessity to talk if you don't want to,' she said. 'But I have to ask — what happened to Harry?'

'The bastard ran out,' Helen said in a low voice. 'There was this banging on the door, and we knew there were several men there. That's when I telephoned you. I'm sorry. I panicked. I didn't know what to do. We tried nine-nine-nine, and they said they'd get to us as soon as they could, but that they were having problems.'

'Darling,' Joanna said. 'Who else were you going to try, save your mother?'

'They didn't manage to break in for

another fifteen minutes,' Helen said, in a low monotone. 'But then the door gave. When they came in, Harry, who'd been making all sorts of aggressive noises and had armed himself with a poker, charged them, broke through them, and ran down the stairs.'

'He could have been going for help,' Joanna suggested, much as she disliked the man.

'He never came back,' Helen said. 'So there I was . . . with these four guys.'

Joanna gave her a hug.

'How was it with you?' Helen asked.

'With me?'

'When you were raped.'

'I was never actually raped,' Joanna said.

'I know. You killed the bastard who tried it. Oh, Mother — there were four of them.' Raisul and Charlie, in the front, sat rigid.

'We understand, darling,' Joanna said. 'You have nothing to reproach yourself with. And it is so good to have you coming home.' She held the girl close. 'So good.'

It was four in the morning before they reached Caribee House, and Michael was waiting for them. 'I have been so *worried*,' he said.

'I know,' Joanna said. 'But what was I to do? I had to go after her.'

'Of course you did. Is she all right?'

'She has been beaten and raped,' Joanna

said. 'No woman is ever all right, after something like that. But she's my daughter. Yes, she's going to be all right, as you put it.'

His shoulders sagged. 'I should've been here.'

'I'm glad you weren't.'

'And the bastards who did it?'

Joanna sighed. 'I don't suppose they'll ever be caught. There was so much going on.'

'I never thought I'd hear you say something like that.'

She raised her head. 'Maybe even I'm coming to realise there are some things you just have to let go. Let's go see the baby.'

He caught her arm. 'But there are some things you don't mean to let go, right?' She checked, looking down at him. He grinned. 'One of the reasons I was delayed in town this evening; friend Amalia is in trouble.' Joanna came back down the stairs. 'I didn't want to tell you till I was sure. But he's overstretched in every direction. Principally to his bookmaker. I had my people have a chat with that worthy, and persuaded him to call.'

'You didn't use heavy stuff?'

'Not in the sense you mean. We simply offered to match Amalia's debts, two to one, if he was called in.'

'Oh, Michael . . . but the cost . . . '

'Not so much as you might think. There

are differing values of wealth. Amalia is on the bottom rung. So what's a man to do? Start looking at his portfolio. And Petherick shares are around the bottom of *that* rung, at the moment.'

'You mean he's sold up?'

'J & J are now in possession of thirty-one per cent of Petherick shares.'

'Michael!' she screamed, and hugged him. 'But Andy . . . ?'

'Oh, sure. He and Townsend still have fifty-one. But I'll bet you they're not the only ones up late tonight.'

Joanna supposed she should be the most miserable mother in the world, because of what had happened to Helen. Instead she was the happiest woman in the world. As Michael had promised she would be. But the happiness was not merely because she felt, she knew, she was going to win in her battle for total rehabilitation. It was compounded because, no matter what had happened, she had reassembled her immediate family.

Now she wanted to go the whole way.

* * *

William and Norma were really not a problem. They both came down to Caribee House the next day. Helen remained in bed, and they did not see her. But there was enough to talk about. The tabloids had, of course, gone wild with the story of how Joanna — EX-CONVICT . . . CONVICTED MURDERESS . . . CITY WHIZZKID AGAIN ON THE LOOSE . . . ANXIOUS MUM CLIMBS LADDER TO RESCUE DAUGHTER — had behaved.

She was even visited by her probation officer, who warned her that she had, technically, broken the law. 'You mean you're going to send me back to prison?' Joanna asked, softly, 'For rescuing my daughter?' The woman had flushed with embarrassment, and soon left.

William, while delighted, was as usual cautious. 'Seems they can't keep you out of the news,' he remarked, as they sat together on the sofa.

'One would think they'd concentrate on the riot,' she remarked.

'Not quite as exciting, perhaps. Have you heard from Gosling?'

'Why, no. Should I have?'

'Well, maybe he didn't know where you were, before. But he'll know now. Did you know that Petherick Shipping is in trouble?' Joanna raised her eyebrows. 'Oh, of course they're suffering like everyone else from high interest rates and what have you. But they're also in real trouble. There's rumour in the City of a hostile takeover bid.'

'Good heavens,' Joanna said. 'I wonder who that can be.'

They gazed at each other, then both burst out laughing at the same time. Then William grew serious. 'J & J,' he said thoughtfully. 'Andy's not a fool, you know, sis.'

'I'm sure he's not.'

'And as long as he and Townsend are sitting on fifty-one per cent . . . '

'There's work to be done. I agree. But we will do it. Every chain is only as strong as its weakest link.'

'Meaning Townsend?'

'He has his fingers in a lot of pies. Some of them are going to get burned.'

William looked across the room to where Michael was chatting with Norma and Raisul. 'And he's going to back you all the way.'

'It's what he wants to do. Now tell me about Tilly.'

William sighed. 'Not so good. Billy has been made redundant again. I believe they'll have to sell their house. She's talking about emigrating to Australia.'

'Does Australia want people like them?'

'We'll have to see. Sis . . . '

'Yes,' Joanna said. 'I suppose I'll have to pick up the pieces. And Billy knows the ropes.

Tell him I want to see him.'

'And Tilly?'

'Her too, if she wants to come.'

* * *

'Townsend,' Michael said, sitting up in bed, surrounded by sheets of prints-out. 'Thomas O'Reilly Townsend. Tot.'

Joanna peered over his shoulder. 'Where on earth did you get all that?'

'I have people working on him. And Gosling. Gosling's finances seem in pretty good shape, with one proviso. He seems to have sunk everything he has into Petherick Shipping. He owns thirty-five per cent of the shares, and with Townsend's backing he therefore controls the company. He doesn't seem to have much outside that, but he has no big outside debts, either. No, Tot is the man we have to work on. Sweep him away, and Gosling is on a hiding to nothing.'

'And?'

'He has some debts. We're working on them, but I don't think they're sufficient to make him sell up. Anyway, he wouldn't dare without Andy's agreement, and that won't be forthcoming for the reasons I've just given. Andy *has* to keep control of Petherick, or he's on his uppers. What we have to do is make

Townsend more frightened of us, even if he doesn't know who we are, than he is of Andy.'

Joanna hugged herself. 'Sounds illegal.'

'We're not going to break any laws. At least, none that can be traced back to us. You prepared to be patient?'

'You bet.'

He kissed her. 'Then we'll just let them sweat a while. Finding out who we are.'

* * *

Patience. It was a great temptation to go down to the City and look at Caribee Building, now renamed Petherick Building. But it had to be resisted. It was a curious summer. The Brixton riots might have ended, but there were riots in several other cities in the country, as heat and unemployment took hold, and yet at the same time the entire country was winding itself up for the royal wedding that promised so much.

William duly brought Billy to see Joanna; Tilly still preferred to stay away. Then he left them alone, Joanna having intimated that what she had to say to Billy was confidential. 'She's proud,' Billy said. He looked a wreck of the good-looking, confident man she had once known; she reckoned he might have a drink problem.

'What's she got to be proud about?' she asked. 'I'm the one who's done all the suffering.'

'It was not leaving her in charge of the children,' Billy said. 'That really hurt.'

And didn't do the children a lot of good either, Joanna thought. 'Now I hear you're emigrating.'

'Well, we'd like to. If all the papers come through.'

'What do you expect to find in Australia that you haven't been able to find here?'

'Work, for one thing.'

'You can have a job, if you're prepared to work.'

He frowned at her, suspiciously. 'Working for you?'

'That's right. I reckon you know I expect utter loyalty, and utter commitment, too.'

He licked his lips. 'Doing what? You back in business?'

'I intend to be. Do you want the job?'

'As long as it's legal.'

'You keep it legal. Your brief is Tom Townsend. I want his shares. I want to find something that will make him sell. This must be done in absolute secrecy. You find me something.'

'And when I do?'

'When you do, I'll have control of

Petherick Shipping, and you'll have a permanent job there.'

'I'll see what I can do.'

'You'll have to do better than that. You have six months, at a thousand pounds a month.'

'A thousand? Did you say a thousand?'

'Yes. Six months. If you don't come up with something by then, you're out. And Billy, if anyone, *anyone*, finds out what you're up to, you're out on the spot.'

Billy gulped. 'Does that include Tilly?'

'Tilly is at the top of the list,' Joanna told him.

* * *

'There's a woman to see you,' Mrs Partridge said.

Joanna was in the study, where she spent a lot of time. She seldom left Caribee House now, leaving the business details of J & J to Michael, who enjoyed going up to London. She only wanted to go to London if she could go to Caribee Building. Besides, she wanted to be near to Helen, who was only slowly recovering from her traumatic experience. She wanted to be around if that creep Harry ever attempted to show up. But he hadn't so far. Now she could tell from Mrs Partridge's tone that she did not approve of the caller.

'Did she give a name?' Joanna asked.

'Yes, madam: Belinda Grant.'

'Belinda!' Joanna cried, and ran into the hall. 'Oh, Belinda . . . ' they embraced. 'But I didn't expect you out so soon.'

'Good behaviour,' Belinda said. 'Did I do right in coming?'

'Of course you did. I promised you a job. You have it.' They hugged again, while Mrs Partridge surveyed them somewhat grimly. 'This is Belinda,' Joanna explained. 'She's going to be my maid.'

Which was easier said than done. Belinda knew nothing about being a lady's maid. But Joanna was happy to teach her. Not only because of her promise, and because Belinda was eager to learn, but because Belinda had other talents to go with her five-foot-eleven-inch height; she was as strong as any man and quite as happy as any man to engage in a punch-up. Joanna's instincts told her that a bodyguard, such as she had had when she and Matilda had been on the same wavelength, might come in very handy over the next few months.

Michael was amused, if just a little cautious. He had, of course, met Belinda at the wedding, and remembered that she and Joanna had been very close. 'Did you ever sleep together?' he asked. 'I don't mean in the sense that you shared a cell.'

'Would it make you mad if I said yes?'

'Not in the slightest.'

'You'd be titillated,' she teased. 'Because like all men you have a weakness for lesbians. Taken together, as it were.' Then she was serious. 'Yes, we slept together, sometimes. But it wasn't like you think. Oh, sure, there was sex. We're both virile human beings. But it was a necessity, from loneliness, despair, if you like. In prison, if you can't reach out and touch somebody, mentally, you go round the bend.'

'I do understand that,' he said. 'You can take her to bed any time you wish.'

'You don't understand,' she said. 'I'm not lonely any more. I have you, I have my children, I have my home, and I have all the future in the world.'

'And what does she have?' he asked, quietly. Perhaps he did understand, after all.

* * *

Joanna decided against going up to town to watch the wedding. So the whole family gathered round the big downstairs television, drinking champagne and eating turkey sandwiches.

'The wedding of the century,' Belinda said.

'I think I'm going to cry.'

It was a week later, when Joanna was on her weekly visit to her hairdresser in the village, that she encountered Alicia. She had just come outside, and was waiting for Belinda. Belinda accompanied her everywhere, but had gone off to do some shopping while her mistress was being attended to, and as usual was late coming back. Something else Joanna could appreciate; like her, Belinda was only savouring the inexpressible feeling of being free after being locked up for several years.

So she was content to wait, and watch the passers-by. She instinctively took a step backwards when the little car pulled in to the pavement in front of her. 'So it's true,' Alicia said, rolling down her window.

For a moment Joanna did not recognise her. Eight years ago Alicia had been trimly attractive; this woman was overweight and had shadows under her eyes. 'Alicia!' she cried. 'How nice to see you. My, you're looking well.' Alicia snorted, switched off her engine and got out. 'What brings you to this neck of the woods?' Joanna asked.

'I was hearing a rumour, that it was you who had bought Caribee House,' Alicia said. 'I wanted to know if it was true. And it is, apparently.'

Joanna frowned. 'Just where did you hear this rumour?'

'Well, it wasn't a rumour. I put two and two together, when I read in the paper how the ex-convict Joanna Johannsson had raced from her home in Berkshire to the rescue of her daughter. There is only one place in Berkshire that you'd want to live.'

'Of course,' Joanna said. 'And how is your friend, Stephen?'

'I have no idea,' Alicia said.

'And no replacement?'

'So you're riding high, wide and handsome again,' Alicia remarked. 'Look, people are beginning to notice us. Why don't we go some place and have a coffee?'

'I'd love to. I'm just waiting on a friend.'

She looked along the street to where Belinda was striding towards them; Belinda always strode. 'Good lord!' Alicia commented. 'Where did you find her?'

'She was my cellmate,' Joanna explained. 'We'd both killed a man, but her lawyer was cleverer than mine, and she got away with manslaughter. Now she's my bodyguard.'

Alicia gulped. 'Well, maybe we'll leave the coffee.' She got back into her car. 'Bodyguard? Anyone would think you were going back into business.' Then she frowned. 'Shit!'

she said. 'You *are* going back into business. J & J. What a fool I've been. You bought my shares!'

'J & J bought your shares,' Joanna said, carefully.

'And you control J & J. You bitch!'

'Have we got trouble?' Belinda asked pleasantly, having come close enough to overhear the last remark.

'I think Mrs Edge is just leaving,' Joanna said.

'The famous Alicia,' Belinda commented. 'I've heard of you, famous Alicia.' Alicia engaged gear with a tremendous scraping, and drove off.

'Actually,' Joanna said, 'we may have trouble.' Because if Alicia could add two and two and get four, so could Andy Gosling.

* * *

The following week, Billy came down to see her. 'Don't tell me you've come up with something already?' Joanna asked, receiving him in the study. Michael, as usual, had gone up to town.

'Could be.' Billy was looking much better. He had bought himself a new suit, and there was a spring in his step.

'So?'

'How high will you go for Townsend's shares?'

'Explain.'

'Well, I did to him what they once did to you. I telephoned him and offered to buy his holding.'

'What did you offer?'

'They're currently trading at three hundred and fifteen pence. I offered to buy him out at four hundred. Was that all right?'

'Six hundred thousand? That's two-point-four million! I'd have to clear that with Michael. What was his reaction?'

'Said he'd think about it. Which is why I reckon I might have to go higher. But he's interested.'

Joanna stroked her chin. If Townsend was interested, he'd hardly go bleating to Andy, because Andy would put the stopper on any suggestion of a sell-out. But two-point-four million . . . she squared her shoulders. Once she had taken that kind of money in her stride. And it would give her control. 'Let me talk with Michael and come back to you. Did you make a date for speaking with Townsend again?'

'We're to meet the day after tomorrow.'

'You mean he knows who you are?'

'No way. I'm Mr Smith.'

Joanna frowned. 'And you never met when

I was running Caribee?'

'No, we didn't. You wouldn't ever give me a seat on the board, remember?'

'As things have turned out, that was a lucky escape for all of us, wasn't it? I'll give you Michael's confirmation, or not, tomorrow.'

'And if it's not?'

'You just don't keep the appointment.'

'Right.'

She telephoned Michael, and as she didn't want to discuss it over the phone, he came down for lunch. 'Then it's in the bag,' he said.

'You mean you'll authorise the expenditure? Suppose he holds out for more?'

'If he goes for it, we've got him. Is Montgomery any good as a negotiator?'

'He was, once. A long time ago.'

'Well, he can go up to five. Only if he has to.'

'Michael, that's three million pounds.'

'I said I'd spend whatever it took to give you back your company, Jo.'

'Oh, Michael . . . I don't know what to say.'

'Then don't say anything. Anyway, my darling, it's a good investment. I reckon that with you back in charge, those shares will soon be back to something like eight. I'll just about double my money.'

She telephoned Billy. 'So, it's all up to you.'

'Jesus,' he said. 'Five hundred . . . '

'Only if you have to,' she reminded him.

'Yeah. Oh, yeah. I'll screw the bastard, Jo. That's a promise.'

'Just get the shares, Billy. What time is your meeting?'

'Nine o'clock tonight. In a pub just off the Portobello Road. The Bell & Jewel.'

Joanna wrinkled her nose. 'Whose idea was that?'

'His.'

'Well, go easy. When will you call me?'

'Hopefully tonight. Up to midnight all right?'

'You call me any time you like, Billy. I won't mind being woken up to hear that news.'

'Excited?' Michael asked at dinner.

'I'm surprised I can eat,' Joanna said.

'What's up?' Raisul asked.

'A big deal,' Michael told him.

'The biggest deal of my life,' Joanna said.

'You mean you could get the company back?'

'That's it.'

'Oh, Mother . . . ' Helen burst into tears, as she was liable to do any any moment. 'I am so happy for you.'

'For us all, darling,' Joanna said. 'And we have Michael to thank for it.'

Michael grinned. 'He hasn't gone for it yet.'

On Michael's recommendation she took a sleeping pill. 'No use just lying there, wondering what's happening,' he said. 'I'll wake you up when he calls.' But when Joanna awoke it was broad daylight and Mrs Partridge was bringing in her breakfast. She sat up, pushed hair from her face. 'Where is Mr Johannsson?'

'He's breakfasting downstairs, madam, with the children.'

'Will you tell him I'm up?' She drank juice and coffee, and Michel came in. 'Nothing?'

'I'm afraid not. But don't be downhearted. There are a million and one reasons why he should not have called during the night.'

'Hm.' Yet she was tense, switched on the television to look at the breakfast news. This was mostly concerned with the contest for the deputy-leadership of the Labour Party, in which Denis Healey had just beaten Anthony Wedgwood-Benn. Joanna was only interested in politics in so far as it influenced share prices and interest rates, and as Labour was out of power they could not affect those issues. She was about to switch off when the newsreader said, 'Police are appealing for witnesses after the fatal shooting of two men last night in a street in north London. The men have not yet been identified, but it is known they had been drinking together in the Bell & Jewel public house. They left together, and got into a Ford Cortina which may have belonged to one of the men. Before they could drive off, however, someone stepped up to the car and shot them both through the head. Both men died instantly . . . '

Joanna clasped both hands to her throat, while Michael, who had been in the bathroom, hurried back in. 'You don't think . . .?'

'Has to be,' Joanna said. 'Oh, my God!'

'Listen, there are a thousand and one thugs in London,' Michael said. 'That sounds like a gangland assassination to me.'

'If you mean it was a hit,' Joanna said, 'I agree with you.' She got out of bed, went to the bathroom herself.

Michael followed. 'Gosling? Would he go that far?'

'As you said the other day, Michael, if he loses control of Petherick, he's on his uppers. That can make a man quite desperate.'

'Jesus! What are we going to do?'

'Find out, firstly, if it was Billy and Townsend who were killed, and secondly . . . ' she hesitated.

'Go on.'

'Who Townsend has willed his shares to.'

Michael gulped. 'Some people would say you have ice water in your veins.'

'Some people already have. I hope you know better. But the fact is, if there is some clause that says those shares go to Andy . . . '

'I'll see what I can discover. And Billy?'

'I know,' Joanna said. 'I want Gosling for murder, as well.'

'That could be hard to prove.'

'If he did it, or ordered it done, we have to be able to prove it, Michael. And there is no one else in the world would want both Billy and Townsend dead, at this particular moment. Can I leave that with you? I have to do something about Matilda.'

* * *

'Listen,' Belinda said. 'I'd like to help.'

'How, exactly?' Joanna asked.

'Well, I have friends who might know something.' She grinned. 'Be able to do something. Please let me help, Joanna. I owe you so much.'

'Don't be a goose,' Joanna said.

'It's true. You've made my life over. And now the thought of that thug ruining yours . . . I want to help you. I have to help you.'

Joanna hugged her. 'You're an absolute sweetie. But this isn't your problem. Don't worry. We'll sort it out.'

Belinda looked sceptical.

William was on the line almost before she had finished speaking. 'Have you seen the news? The bodies have been identified.'

'I saw the news,' Joanna said.

'Jo, was Billy doing something for you?'

'He was working for me, yes. Have you seen Tilly?'

'No. But . . . '

'Give me her address.'

'I'd better come with you.'

'No,' Joanna said. 'This I have to do for myself.'

It was a tiny, untidy flat. The door was opened by Tilly's eldest, Miriam — she was named after her grandmother — a girl of fifteen, who stared at her famous aunt with wide eyes. 'May I come in?' Joanna asked. The girl bit her lip. She had been crying, that was obvious. 'I'd like to see your mother,' Joanna said.

The girl stepped aside. 'She's in the bedroom.'

George, two years younger than his sister, peered at her from a littered lounge. Joanna smiled at him, and opened the bedroom door. Matilda was sprawled across the bed, only half dressed, staring at the television set. A tumbler of gin stood on the table; it was a quarter to eleven in the morning. 'Go away,' she said. 'I told you to go away.'

'If you're referring to the children, I think that might be a good idea,' Joanna said. 'Would you like me to take them home with me? They could stay there until things settle down.'

Matilda rolled on her back. 'What do *you* want?'

'To say how sorry I am.'

Matilda sat up. 'Billy was working for you! He wouldn't tell me. But now I'm sure.'

Joanna sighed, and sat beside her on the bed. 'Yes, he was working for me.'

'And people who work for you wind up dead, right?' Joanna really didn't have a reply to that. 'Even William should have been dead,' Matilda said. 'It's a miracle he survived that bullet.'

'I know,' Joanna said.

'But you don't care.'

'I do care,' Joanna said. 'I can't give you back Billy. But I can take you home, and your children, and look after you. We're family, remember?'

* * *

William and Norma came out to dinner, the first time in a very long time the entire family had sat down to dinner together; even Helen came down. But Belinda was missing. 'She went out,' Mrs Partridge explained. 'Just left. Said she had someone to see.'

Michael looked quizzical. 'Just how much do you know about that young woman's background?' he asked.

'Actually, very little,' Joanna confessed. 'Save that she is a self-confessed killer.'

'Good Lord,' Norma commented.

'In her own milieu,' Joanna said. 'Which was petty crime.'

'Or not so petty,' Michael said. 'I've been doing some investigating. That chap she is supposed to have cut down in a lovers' tiff was a well-known mobster.'

Joanna frowned. 'Meaning what?'

'My investigator thinks it was a contract. And that her lawyers, and a good number of her witnesses, were employed by the mob, which is why she got a reduced sentence for manslaughter rather than murder.'

'Holy shit!' William commented.

'But . . . she's absolutely faithful to me,' Joanna said. 'I'd swear that on the Bible.'

'And I'd believe you,' Michael said. They gazed at each other, then Joanna got up and left the table to go into the study. Michael followed her. 'What are you going to do? I thought you hated the guy? That you wanted only to bring him down?'

'I do. But I'm not having another death on my conscience,' Joanna said, already dialling. 'Hello,' she said. 'Is Mr Gosling at home. Tell him Joanna Johannsson is calling, and that I need to speak with him, most urgently. The butler,' she whispered at Michael, standing anxiously by.

'Joanna!' Andy sounded as confident as ever. 'Long time no speak? How was Liddleton?'

'The experience of a lifetime. Andy, I have got to see you, now.'

'Do you, now. Is it to do with buying, or selling, shares? I know all the tricks that you have been up to, Joanna. Did you seriously take me for a fool?'

'I never took you for a murderer, Andy.'

There was a moment's silence. Then he said. 'You have just uttered the most complete slander.'

'And I am sure you are recording this conversation,' Joanna said. 'Now let me say again, Andy, either you come down here, or I shall come to you. But it has to be now.'

'And I say, forget it.' He hung up.

'We'll go up to town anyway,' Joanna said.

Michael nodded, and called for Charlie.

The phone rang. 'Maybe he's changed his

mind,' Joanna said, and picked it up. 'For you.'

Michael took it, listened, frowned, and then grinned. 'That's great. Keep close.'

'Townsend?' Joanna asked.

'One of my people, yes. Townsend's will was read this afternoon. Seems he had a live-in friend.'

'Male or female?'

'Male. To whom he left everything. The word from my agent is that the shares could be up for grabs.'

'And they'll be grabbed by Andy, if we don't do something.'

'If your suspicions are correct, Jo,' Michael said, 'we might be a whole lot better off not doing anything.'

'It's a temptation,' Joanna said. 'But would you believe that I have never, in all my life, deliberately been involved in anyone's death? I don't want to start now, not even with a slug like Andy Gosling.'

'I hoped you'd say that,' Michael agreed.

Charlie raced through the London suburbs to reach Andy's Kensington flat; it reminded Joanna of her equally mad drive to rescue Helen. And this time? To rescue the man she most loathed in all the world? Or the woman who had become her most faithful servant? Charlie found parking about a hundred yards from the flat, and all three of them leapt out and ran along the pavement. It was a third-floor flat, and lights glowed in the windows; it was now quite dark.

Joanna pressed the street bell, and again, but there was no reply. 'Shit!' she muttered.

'I can open the street door, madam,' Charlie said.

She looked at Michael. 'Maybe we'll all be able to share a cell,' he remarked.

'Do it.'

Charlie broke the glass with his elbow. It made a sharp noise, but there was no one on the street. Carefully he reached through and released the latch. 'No burglar alarm?' Michael wondered.

'We're not as sophisticated in London as you people are on the other side of the Atlantic,' Joanna said.

The door swung in, and they hurried up the stairs. There was no answer when they knocked on the flat door, either. Joanna looked at Charlie. 'If you have a credit card, madam . . . ?'

Michael produced one, and a moment later they were in the flat, looking around them in horror. The lights were still on, and just inside the doorway a man lay on his back stabbed through the heart. He was no one Joanna had ever seen before. But on the far side of the room Andy Gosling lay, also on his back, and he too had been stabbed, several times. 'Don't touch anything,' Michael advised.

The three of them stood together in the centre of the room. 'What do we do?' Joanna asked.

'Get the hell out of here, and back out to Caribee House,' he advised.

'What do we do when she comes home?' Joanna asked, as Charlie drove through the night.

'I don't think she's going to do that,' Michael said.

'But . . . that poor girl. She did it for me.'

'As she killed before, for her previous employers.'

Joanna shuddered.

* * *

'It's a tangled world,' remarked Inspector Lawton. 'I understand, Mrs Johannsson, that Mr Gosling was a business partner of yours.'

'A long time ago,' Joanna said. 'He took over the company when I was sent to prison.'

'But you have been trying to get it back.'

'I have. I think I have done so. Or am about to do so.'

'With Mr Gosling's consent?'

'No,' Joanna said. 'It was to be a hostile takeover.'

'Which will be assisted by Mr Gosling's death.'

'Are you accusing me of something, Inspector?'

'No, no, Mrs Johannsson. It's just all, well, very coincidental. No doubt it will all be cleared up when we arrest whoever committed the murders.'

'I'm sure it will,' Joanna said. 'I assume you have leads.'

The inspector closed his notebook with a snap. 'We have some evidence that Mr Gosling entertained a young woman in his flat shortly before he was killed. That is to say, we have a witness who says he saw a young woman entering the flat, and another witness who says she saw a young lady leaving the flat about half an hour later.'

'Then you have a description?' Joanna's heart was pounding quite painfully.

'Nothing of any value. Tall, well-built, dark-haired . . . ' he regarded Joanna speculatively, considering the short, slender, yellow-haired figure in front of him. 'Unfortunately, the woman appears to have disappeared into thin air.' He stood up. 'I'm sorry to have troubled you, Mrs Johannsson. Loose ends, you know.'

'That poor girl,' Joanna said, when Michael had seen the Inspector out.

'Why poor? She's doing what she does best.'

'And when she returns here, asking for help?'

'I told you, she's not going to do that. She reckons she's paid her debt to you. To society, if you like. She'll have gone back to her own kind.'

'And that's a load off your mind.'

'Yes,' he said seriously. 'It is. She, and Andy, were your last links to your past. Now there's only the future to look forward to. Why don't we join the family for dinner? They're all here. Your old friend Peter Young is here as well. You'll want to talk to him about restructuring the company.' He winked. 'And changing the name back to Caribee Shipping. It's all yours, my darling.'

She looked up at him. 'Yes,' she said. 'Thanks to you, Michael. I shall never be able to thank you.'

'Thank me by being you.'

'Yes, but I'm not me anymore. I feel sort of . . . well, it's difficult to explain.'

He waited.

'So many people have passed by, and on, and I'm still here. What's more, I'm back on top, and they . . . what I'm trying to say is,

I'm not the woman who used to square her shoulders and stick out her chin and say to herself, get out of my way, world, I'm coming through. I'm too aware of how near I came to disaster, so often, and of how many people I hurt while careering along. I don't even hate Mrs Anstey or Angie anymore, would you believe it? Maybe I've grown up.'

He took her into his arms. 'And that is the greatest thank you of all,' he said as he kissed her.

THE END

Other titles in the Ulverscroft Large Print Series:

BEYOND THE NURSERY WINDOW

Ruth Plant

Ruth Plant tells of her youth in a country vicarage in Staffordshire early in this century, a story she began in her earlier book NANNY AND I. Together with the occasional dip back into childhood memories of a nursery kingdom where Nanny reigned supreme, she ventures forth into a world of schooldays and visits to relatives, the exciting world of London and the theatre, the wonders of Bath and the beauties of the Lake District. She travels to Oberammergau, and sees Hitler on a visit there. On the threshold of life the future seems bright and war far away.

THE FROZEN CEILING

Rona Randall

When Tessa Pickard found the note amongst her father's possessions, instinct told her that THIS had been responsible for his suicide, not the professional disgrace which had ruined his career as a mountaineer and instructor. The note was cryptic, anonymous, and bore a Norwegian postmark. Tessa promptly set out for Norway, determined to trace the anonymous letter-writer, but unprepared for the drama she was to uncover — or that compelling Max Hyerdal, whom she met on board a Norwegian ship, was to change her whole life.

GHOSTMAN

Kenneth Royce

Jones boasted that he never forgot a face. When he was found dead outside the National Gallery it was assumed he had remembered one too many. The man he had claimed to have identified had been publicly executed in Moscow some years before. The presumed look-alike was called Mirek and his background stood up. The Security Service calls in Willie 'Glasshouse' Jackson — Jacko — as they realise that there is a more sinister aspect. Jacko and his assistant begin to unearth commercial and political corruption in which life is cheap and profits vast, as the killing machines swing into action.

THE READER

Bernhard Schlink

A schoolboy in post-war Germany, Michael collapses one day in the street and is helped home by a woman in her thirties. He is fascinated by this older woman, and he and Hanna begin a secretive affair. Gradually, he begins to be frustrated by their relationship, but then is shocked when Hanna simply disappears. Some years later, as a law student, Michael is in court to follow a case. To his amazement he recognizes Hanna. The object of his adolescent passion is a criminal. Suddenly, Michael understands that her behaviour, both now and in the past, conceals a deeply buried secret.

THE WAY OF THE SEA AND OTHER STORIES

Stanley Wilson

Every story in this collection was written by Stanley Wilson with radio in mind. The BBC has broadcast all of them, and many have been used overseas. All have appeared in magazines or newspapers. The stories range the globe and beyond, from India to Canadian backwoods, from an expedition up the Amazon to a hundred years' journey to the planet Eithnan, from the Caribbean to a rain-sodden English seaside promenade, and from a fishing trawler to a hospital ward. There is frustration, there is tenderness, there is horror, there are tears, but there is laughter as well.